THIEF
RIVER
FALLS

THIEF RIVER FALLS

BRIAN FREEMAN

🐦 THOMAS & MERCER

Published by Thomas & Mercer, Seattle
www.apub.com

Amazon, the Amazon logo, and Thomas & Mercer are trademarks of Amazon.com, Inc., or its affiliates.

ISBN-13: 9781542093361 (hardcover)
ISBN-10: 1542093368 (hardcover)

ISBN-13: 9781542093385 (paperback)
ISBN-10: 1542093384 (paperback)

Cover design by Rex Bonomelli

Printed in the United States of America

First edition

For Marcia

THIEF RIVER FALLS

The Award-Winning Thriller
from Bestselling Author

LISA POWER

Start reading the book now with this exclusive excerpt!

Down, down, down comes the rain of black dirt, landing in showers on the boy's small body and slowly burying him in the ground.

Already, two inches of heavy earth weigh on his arms. His skin is cold. His face is wet with tears and blood. Nervously, he cracks his eyes to look up while he can still see anything at all. It is dark in the hole, where the glow of the moon can't reach him. The men are shadows above him, working like machines. He hears the scrape of metal and rock as they wield their shovels. They whisper to each other, and he can hear their words over the loud noise of their breathing.

"I hate this, man. He's just a kid."

"Do you think I like it? There's no other way."

"Yeah, but a kid. That's not why we did this."

"Be quiet and finish the job. We're wasting time."

"What if someone finds them, man? I'm telling you, we didn't dig deep enough. Someone might find both of them, and then what happens?"

"There's no *time*, do you hear me? Hurry."

Both of them.

Yes, the boy is not alone in the black hole. There is a man under his own body. The two of them are trespassers in a grave where they don't belong. The man beneath him is warm, but he doesn't breathe. He has arms and legs, but he doesn't move. The man with him is dead, but the boy is still alive.

The ones with the shovels do not know this. They think they've killed him. The boy wants to cry, to whimper, to scream, but he has to stay quiet. He must be frozen like a statue if the men look down. An urgent voice whispers in his head and tells him exactly what to do.

It's his mother's voice.

They think you're dead, my sweet. You must play dead. You must be dead.

Then, as if sensing his fear, she adds, *But trust me, you're not going to die.*

He wants to believe that. His mother wouldn't lie to him. Even so, panic wriggles up his body like a fat, hungry worm. The men shovel, the earth grows deeper, and all the boy wants to do is thrash and squirm and kick it all away from him. He can taste the damp ground in his mouth now, and he wants to gag, but if he does that, the men will jump down in the hole with the shovels again. They will hit him like they did before, much harder, and this time, he won't wake up.

No.

He must wait.

The hole fills in around him, encasing him the way a fish gets trapped in lake ice. How deep is he now? Three feet? Four feet? His mother tells him again, *You are not going to die, my sweet.* And yet soon he is completely underground. The moon and sky disappear. The earth feels like a huge animal sitting on top of his chest. He can't move his arms or legs. Even his lungs struggle to push enough soil away to breathe. As he does, he inhales dirt and spits it quietly out. He must do something. He can't wait any longer.

Are the men still there?

He can't hear their voices anymore or the scrape of the shovels. Everything is silent. Maybe they're done. Maybe they're gone.

It's time, my sweet.

His stiff fingers curl like claws. He becomes a mole now, tunneling in the loose ground. He digs with both hands, inching toward the surface, pushing away the earth where he is buried. It is slow work. He chokes and coughs in the foul air. His whole world is black and dark and cold, and he is oh so tired. His head hurts where the men hit him. He wants to sleep. His mind floats, drifting off like a balloon in the air, dragging him up into the clouds.

You must keep going.

"But I'm scared," he tells his mother.

I know.

"I can't do it."

Yes, you can.

"No. No, I can't. I want it to be over."

Don't give up, my sweet.

But it would be so much easier to give up. The work is too hard, the earth too heavy, the surface too far away. If he stops, if he lets the ground win, he can see his mother again. They will walk off together. He will feel her arms around him. If he frees himself, he's still alone. Without her.

The little mole stops tunneling. His aching fingers rest. Tears leach from his eyes into the blood and dirt caking his skin. The boy sobs. He needs comfort, needs to hear her voice again. Her real voice, not the one in his head.

"Mom?"

I'm right here, my sweet . . .

1

Down, down, down came the rain.

Lisa Power listened to the hammering thunder on the roof of her pickup truck. The drumbeat had a hypnotic quality. It had been raining for hours, one of those endless fall rains that sucked all the color out of the world and turned your life into a black-and-white movie.

Rebecca. The Ghost and Mrs. Muir. Sunset Boulevard.

That was how Lisa felt right now, like a heroine in a sad old story.

The drive from Thief River Falls had taken much longer than usual because of the rain, but she was finally home. She pulled her truck inside the detached garage and shut off the engine. She climbed out of the pickup and stood in front of the open garage doorway, where a waterfall overflowed the gutters. Her arms were limp and weak at her sides. Her brown eyes were wide open, and her wet brown hair was pasted to her face. She stared blankly at the rural highway at the end of her long driveway, but there were no headlights to be seen to the north or south. No trains rattled along the railroad tracks that ran parallel to the highway. Beyond the road, flat, empty fields stretched for miles into the night, and the black sky simply flooded rain onto a desolate landscape.

At times like this, Lisa felt as if she were the only human being living on the moon. She'd driven for more than an hour and not seen another soul.

She tried to find the energy to walk through the rain to her house. She was already drenched, her clothes soaked and muddy. Like a robot, she hiked through the downpour and braced herself against the wind that pushed her around like a doll. She'd forgotten to leave a light on, so her house was dark. The outbuildings around her made faint silhouettes against a black sky, the old barn barely standing upright in the overgrown field, the windowless shed playing music with its metal roof, the writer's cottage looking forlorn in the empty flower garden. Towering spruces dotted the land, bending and swaying in the storm. They shook their branches like a dog spraying water off its fur.

Lisa was almost at the white front porch when she heard a whisper.

"Mom?"

The voice was as clear in her ears as if a child were standing next to her. She froze, and her head snapped around. She squinted into the rain, trying to pick out someone hiding in the shadows. But no one was there. She was hearing things, a trick of the night. She waited awhile, just to be sure, but the only noise now was the wind screeching at her like a banshee telling tales of the dead.

Lisa climbed the porch steps and opened her front door. Inside, she closed her eyes, leaned back against the door, and dripped on the welcome mat. When she turned on the hall light, the brightness made her head throb the way migraines always did, so she turned it off again. She didn't need light. In this house, she could see in the dark. She knew every inch of it. This was her castle in the middle of nowhere, a place where she could pull up the drawbridge and keep out the world. She'd bought and renovated the old house on a large plot of abandoned farmland. Or maybe it was fairer to say that Reese Witherspoon had bought it for her when she acquired the film rights to Lisa's fourth novel.

That was a phone call she would always remember. She could still hear that famous, unmistakable voice on the phone, telling Lisa how much she loved her book and wanted to play the lead role herself. In the tally of best days of Lisa's life, the day of Reese's call would be near the top.

Two years ago.

Before all the tragedies began. Before the Dark Star came into her life.

Lisa was wet and cold, and she needed a shower. She peeled off her clothes, kicking off her boots, unbuttoning her flannel shirt, unzipping and stepping out of her messy jeans, and wriggling out of her soaked underwear. Naked and shivering, she padded to the cold wrought iron staircase that twisted up to her bedroom, which took up most of the second floor. She went straight into the bathroom, still not turning on any lights. She had a walk-in shower made of opaque glass blocks, and she stood under the hot water, pummeled by body sprays that washed away the dirt and pinked up her skin. The warm, wet darkness enveloped her, and she inhaled steam as if it were fine whiskey spreading fire through her whole body. She lost track of time as she stood there.

When she finally returned to her bedroom, she wandered to the wall of windows overlooking the highway. There was no letup in the rain. Seeing the ghost of her reflection in the glass, Lisa Power stared at Lisa Power. She was bony and not too tall. She had shoulder-length brown hair that usually had a mind of its own, like an unruly nest. Her face was pretty, but she'd always believed that her nose was a little bit too big for the rest of her features. Her pale lips were slightly open, as if she were always deciding what to say next. The faint creases in her forehead reminded her of her age, thirty-nine years old. But everyone who met her talked about her eyes, those big, wide, impenetrable brown eyes. As a writer, Lisa had always believed that she could look at someone's eyes and know exactly what they were hiding, but that wasn't true of her own. Right now, the woman looking back at her in the window was a stranger.

The time on her bedroom clock finally registered with her. It was after ten o'clock in the evening in Minnesota. That meant in California it was now after eight o'clock.

"Oh, crap," she said. She was late.

She rushed to put on clothes and then dried her wet hair as best as she could. She had to turn on lights to do so, and the brightness sharpened the pain behind her eyes. When she was as put together as she was going to be, she hurried downstairs to the finished basement. She had a specially constructed theater there, with a large custom screen and a row of plush movie seats. Near the screen, she kept a whiteboard where she'd written down the dates, times, and phone numbers for her call-in book clubs.

Tonight's discussion was right there on the list. *October 10. Palo Alto, 8:00 pm PDT, contact Aria Dhawan.*

Lisa booted up a laptop and loaded the video software that connected to the oversize screen. She dialed the number she'd written down for the California book club, and as the phone rang, she took a seat in the centermost chair of the theater. She forced herself to relax. She did these discussions several times a month with book clubs around the country, and they were always the same: the same questions, the same women, the same wineglasses, the same jokes, the same compliments. No one invited her to a book club if they didn't enjoy her books, and yet these things always made her cringe. She could see her image on camera in a little box in the corner of the screen, and she had to remind herself: *smile.*

Seconds later, a high-definition image of a Palo Alto living room filled the screen. Seven thirty-something women, fit the way only young Californians could be, erupted with happy smiles when they saw her. They were spread across modern furniture in a high-rise apartment that overlooked San Francisco Bay, and they already had their glasses of chardonnay in hand. In the middle was the hostess—smart, jet-black hair; red glasses on her face; a woman with the upscale look of a young executive at a tech giant.

"Ms. Power?" the woman said. "Welcome. I'm Aria Dhawan. It's so kind of you to join our book club tonight. I have to tell you, we all just loved *Thief River Falls*. We don't typically read thrillers in our group, but we made an exception for this book because of the recommendation from Reese, and we're very happy we did."

"I'm so glad," Lisa replied.

"The ending made me cry, but there was something uplifting about it, too. When the boy Purdue comes back as the woman is dying? That was so moving. I don't have children myself, but it was definitely a mother's book."

"Yes, believe me, I cried when I wrote that scene, too."

"Well, we have a lot of questions for you, but I know it's late there, so we promise not to take up too much of your time."

"That's okay. This is what I do. When I'm not writing, that is."

One of the other women put down her wineglass and jumped into the conversation. "The setting of your book is so remote! And the name of the town is very romantic. Is Thief River Falls a real place? Is that where you live?"

Lisa forced another smile. Always the same questions.

"Oh, yes, Thief River Falls is a real place. It's located in far north-western Minnesota, not too far from the Canadian border. And yes, I lived there my whole life until very recently. I purchased a house about an hour north of town last year, but you'll still find me in Thief River Falls several times a week."

"You must be famous there," one of the other women said.

"Or infamous. I was a little nervous about bringing so much mayhem to my hometown, but my neighbors didn't seem to have a problem with it. I'm not so sure about the chamber of commerce, though."

The women laughed. They always did.

Lisa knew which laugh lines to use and which stories tugged at people's heartstrings. For nearly every question at a book club or library visit, she had an answer memorized, because she'd talked to so many readers over the years who all wanted to know the same things.

Where do you get your ideas?

"I wish I could tell you. I see the world—people, places, whatever—through the lens of thrillers. I always have, since I was a girl. To me, everything in my life is about plots and characters. It's a little scary sometimes."

Was it hard to break through as a writer?

"Incredibly hard. It took me years to sell my first book. I didn't make a living at it until *Thief River Falls*, which was my fourth book. That's only because of Reese and the movie deal. Until then, I was working full time as a nurse at the local hospital."

Where do you write?

"Well, I built a little writer's cottage for myself at my new place. I used to live in a very small two-bedroom house next door to my parents, and there wasn't much room. So either I'd take my laptop up to the attic and hang out with the spiders, or I'd be out in the backyard working next to the kiddie pool and the jungle gym."

She didn't need to think about the answers she gave. They just rolled off her tongue. Sometimes she had to stop herself to let them get the questions out of their mouths before she began answering.

And then there were the questions she hated. The personal ones.

"Are you married?" one of the Palo Alto women asked.

Lisa got that question every time. She wondered if male writers did, too. As always, she had a throwaway line ready to be delivered.

"No, I'm not married. That's one downside of living in a remote area. There are a lot of farm animals around here, but not much in the way of single men."

More laughter.

They were a good group. She could feel their intelligence. She thought about telling them the truth: *I was engaged once, but Danny died more than ten years ago. That was two months before our wedding.* She thought about pouring out her soul and confessing everything that had happened to her in the past two years. About the Dark Star and how it had taken away her family. But people didn't want to hear those things, and Lisa didn't need the sympathy of strangers. She wanted to be done answering questions for the night. All she wanted now was to go to bed and sleep.

She grabbed a hardcover copy of *Thief River Falls* from the theater seat next to her. She kept the book there for these moments, because it was always a good way to hurry the video chats along to their conclusion.

"Would you like me to read a little from the book?"

The women on the screen murmured their enthusiastic approval. People liked hearing her read. Lisa enjoyed it, too, because it gave her the opportunity to act out the characters. It helped make the people in the books real to her. Human, three dimensional, full of emotion, not just creations on a page.

She turned to the prologue, which was where she always started. But before she could begin, a voice interrupted her.

"Actually, I have a question for you."

Lisa looked up at the screen in surprise. The voice belonged to a man, but she saw only women in the Palo Alto condo. "I'm sorry; who's that?"

Aria Dhawan glanced sideways at someone standing out of camera range. "Oh, that's my husband. Sometimes he lurks at our discussions. You should be honored—I don't think he's ever asked a question of one of our authors before. Come on, Rohan; if you've got something to say, at least let the woman see you."

Lisa waited, and Rohan Dhawan wandered into view. He had red wine where the others drank white. He was older than his wife, well into his forties, with thinning black hair that left only a few tufts on his forehead and a neatly trimmed beard. He was tall and thin, wearing a black sport coat that fit him loosely, a black T-shirt, and tan khakis. The clothes were casual but expensive. He had thick, inquisitive eyebrows, and his dark, unblinking eyes bored through the screen. Even two thousand miles away, those eyes, combined with a condescending little smirk, made Lisa uncomfortable.

"Ms. Power," he said politely.

"Mr. Dhawan. What's your question?"

"I wanted to know if you have ever been afraid that someone will bring your books to life."

Lisa blinked with surprise. "I'm not sure I know what you mean."

"I mean your books are about violence. Killing. Terrible things happen. Aren't you concerned that some deranged person might be inspired to do evil by what you write?"

Lisa's head throbbed. The brightness of the screen made her want to close her eyes. Her migraine was back. "Actually, my thrillers *aren't* about violence, Mr. Dhawan. There's violence in them, but that's not the point of the books. They're about people."

"And yet they could be considered a road map to murder, could they not? In the wrong hands, that is."

"Rohan," his wife murmured, disapproval in her voice.

"No, it's a fair question," Lisa replied, straining to keep a smile on her face. "I guess I'd say that if someone's inclined to do evil, they don't need me or my books to carry it out. They can get plenty of inspiration from the real world."

"I'm sorry, Ms. Power, but isn't that a bit of a cop-out? You titillate people with the reality of what you create. That's the point of a thriller, isn't it? You want us to think your plots could really happen. Would it be so surprising if someone took it too far? It has happened to other writers, has it not? What would you do if some copycat killer came along and decided to bury a child alive because of something he read in your book?"

"Rohan," his wife interjected.

"Truly, Ms. Power," the man went on, grilling her like a prosecutor with a hostile witness, "is that something you could live with? Wouldn't you feel at least partially responsible?"

"No. No, I wouldn't." Lisa stood up. She felt dizzy and short of breath. "I hate to cut this off, but I'm afraid it's late, and I have a terrible headache."

"Ms. Power, I'm very sorry," Aria began. "Please excuse my husband—"

"That's all right. My apologies for ending so abruptly. Good night."

Lisa reached down to the laptop with trembling fingers and ended the call. The video disappeared immediately, and all she could see in front of her now was the huge bright-white screen, so white that it hurt her eyes. She felt herself breathing quickly, hyperventilating.

She tried to walk, but the whole world spun like a carousel, and she found herself collapsing to her knees.

Down, down, down . . .

2

Lisa awoke sometime later in bed, dreaming that someone was outside her front door. It was after midnight. The last thing she remembered was getting up off the floor in the basement theater and coming upstairs and changing into her nightgown. Outside, through the floor-to-ceiling windows of the bedroom, she could see that the rain had finally stopped. The clouds had cleared out, leaving an open sky, and the moon was a bright searchlight, casting its milky glow across her body. She lay atop the heavy blankets. The house was so silent that she felt lonely.

Then it happened again.

Downstairs, someone pounded heavily on her front door. She realized that the noise hadn't been part of a dream; it was real. She heard a muffled voice shouting her name from the porch.

"Ms. Power! Are you home? We need to talk to you."

Lisa didn't recognize the voice. It wasn't anyone she knew, and strangers typically didn't show up here unannounced in the middle of the night. She slipped out of bed, but she stayed away from the windows, where the curtains were open. She had never felt a need to close them for privacy, because her nearest neighbor was two miles away. But right now, she was conscious of the white moonlight that would make her visible to anyone outside. Until she knew who was there, she didn't want to announce the fact that she was home and alone.

She crept to the bedroom wall and nudged just far enough past the edge of the window frame to look down. The slant of the roof made it impossible to see who was on the porch, but she could see a vehicle parked in her gravel driveway. It was a black SUV, and she could make out large gold lettering on the doors. Someone from the county sheriff's department was paying her a visit.

But not the sheriff in Kittson County, where she lived.

The SUV was from south of her in Pennington County, where the county seat was Thief River Falls.

As she watched, a police officer stepped down from the porch. She could hear the crunch of his boots as he walked into the middle of her front yard. He wore a deputy's uniform, but the wide brim of the man's hat made it impossible to see who it was. He turned around to stare up at the house, and Lisa instinctively backed away to make sure he didn't see her. She didn't know why she was hesitating about opening the door to the police. She knew most of the deputies in Pennington County, and they knew her.

And yet something about this man didn't feel right. His arrival made her uneasy.

She knelt beside the wall until she was stretched out flat on the ground, and then she crawled forward to spy through the bottommost corner of the window. She still couldn't see the deputy's face, but she saw something else. In the shimmering moonlight, she could see his hand, as bone white as the hand of a skeleton.

He was holding a gun.

He had his gun out of its holster.

A second voice cut through the nighttime quiet. "Is she there?"

"No, I don't think so."

She watched another deputy join the first, emerging from the overgrown field on her land. The low brim of this man's hat, too, covered his face. Their voices were unfamiliar. She didn't know them.

The second man had his gun in his hand, too. *Why?*

"Check the garage," the first cop instructed his partner. "See if her truck's inside."

Lisa watched the other cop approach the door of her garage. He tugged on the door handle, but it was locked and wouldn't open. She found herself grateful that the garage had no windows that would let the man shine a flashlight inside and see that her truck was parked there. She didn't want them to know that she was home.

"I can't tell," the second man called. "Did you check to see if the front door's open?"

"I will."

The other police officer headed back to the porch. Lisa heard the thump of his footsteps, and she gasped quietly. She squeezed her eyes shut and felt her whole body tighten into knots. She couldn't remember if she'd locked the door when she got home. Half the time, she forgot.

Directly below her, she heard the rattle of the doorknob and the thud of someone pushing heavily on the door from outside.

Then the cop called to his partner again. "No, it's locked."

"What do you think? Should we break in?"

The first police officer didn't answer immediately. Lisa felt her breath coming faster, and she sweated in the warm, humid bedroom. She tried to grasp what was happening. Two cops, two strangers, both with guns in their hands, were debating whether to *break into her house*.

She heard footsteps descend the porch steps and scrape along the gravel again. When she peered into the yard, she saw the two police officers meet near their squad car. They were both solidly built, one taller than the other. Their faces were invisible.

"Should we break in?" the second cop repeated.

"No, not right now. We'll come back when it's light."

Under the white moonlight, both men holstered their weapons. She watched them climb into either side of the SUV, and the engine roared to life, and the headlights came on like two shining eyes. The cops turned around in her yard and drove to the highway. The vehicle headed south.

South toward Pennington County. South toward Thief River Falls.

Lisa felt a sickness in her gut, driven by fear. She hadn't eaten in hours, and she felt acid bubbling up out of her empty stomach, burning her throat. She scrambled to her feet and ran to the bathroom, where she threw open the toilet lid and retched through a series of dry heaves. Nothing but yellow liquid came out of her mouth. The effort of throwing up exhausted her. She rested for a while with her head leaning against the marble counter on the sink, and then she got up and rinsed out her mouth and walked unsteadily back into the bedroom.

She tried to decide what to do.

Call the police. That was her first instinct.

But the police were the ones who'd been here. From the wrong county. With their guns out. Searching her property, testing the locks on her house, debating whether to force their way inside. No, she wasn't ready to call the police yet, not until she knew what was going on.

Call Laurel.

Laurel March was her best friend.

It was the middle of the night, but Laurel wouldn't care about being awakened. Laurel was the calm head whenever Lisa found herself in the midst of a panic attack. Lisa didn't think she would have survived the last two years of the Dark Star without Laurel's help. She couldn't count how many times she'd gone to her friend to talk, cry, scream, and pray.

Call Laurel. Together, they would figure out what was happening.

Lisa grabbed her cell phone from the nightstand beside her bed. Before she dialed, she went back to the tall bedroom windows. She didn't bother hiding now. Her eyes checked the highway to be sure the police were gone and hadn't come back. Then she turned her stare down to the ground.

She wasn't alone. Right there, under the bright, bright moonlight, someone was standing in her yard. Looking up at her.

It was a young boy. He couldn't have been more than ten years old. When their eyes met, he turned and ran.

Lisa rushed outside from the house, and the night air assaulted her. The storm was over, but the ground was wet, and cold wind blew down from Canada across the flat fields with the speed of a train. She shoved her hands in the pockets of her cream-colored trench coat. Her long brown hair swirled around her face in tangles.

"Hello?" she shouted, trying to make herself heard over the wind. "Are you there? Do you need help?"

No one answered.

She had a flashlight in her hand, and she used it to examine her yard through a cone of white light. She walked completely around the perimeter of her house and did the same at her detached garage. She hiked all the way down the driveway to the rural highway and looked for a child on the shoulder, but the road was deserted in both directions. There were no other houses close to hers and no lights to be seen anywhere.

"I won't hurt you," she called. "I want to help. Where are you?"

The boy couldn't have gone far. She'd grabbed her coat and dashed out of the house immediately after seeing him. And yet there were hiding places everywhere. He could be sheltered among the evergreens, crouched in the tall weeds, or taking cover inside one of the outbuildings.

Lisa walked back from the highway, dodging silvery pools of standing water from the rain. She went to the place where her green lawn ended and the wind rippled across acres of open fields. The beam of her flashlight lit up only a small area around her. She listened, but the rustle of brush and branches drowned out every other sound. She shivered as another gust of northern wind almost lifted her off her feet.

"My name is Lisa," she called. "I'm a friend."

Nearby, metal banged sharply against metal. She swung the flashlight in that direction and saw the aluminum door of her machine shed swinging back and forth in the gales. She headed toward the shed across the wet grass, not knowing if the boy had taken refuge inside or if the police had opened the shed to search it.

Search for what?

She held the shed door tightly as it shuddered in her grasp. With her other hand, she lit up the interior with her flashlight. She saw her riding lawn mower, its blades stained green; the snowplow attachment for her truck; a pegboard with saws and drills hung on hooks. Bags of fertilizer were stacked on wooden shelves, giving off a sweet smell and leaching orange dust onto the metal floor.

No one was inside.

Lisa closed the door and relatched it. She kept a rusty padlock for the latch hung on a nail by the door, but she'd never bothered to use it.

The next place to search was the old barn. She rarely went inside the barn because the interior was unsafe. Sooner or later, she assumed she would wake up to find that it had collapsed under the weight of winter snow. It was situated deep in the fields, almost a hundred yards from the house. The rutted access road was still visible, although the weeds of two seasons had grown across the dirt. Because of the rain, the road was like a river, and she had no choice but to hike through the water, which was deep enough to get inside her shoes. She tucked in her chin as she marched into the cold wind.

Halfway to the barn, where a swell in the ground left a stretch of mud that hadn't flooded, she saw footprints reflecting the white of the moon. They were small, definitely belonging to a child. The boy had come this way. The footprints were far apart; he was running. Lisa ran, too, wanting to catch up with him. The barn loomed ahead of her. The red paint on its walls had faded and peeled, and the shingles on the rounded roof were black with dirt. Some of the crossbeams had warped, and storms had broken many of the windows, making the field around the barn a minefield of glass and nails. The two-panel door hung open, and more small muddy footprints led inside.

"I'm coming in," she called. "Don't be scared."

She walked carefully through the barn door into the darkness. The wind whistled through open cracks in the walls. She shined her flashlight on the floor and saw dead leaves, cut straw, and rusted tools. Amid the dust, she also saw a few fresh drips that were bright red.

Blood.

"Are you hurt? Let me help you."

The flashlight cast shadows behind the tall wooden posts that supported the roof. A row of stalls with metal gates divided the long wall next to her. There had been horses kept here once upon a time. She moved down the corridor, checking each stall, and her flashlight lit up dead things decaying inside. Birds. Rats. Snakes. Huge spiderwebs drooped from the rafters. The roof leaked, and puddles glistened on the floor. Green moss spread up the walls.

"Where are you? I know you're here."

In the stall ahead of her, she heard a noise. She came quickly around the half door and lit up the interior, and the light made a devilish red reflection in two animal eyes. A black cat, its back arched, its fur pricked up, unleashed an angry hiss from the corner of the stall. Lisa screamed as the cat leaped at her, scrambling over her shoulder and tearing panicked scratches with its claws. She stumbled backward and spun around as the cat jumped down and stampeded into the shadows.

Her heart raced. Her shoulder stung. She closed her eyes to settle her nerves.

When she opened her eyes again, she had to stifle another scream by squashing her hand over her mouth. "Oh!"

In the white beam of the flashlight, a young boy stood like a soldier at attention with his back against one of the barn's support posts. He wore only a T-shirt and jeans, both of which were soaking wet against his skin. He shivered, freezing. His mouth hung open, and his blue eyes were wide with terror. He had fair blond hair, but it was hard to tell, because his head and face were matted with dirt and blood. He eyed the open barn behind her and looked ready to run, just like the cat.

Lisa recovered from her own fright and took a step away to give the boy space. "It's okay. I'm not going to hurt you. I want to help."

The boy didn't say a word.

"I'm a nurse. When people are hurt, I help them get better. Can I take a look at your head and see if you're hurt?"

She reached out a hand, but the boy recoiled. He shut his eyes and twisted his face, as if the slightest touch would be torture.

"That's okay. We don't have to do that right now. The thing is, I'm really cold, and you look really cold, too. My house isn't far away. It's nice and warm there. I can even make a big fire in the fireplace for us. Wouldn't you rather go inside instead of staying out here?"

The boy opened his eyes. There was a tiny softening in his face as he looked at her, the first small glimmer of trust. As scared as he was, he was also tempted by the promise of a warm house and a crackling fire. Lisa squatted down until they were eye to eye and gave him the biggest smile she could.

"Listen, you're probably thinking, this woman's a stranger. And we all know you're not supposed to go anywhere with strangers, right? That means the first thing we should do is get to know each other. I'm Lisa. Can you give me a 'Hey, Lisa'? Can you do that for me?"

She won a shy smile from him. His lips moved, and he murmured, "Hey, Lisa."

"Look at that—you can talk! There we go! Now what about you? What's your name?"

He was silent again.

"Please?" she said. "Just tell me your name."

The boy shook his head over and over. Then he spoke again, and his voice was even softer than before. Like a whisper.

"I don't know," he said.

3

The fire cast a warm glow throughout the rustic den at the back of Lisa's house. The wall surrounding the fireplace was made entirely of rough flagstones, and varnished log beams filled the other walls and stretched overhead across the ceiling. A faux fur rug was spread in front of the hearth, and the boy sat there, wrapped up in a quilt that Lisa's mother had made several years earlier.

His blond hair shone almost white. His skin was scrubbed, pink and clean after his shower. His clothes were in the washing machine. She'd found a cut behind his ear but concluded that the injury itself wasn't deep or serious, just a flesh wound that had bled profusely. However, the boy couldn't tell her what had actually happened to him. He had no identification on him, nothing that would tell her who he really was.

Lisa watched from the doorway without letting him know that she was there. He seemed entranced by the flames, and he hummed, which was a comforting noise like the purr of a cat. His blond hair was wavy and unkempt and needed a cut. He had beautiful blue eyes, the kind of eyes that would make him a heartbreaker when he grew up. He was still scrawny like a little boy, all knees and elbows, his wrists as thin as matchsticks. His teeth were a little crooked and would need braces eventually.

What she noticed most about him was his serious face. He looked as if he was always thinking about things and trying to figure out their meaning. When he went into a room, his gaze moved around to every piece of furniture, every picture on the wall, every book on the shelves. He didn't say much, but he seemed endlessly curious. Lisa could relate to that, because she'd been the same way as a girl, an introvert who noticed everything around her, like a silent spy.

She walked into the den. The boy heard her footsteps, and his head flew around, as frightened and alert as a startled rabbit on the lawn. She worried that he scared so easily, because it seemed out of character with everything else about him.

Lisa gave him a reassuring little wave. "It's just me."

She joined him on the deep rug and crossed her legs. She put out her hands, warming them near the fire. The boy studied her with that deep, intense stare that was full of questions.

"So can we talk a little bit?" she asked.

The boy shrugged. "Sure."

"How's your head? Does it hurt?"

"No."

"I'm washing your clothes. They'll be clean soon."

"Okay."

"Do you remember anything about what happened to you?"

"No," he said, shaking his head with his mouth squeezed into a frown, as if he didn't like disappointing her. "I don't."

"That's okay. Let's not worry about that yet. What about your name? Do you remember what your name is?"

"No. I don't know that, either."

"Hmm. So you're a mystery boy, huh? Well, we need to do something about that, because everybody needs a name. You don't want me to be saying 'hey you' all the time, right? Let's give you sort of a secret agent name, at least until we find out who you really are. Okay? How about I call you Purdue?"

"Purdue," the boy murmured. "Why would you call me that?"

"It's from a French word that means 'lost.' And right now, you're sort of a lost boy, aren't you?"

"I guess."

"Well, the name *Purdue* is very special to me. I wrote a book about a little boy who was lost, sort of like you. And his name was Purdue."

"What happened to him?"

Lisa thought, *He was buried alive.*

"He was rescued by a very brave woman and lived happily ever after," she replied. "Of course, he had a lot of adventures along the way. That's the way my books go. But the main thing is, he ended up figuring out who he was and where he was supposed to be. I'm going to make sure that happens for you, too. Okay?"

"Okay." The boy's face had that same serious expression again. "Do I look like this other Purdue? The one you wrote about?"

"No, you don't look like him at all. The boy in my book had dark hair and came from Missouri and had a southern accent. Y'all don't talk like a boy from Missouri, now do y'all?"

This time the boy smiled. "No."

"No, you don't. But I don't think my Purdue would mind if you shared his name for a little while."

He nodded. "Okay."

"Very good. You are now officially Secret Agent Purdue. And our mission is to figure out who you are and where you came from and where you're supposed to be. Got it? You say you don't remember what your name is or how you got hurt, so I guess we need to start somewhere else. The first question is, What *do* you remember?"

Purdue sucked in his lips and held his breath, as if he were trying to get rid of hiccups. When he finally exhaled with a loud whoosh, he shook his head in frustration and looked upset with himself. "Nothing. I can't remember anything."

"Well, let's start a little closer to home and see if we can't jog something loose. When I saw you and you saw me, you were standing in the middle of my yard. How'd you get there?"

"A truck," Purdue answered immediately. His eyes widened, as if he'd surprised himself with the answer.

"A truck. That's great. See, you're remembering things already." Lisa cocked her head. "Was it *my* truck? I have a pickup, and I drove home from Thief River Falls earlier this evening. Were you hiding in the back of my pickup?"

"I don't think so."

"Are you sure?"

"After I was in the truck, I walked a long way before I got here," Purdue explained.

"You walked? From where?"

"I don't know. I was in this truck, and we drove for a while. I'm not sure how long. I think I fell asleep. Then I woke up, and the truck was stopped. I got out, and nobody else was around. So I started walking."

"Were you alone?"

"Yes."

"Why were you in the truck?"

"I don't know."

"Who was driving it?"

"I don't know."

"Did you get into it yourself, or did someone put you there?"

"I don't remember. I'm sorry."

"You don't have anything to be sorry about. This isn't your fault. You said you got out of the truck, and nobody else was around. Where were you? Were there buildings nearby?"

"A house, I think."

"This house? My house?"

He shook his head. "No. It was somewhere else."

"Was anyone home? Did you ring the doorbell?"

"No. I was scared. I didn't know what was going on. My head hurt. I just felt like—I just felt like I had to get away. I had to run. If I didn't run, something bad was going to happen to me."

"Like what?"

"I don't know. Something bad."

"Okay, so you started walking. Where did you walk? Were you on a road?"

"No. I went through the fields. The rain was pouring down, so it was all muddy. I walked for a long time, and I was really cold. It was dark so I couldn't see where I was going. Then I saw lights, so I went that way. It was your house. And there you were in the window."

"That's all you remember?"

"Yes."

Lisa sat back, trying to make sense of it, but there was no sense to be made. This boy had sprung from nowhere. He was truly *perdu*. She saw no deception in his face to suggest that he was lying or hiding the truth. His life had begun on a truck, with no past that he could remember, and he'd wandered through the rain in the middle of the night until he found himself at the home of Lisa Power. Amid the cold remoteness out here, he was lucky to be alive.

"You've done really well, Purdue," she reassured him. "You already remember a lot more than you thought you did. With time, I'm sure more will come back. You've got a life. You came from somewhere. We'll figure it out."

Purdue surprised her by reaching out and hugging her tightly with his skinny arms around her neck. He was warm from the fire, and he smelled of the lavender aroma of her soap and shampoo. "Thank you, Lisa."

"You're welcome, Purdue."

He sat back, cuddled up in the quilt again. "What happens now?"

"Well, I've cleaned up that wound on your head, and it doesn't look too bad, but I'm worried about the fact that you don't remember anything. You're okay on the outside, but I want to make sure there's nothing wrong on the inside, too. So what I'd like to do is take you to the hospital so they can run some tests and make one hundred percent sure that you're okay."

Purdue's hand shot out and squeezed her wrist. He shook his head frantically. *"No."*

"Why not?"

"I don't want to go to the hospital. People die there."

"Well, sure, but people get better there, too. I was a nurse for years before I started writing books, and I worked with some great people at a hospital about an hour south of here. I'd like to take you there."

The boy shook his head again, even more firmly than before. *"No. No, we can't.* Please don't take me there. Please. You can take care of me! I'm safe here with you."

Lisa sighed. She didn't want to agitate the boy any more than he was. "Tell you what, you've had a long day. You must be really tired. Your clothes are probably dry by now, so I'll go get them, and then you can sleep for a little while and get your strength back. I've got a friend who can help us decide what to do next, and we can talk about it in the morning. Okay?"

Relief flooded across his face. "Yes. Thank you!"

"I'll be right back with your clothes," she said.

Lisa pushed herself to her feet. She could feel that her face was flushed from the heat in the room. She left the boy by the fire and headed back to the doorway that led to the rest of the house, where the air was cooler. Before she left, however, she thought of another question and turned back.

"Hey, Purdue?"

He looked up at her with big eyes. "Yes?"

"I know you may not remember, but can you think of any reason why the police might be looking for you? I mean, is it possible that someone took you who wasn't supposed to do that? Like maybe the person who was driving the truck?"

She saw a shadow flicker across his face. "I don't know."

"It's just that the police came to my house earlier," she said. "I didn't know why, but now I wonder if it could be because of you."

"The police were *here*?"

"Yes. They left, but they'll be back in the morning. I can talk to them and find out what's going on."

Purdue said nothing. The shadow returned to his face, and this time it stayed.

"Anyway, I'll be right back," Lisa said.

She gave the boy another smile and then wandered through the house to the wrought iron stairs and climbed to the laundry room adjacent to her bedroom. She opened the dryer door and bundled up the boy's clothes in her arms. She brought them back to the den, but when she came through the doorway, she saw that the quilt had been left in a crumpled pile on the floor. The fire still crackled, but no one sat in front of it. The boy was gone.

"Purdue?" Lisa called. She dropped the clothes on the rug and crossed the room to the glass door that led to her back porch. It was ajar, with cold wind rushing in. She headed onto the deck under the moonlight and called again. "Purdue, where are you? What's wrong?"

At first, she heard nothing to tell her where he was. Then, under the murmur of the wind in the fields, her ears honed in on a low, desperate whimper. He was crying. The noise came from behind her. She turned around and squinted into the farthest shadows of the deck, which was crowded by patio furniture and the square body of an outdoor spa. She spotted Purdue huddled next to the wall of her house, his hands wrapped around his knees. He was barely visible, naked and cold in the darkness.

When she got closer to him and reached out her hand, he cringed, as if he was afraid of her now, too.

"Purdue," she murmured. "What's wrong? Why did you run?"

Tears dripped from his eyes, and mucus dripped from his nose. "Don't give me to the police, Lisa. Please."

"Why not?"

His hair fell across his face, and his low voice gurgled from the back of his throat when he tried to speak. "Kill the boy."

"What?"

"I heard men talking," Purdue told her. "They were policemen, and that's what they said. *Kill the boy.*"

4

Purdue slept.

Lisa put the boy in her own bed, rather than in one of the smaller bedrooms downstairs, and she tucked him under the down comforter. His head sank into the mountain of pillows. She turned off the lights but stayed in the bedroom where she could watch him. She pulled a cushioned chair near the windows so she could keep an eye on the front yard, and she draped her mother's quilt over her knees.

She knew she wouldn't sleep herself.

Her fingers caressed the squares that were sewn together on the small satin quilt. Her mother had made it for her a decade earlier. All the patterns were in different shades of blue, decorated with whimsical cartoon animals. A whale. A unicorn. A pelican. A giraffe. Her mother had been quirky and artsy when it came to crafts, and Lisa attributed her own love of creating things to her mother's genes.

Madeleine Power. Her mother, born in France in a small coastal town outside Marseille, pretty, religious, spirited. She'd met Lisa's father when they were both teenagers and he was an American traveling through Europe with a church choir group. They'd fallen in love, and she'd followed him home to this barren part of the world without a look backward. Sometimes Lisa tried to imagine the courage it had taken for an eighteen-year-old French girl to uproot herself and marry a young Minnesota factory worker thousands of miles from home. But that was her mother—utterly fearless. She'd filled her loneliness by having a large family. First Lisa and her twin brother entered the world, then three more boys over the course of the next eight years, all of them squeezed together in a matchbox house on Conley Avenue in Thief River Falls.

As the only two women in the family, Lisa and her mother had been so close as to be inseparable. She'd lived at home with her parents until she was almost thirty. Even when she'd finally moved out, it was to a rental house right next door, where she could still talk to her mother through the open windows and hear Madeleine singing French songs as she baked.

It was Madeleine who'd read her daughter's stories at age five and told her that one day she would be a writer.

It was Madeleine who'd been seated next to her at the Grand Hyatt in New York, cheering and whistling when Lisa's book was named the thriller of the year.

It was Madeleine who'd cradled her when the call came about Danny, who'd held Lisa as she cried inconsolably, who'd whispered that even in the wake of terrible grief, life would go on. *La vie continue. Il doit.*

It was strange how Lisa's life had always changed with phone calls.

A phone call from the fire chief in Kern County, California, to break the news about Danny.

A phone call from Reese Witherspoon to make her book into a movie.

A phone call from the police in Crookston, Minnesota, to let her know that there had been an accident on a slippery, snow-swept road, that a semi had gone through a stop sign on the rural highway, that we are very sorry but your mother, Madeleine Power, was killed in the collision.

So began the chain of events that would pick apart Lisa's whole world, like loose threads unraveling.

The Dark Star.

The quilt slipped from her knees. She got out of the chair, because she couldn't sit still anymore. Her eyes were teary. She stared out the bedroom windows, watching the flat, empty earth that went on forever in the darkness. Maybe leaving her hometown and buying a place here, away from people she knew, had been a mistake, but at the time, she'd felt as if she needed to escape.

That was what her twin brother, Noah, had done, too.

Escape. Run away.

Lisa walked over to her bed and stared down at Purdue, lost in the white blanket and white pillows. He looked small and fragile that way, as if she could blink and he would disappear. Instinctively, she reached down and ran her fingers through his thick hair. He murmured and sighed in his sleep.

The echo of his words rippled through her memory. *Kill the boy.*

She didn't know whether to believe what he'd told her. He gave no indication of lying, and he was injured and clearly terrified of something. And yet it was so easy for children to misread and misunderstand things. Whatever trauma he'd suffered had interfered with his memory, and maybe he'd filled in the gaps with fantasy. She would have assumed that was true if police officers hadn't showed up outside her house with their guns in their hands.

Purdue's clothes lay where she'd folded them on the corner of the bed. She realized she hadn't searched his clothes to see if there were any clues in them about who he was or where he'd come from. She picked up the little bundle, grabbed her phone from the nightstand, and carried all of it out of the bedroom, letting Purdue sleep. Downstairs, she went into her kitchen, turned on the lights, and poured herself a double shot of Absolut Mandarin. When she tasted it, the cold, sweet vodka on an empty stomach went straight to her head.

She examined Purdue's white T-shirt and white athletic socks. They were standard issue, the kind she would find at any Walmart, including the supercenter in Thief River Falls. His jeans were more interesting. They were stonewashed and featured zippered pockets on the front and back. When she felt the pockets with her fingers, she realized he had things zipped inside, and it gave her hope that maybe some of his secrets were hidden there, too.

Lisa unzipped one of the front pockets and fished out the contents. It was money, a handful of loose change and a few folded dollar bills that were wet from having gone through the wash. She checked the opposite pocket and found a long silver key that looked like it was made for an automobile. There was just the one key and nothing else. She found it strange that Purdue, who was many years too young to drive, had a car key in his jeans but no key for a house.

His back pockets were empty. No wallet. No school ID. No phone. Nothing that would make him anything other than Purdue.

She spotted one more pocket on the side of the boy's jeans near the knee. It was tiny, barely big enough to hold a credit card, but she realized that something was wedged inside. She yanked open the zipper and scooped out what was in the pocket with one finger. When she held it up, a metal cylinder gleamed in the light. Seeing it, Lisa inhaled sharply.

It was a spent cartridge from a gun.

She held the brass in front of her face and rolled it around in her fingers. The mental image of it being used made her twitch. The bang of the shot. The recoil. The ejected brass flying from the gun.

She wanted to know where Purdue had found it.

She wanted to know who had fired the gun and where the bullet had gone.

At that moment, Lisa realized it was all true. Purdue was in danger.

She finished her vodka in one swallow, and then she gathered up Purdue's clothes and turned off the kitchen lights. She wanted the house completely dark if anyone showed up here. After she crossed the foyer, she checked the security of the lock and dead bolt on her front door. She went upstairs, where Purdue was still sleeping, and put his T-shirt, socks, and jeans back on the bed. She stuffed the money and car key back into his pockets, but she kept the spent cartridge herself. Then she went into her large walk-in closet and shut the door behind her.

Lisa changed clothes. She anticipated a long, cold day ahead. She found heavy wool socks in a dresser drawer and a pair of dark corduroys.

She grabbed a jean shirt, buttoned it, and left it untucked. She had a white down vest on a hanger, and she took it down by the collar. Finally, she went to the bureau at the far back of the closet and found her gun safe shoved to the rear of the highest shelf. She pulled it into her hands and undid the combination lock and flipped open the top.

Her Ruger 9 mm semiautomatic pistol was inside, along with a loaded ten-round magazine. It was in perfect condition, only a year old. She'd bought it when she moved to this house, because help was far away when you lived out here and strange things had a way of happening so close to the border. Once a month, she fired at the range, and she was obsessive about keeping the gun clean and lubricated. She'd grown up with guns in her family. Pistols. Shotguns. Hunting rifles. Firearms were one of the prerequisites of country life. Even so, there had never been a time when she felt as if she needed to keep her pistol on her person when she was out and about.

Not until now.

Now her gut told her, *Stay armed.*

She shoved the magazine into the pocket of her corduroys, and then she zipped the Ruger into the right-hand pocket of the down vest. She took the vest with her as she left the closet. Purdue was still asleep, a little boy in a sea of white. When she went back downstairs, she hung the down vest on the hook by the front door, so she could grab it whenever they left the house.

She went into the kitchen again. She kept the lights off.

Her phone was on the table. She stared at it, debating what to do. Her gaze shifted to the clock, and she saw that it was nearly four in the morning. Sunrise was still more than three hours away. She'd heard the police saying they would be back when it was daylight.

Lisa took the phone and dialed Laurel March. It was the middle of the night, and she assumed her friend would be asleep, but Laurel answered the phone immediately, sounding as if she'd already been awake.

"Hello?" her friend said. "Lisa, is that you?"

"Yes, it's me. Laurel, thank God you're there. I'm sorry to call so late, but I need your help."

5

The nightmares came for Denis Farrell, just as they had the previous several nights. Whenever he closed his eyes, his dreams tortured him. This one was the worst. He lay in a surgery room on the operating table, dressed in a three-piece suit and tie as if this were just another day at the office. A dozen doctors and nurses in scrubs surrounded him, but masks covered their entire faces, so he couldn't see who they were. One of the doctors loomed over his body, knife in hand. The knife was on fire, a yellow flame dancing all along the metal of the blade.

"I'm awake," Denis protested in the dream.

The surgeon acted as if he didn't hear him. As Denis watched, the doctor slowly brought the flaming knife down to make an incision in his body.

"I'm awake!" he screamed.

But his warning had no effect. The blade seared through his skin, cutting him open from the hollow of his neck to the base of his stomach. Black flaming blood leached from his insides onto his clothes. His shirt and tie caught fire, billowing and steaming along with blood that spurted like a geyser. His organs bubbled and burned deep inside his body. When he breathed, he exhaled fire from his mouth like a dragon. The flames flew up the surgeon's gown, until the doctor was nothing but a column of fire. With each breath, Denis's mouth expelled more flames, lighting up the others in the room. Fire shot up every doctor, every nurse, like they were dry kindling. And then the walls caught fire. And the floor.

His whole world was flame and pain.

Denis cried out and jolted upward in bed, wide awake now. He was bathed in sweat. The sheets beneath him were soaked. His heart pounded so fast that he was afraid he was having a heart attack. He stretched out his arm to take his wife's hand, but he realized that he was alone. Gillian was gone. The pillows and sheets on her side of the bed hardly looked slept in at all.

He found the strength to roll his legs out of bed. He stood up unsteadily and went to the bathroom and splashed water on his face, and he ran his wet hands through the thick, wild nest of gray hair on his head. A glass night-light, a gift from his grandson that was painted with the image of a hummingbird, made him look like a shadowy monster in the mirror. His old tanned skin was a web of wrinkles, and dark half moons sagged below his blue eyes. He hadn't shaved in days, leaving him with scraggly stubble. He wore a graying V-neck undershirt that made him look like an old man. The fact is, he was an old man. He was seventy years old, and he could see every one of those years written in his face and feel them weighing down his bones.

It was the middle of the night, but Denis got dressed for the workday. He wasn't going to sleep again. Throughout his life, he'd carefully laid out his clothes for the next day before getting into bed, so his suit was waiting for him. He put on a blue Arrow shirt and wool dress slacks, and he knotted a paisley tie carefully at his neck. He sat down on the bed and bent over with difficulty to tie the laces on his brown leather shoes, and then he slipped his arms into the sleeves of his suit coat. In the bathroom, he tried to tame his hair with a brush. These were the routines that shaped his life day after day, and right now, they were the only thing keeping him sane.

Denis used the railing on the steps to help him as he limped downstairs. The house was cold. The lights weren't on in the living room, but there was enough of a moon to show him Gillian's silhouette in an armchair by the floor-to-ceiling window that looked out on the backyard. Like him, she was dressed. Her posture was rigid. He spotted a glint of crystal in her hand, which was the last thing he wanted to see. It meant she was drinking again. Ten years ago, she'd nearly drunk herself to death before finally emerging from her downward spiral, and since then, not a drop had crossed her lips. Now the bottle was open again, and there was no such thing as a little slip with Gillian. She'd made the decision, knowing what it meant.

"You couldn't sleep?" he murmured in the darkness.

"I don't think I'll ever sleep again." Her voice was harsh.

"Yes, I know. I'm sorry."

He heard the clink of ice cubes as she finished her drink. Languidly, she reached to a bottle of gin on the end table and refilled her glass. It was as if she was daring him to say something, to try to stop her. He couldn't pretend he didn't hate what was happening to her, even if he understood the reasons.

"Drinking isn't the answer," he said.

"Really? Because I think it's the only answer."

"I can take away the bottle, Gillian. Pour it out. I can make sure no one in this town sells you anything. You know that."

"Go ahead."

They both knew it was a hollow threat. Yes, he could try to choke off her supply, but she had her ways around that. The last time, every liquor store in Thief River Falls had been under strict orders to keep the booze away from Gillian Farrell, but regardless, he would find the recycling bin stocked every week with the broken glass of half a dozen empty bottles.

"You're not just hurting yourself by doing this," he said.

"Oh, I'm sorry. Is this hard on you, Denis? Forgive me." The sarcasm in her voice was as hot and sharp as the knife in his dream.

"You can't blame me for what happened."

"I never said I did."

"No? You're acting that way."

"As usual, you make everything about you. This has nothing to do with you."

"It wasn't my fault," he reiterated. "I did everything I could. We both did. In the end, this was up to God."

"Don't talk to me about *God*," his wife snapped. "I don't want to hear about him. Maybe you think you're closer than everyone else, but you're not, are you? All that power over life and death, Denis, and in the end, you're just as impotent as the rest of us."

He shook his head in frustration. "You're not the only one grieving, Gillian. Don't you realize I'm as devastated by this as you are?"

"You? Devastated? When has that ever been the case? You'd have to be human, Denis. You'd have to have emotions."

"That's terribly unfair."

Gillian took another long drink before answering. "Honestly, I don't care about being fair right now."

Denis knew there was no point in arguing with her. She was drunk and going to stay that way. He left her alone with her bottle of gin, and he limped down the hallway to his sanctuary, his library, his office. It was a big room with dark furniture and dark carpet, and it smelled of tobacco and leather. Two walls were made of built-in bookshelves stocked with hardcover first editions that he'd collected throughout his life. A third wall had glass doors that led to the green grass of their backyard and down the slope to a horseshoe bend in the Red Lake River.

He sat behind his huge walnut desk and switched on the brass lamp, which gave a dim yellow glow. An oil painting on the opposite wall mocked him. So did the framed photograph on his desk. Art lasted forever, but people didn't. He took the picture in his hand, stared at it for a while, and then turned it facedown. He put his palms flat on the desk, which was neatly arranged with file folders. There was plenty of work to do, but he didn't have the spirit to do any of it.

Some people dealt with grief by crying. Some ran away. Some, like Gillian, drank their troubles down. Denis dealt with his grief by getting angry. He liked control, he liked power, and grief took those things away. Gillian was right; he felt impotent. When he felt that way, he had a need to strike back at whatever was causing his pain. He had to find someone to blame. Not that it took any of the grief away.

Denis unlocked the bottom drawer of his desk. He kept his most important papers there. His financial accounts, statements, and passwords. The deed to the house. His will, which would need to be changed yet again. He dreaded the thought of another meeting with his attorney, his life's tragic events reduced to a series of codicils.

A gun was in the drawer, too. A revolver, practically antique, with a hardwood grip. It had belonged to his father and then his grandfather before that. Denis stared at it and could almost hear the gun calling to him. He thought about taking it out, caressing the black steel of the barrel, easing back the hammer. He'd always kept it loaded for a circumstance just like this. For the end of the road. He'd never intended to go out slowly, wasting away to nothing, losing control over his body and mind day by day. No, when the time came, this was the way to go about it.

He wondered, Was this the day?

Gillian wouldn't miss him if he left her. Some relationships recover from loss, and some don't, and theirs fell into the latter category. If he asked her about it, she'd probably tell him to do whatever he wanted, but to do it outside, please, where the blood wouldn't get on the carpet and the walls. That was the extent of her concern with whether he lived or died.

No. It wasn't that day yet.

Denis closed the drawer and locked it again. He got up from behind the desk and went to the outside door. His hand-carved walking stick hung on the handle. He opened the door and leaned on the cane as he proceeded into the yard. The grass was sodden below his shoes from the long day of rain. There was a fall chill in the night air, but he didn't bother with a coat.

He never did. He hiked past Gillian's flower garden and past the fire pit and mature oak trees out to the boat dock that jutted into the water. The shifting dock was treacherous underfoot, but he didn't care. He walked to the very end, where the river slouched past him at a lazy pace. He stared into the water and then up at the sky, as if he could find answers there. But there were no answers anywhere. Not tonight.

He took his phone from his pocket. Typically, he kept it powered on all the time, because emergencies were commonplace in his job day or night. But he'd switched it off earlier in the evening and left it that way. He turned it on again by habit, and when the phone acquired a signal, he heard the buzz that told him he had messages. Voice mails. E-mails. Texts. People were trying to reach him, but he had no stomach to talk to them. Everything could wait until daylight. He switched the phone off again and dropped it back in his pocket.

But they wouldn't leave him in peace. He couldn't get away from who he was. Behind him, on the east end of Eleventh Street where he lived, he heard the noise of a car engine, which was unusual in this neighborhood late at night. The car stopped in front of his house. He waited, knowing that whoever it was, they were here for him. Not long after, the beam of a flashlight swept across the backyard.

Denis glanced over his shoulder to see who was there. He saw a young man in a deputy's uniform making his way toward the river. Garrett was his name.

"Mr. Farrell," the police officer called.

Denis didn't answer and made no effort to leave his place by the water. Soon heavy footsteps made the boat dock shudder. The cop came up behind him and then stopped when he was a few feet away, as if awaiting permission to come closer. Denis finally turned around and made an impatient gesture with his cane. He didn't want to be disturbed.

"What is it?"

The cop was stocky and big shouldered like most cops, but he looked ready to sink into the ground. Denis had that effect on people.

Deputy Garrett shifted nervously on his feet, and the sway of the dock nearly threw Denis into the river.

"Be careful!" Denis snapped.

"Yes, sir. Sorry, sir. I apologize for bothering you tonight. I know this isn't a good time."

"What is it?" Denis demanded again.

"We've been trying to reach you," Garrett told him.

"My phone's off."

"Yes, we figured that. I'm sorry."

"So why are you here?"

"Well, I know this is the last thing you need right now, but I'm afraid we have a problem. We thought you should know."

"A problem?"

"It's about the boy."

Denis felt a roaring in his head. "What about him?"

"The thing is, the boy is . . . well, the boy is missing."

Denis blinked. He heard the words but didn't understand them. "Missing? What does that even mean, *missing*? How is that possible?"

"Well, we don't really know yet, but we can't find him. He just . . . disappeared. We've been looking everywhere, but so far, we're not sure exactly what happened."

"How long ago?" Denis asked sharply.

"Several hours," the cop replied.

"*Hours?* And you're only telling me about this now?"

"We didn't want to interrupt you, sir. We wanted to take care of it without worrying you, but given the situation, we all thought that—"

Denis silenced him with a wave of his hand. He closed his eyes, needing to think clearly. His anger flooded back and gave him a focus. "I don't want excuses, Deputy Garrett. This is unacceptable. I don't care what you have to do, but you need to *find that boy*. Am I clear? Find Harlan and bring him back."

6

Lisa flinched with concern when she saw headlights on the highway, but as the car turned and headed up her driveway, she recognized the red Ford Bronco that Laurel March drove. Relief flooded through her at the thought of her friend arriving. She ran to the front door and hurried down the porch steps and greeted Laurel as she got out of the SUV. Lisa threw her arms around her in a tight hug, and Laurel hugged her stiffly back. They stood like that together in the cold for a silent minute.

"Thank you," Lisa murmured. "I really appreciate your coming over here like this. I'm sorry it's so late."

"Don't worry about that," Laurel replied. "I've told you before, I'm always around when you need anything. Day or night. Now let's go inside where we can talk."

"Can I ask you a favor first?"

"Of course."

"Can you park your Bronco behind the house? Where no one can see it from the highway?"

Laurel cocked her head. "Okay, but why?"

"I don't want anyone to know that someone's here if they drive by. I've been keeping the lights off."

Laurel didn't protest or ask for an explanation. She got back into her SUV and started the engine again. Lisa heard the radio boom to life, playing a song she knew called "Little Talks." Laurel routinely traveled all over the northland for her work, and she liked loud music to keep her company as she drove. She could also provide a half-hour analysis of the lyrics of just about any song. Lisa watched Laurel drive the Bronco onto the wet grass and continue past the house until the vehicle was invisible. Then the music shut down, and Laurel walked back to where Lisa was standing.

"There you go. Is that better?"

"Thanks. I know I sound paranoid."

Laurel didn't say anything to that. Lisa kept an arm around her friend's shoulder as they headed into the house. Inside, Lisa locked the front door and led Laurel into the kitchen. They'd sat together in this room many times over the past two years. The only light came from the clocks glowing on her stainless steel appliances.

"Do you want tea?" Lisa asked.

"Sure."

Lisa heated an electric kettle. When the water was boiling, she poured it into two mugs and dropped a pouch of pomegranate tea into each one. She brought the mugs to the wooden table and sat across from Laurel.

"I know I was cryptic on the phone," she said.

"Yes, you were, but I'm here now, so fill me in. What do you think is going on?"

Lisa shook her head. "I wish I knew. A boy showed up outside my house. He's alone and on the run, and I'm pretty sure he's in trouble. He may be caught up in something dangerous."

"Start at the beginning. Tell me everything."

Lisa got up from the table and paced restlessly. She took a minute to gather her thoughts and then told Laurel what had happened in the past few hours. About the police and their guns and their thoughts of breaking into her house. About hunting for the boy in the backyard and finding him hiding in the barn. About his inability to remember who he was or what had happened to him. About the spent cartridge she'd found in his pocket.

When she was done she sat down again, feeling breathless. Her headache throbbed.

"Normally, the first thing I'd do is call the police," Lisa said, "but the boy says the police may be involved in whatever's going on. I don't want to risk doing the wrong thing or talking to the wrong person and putting Purdue in more jeopardy."

"Purdue? As in *Thief River Falls*?"

Lisa gave a short little laugh. "It seemed appropriate."

Laurel nodded, because she understood the irony. She eased back in the chair and sipped her tea without saying anything right away. That was how she always was. She didn't rush in; she didn't speak without thinking through what she was going to say. Laurel conveyed a sense of unflappable calm that Lisa envied, because her own emotions bubbled right below the surface and were always threatening to overflow.

They'd known each other casually for years, enough to say hello and share an occasional lunch. Both of them had worked at the hospital in Thief River Falls, and Laurel still did on a part-time basis. After Lisa's mother, Madeleine, died in the accident, Laurel had offered to listen if Lisa ever needed to talk. Lisa had resisted for a while, but then she'd decided she needed a friend outside the family, and Laurel had proven to be someone with good ears and a kind heart. They'd grown closer as things in Lisa's life got worse.

First her mother.

Then her father. Then her brothers.

Laurel was older than Lisa. She'd turned fifty in July, although she hid it behind careful makeup. She was tall and slightly heavyset, with a long, elegant neck. She kept her hair shoulder length and sandy blond, with bangs all the way across her forehead. Her nose and chin were both sharp and pointed. Her pale eyes were as intense as lasers, and she rarely laughed, no matter how much Lisa tried to draw her out with inappropriate jokes.

The most she ever got from Laurel was a gentle smile and a little shake of her head. They were opposites in most ways, but Lisa had always felt that she could trust Laurel with her secrets and her life.

She watched her friend puzzle through what she'd told her.

"Is Purdue familiar to you at all?" Laurel asked. "Can you describe what he looks like? Does he remind you of anyone?"

"You mean, have I seen him before in TRF? No, I haven't. I've spoken at the school several times, but I don't remember seeing him there. He's a beautiful child. A little small for his age. Sunny blond hair, amazing blue eyes. And such a strange, serious expression all the time. He's a smart one. You can probably tell that I like him. I don't always do well with kids, but Purdue and I seem to click. I guess he brings out the mother in me."

"Is that so bad?" Laurel asked. "You shouldn't run away from that feeling."

Lisa laughed. "Me? We both know I'd make a terrible mother. My books are my kids, and it's better that way."

"I don't know that at all. That's simply wrong."

"You're sweet," Lisa said. She took a sip of tea, but it was already cold.

"The boy," Laurel went on. "Is he here? Where is he now?"

"He's upstairs sleeping. I put him in my bed."

"Can I see him?"

"Sure, but try not to wake him up. I told him I was going to bring over a friend to talk about what we should do next, but I'm afraid he might be frightened to find a stranger in the room."

Laurel got up and left the kitchen. Lisa stayed where she was in the darkness. She listened to the thump of her friend's shoes in the hallway and felt the subtle shifting of the house as Laurel went upstairs. Not long after, the footsteps started downstairs again, and Laurel came back into the kitchen.

"He's a sweet kid, isn't he?" Lisa said. "I don't like to think about what he's been through."

Laurel looked thoughtful as she sat down. "When did you first see him?"

"Right after midnight. I saw the police officers first. There were two deputies from Pennington County, but I didn't recognize them, which is odd. I know pretty much everyone over there. Mostly, I was concerned because they had their guns out."

"Are you sure about that?" Laurel asked. "It was dark. Maybe you didn't see what you think you saw."

Lisa shook her head. "There was a bright moon. I saw it clearly. Seeing the guns made me wonder if they were really cops at all, although the county vehicle looked legit. Anyway, after they left, that's when I spotted Purdue in the yard. I think he may have been hiding from them."

"Did anything else unusual happen today?"

Lisa shrugged. "You mean before now? Not that I recall. I was in Thief River Falls all day. I got home pretty late in the evening."

"What were you doing in town? Where did you go?"

"I was shopping. I still have a long list of things I need for the house. I got back after nine, and then I did a call-in book club with some readers in California."

"Do you remember anything else about the day? Anything at all?"

"No. Look, I know what you're getting at, because that was my first thought, too. I wondered whether Purdue stowed away in my pickup sometime during the day while I was in town, but he says no. He claims he was in a different truck and escaped when it stopped. I also don't think he came here specifically to find *me*. It was just luck that he wandered across the fields and found my house."

"Luck?"

"Well, luck or fate or whatever you want to call it. Anyway, the question is, What do I do with him? The boy's here, and he's all alone. I want to help him. I feel like he needs protection."

"How about we talk to the police together? You and me. There's safety in numbers."

"I appreciate that, but I want to have some idea what's going on and who's involved before I do that. Until then, I think it's better that no one know he's here."

"What about going to the hospital?" Laurel asked. "You know everybody there. They're your friends."

"Sure, but if we take him there, they'll have to report it. Plus, I think he'll run. Hospitals scare him for some reason. He said if he goes there, he'll die. Why would he say that? What happened to him? There are too many mysteries here, Laurel. I want to get some answers before I'd feel comfortable handing him over to anyone else."

"And how do you plan to do that?"

"Honestly, I don't know. That's why I called you. I don't know what else to do, and I don't have anybody else who can help me."

Laurel reached across the table and took Lisa's hand. "Well, I'm glad you called. I'm always here for you. But it's *not* true that you don't have anyone else in your life. You have a brother, too. Have you called Noah?"

Lisa shook her head. "That's not an option."

"When did you last talk to him?"

"Not since he left. You know that."

"So more than a year ago?"

"Yes."

"Has he left messages for you?"

Lisa shrugged. "When he does, I delete them."

"But you still have his number, don't you?"

"Assuming he hasn't changed it. Look, Laurel, I don't even know where Noah is now, and I don't care. He bailed on me. He couldn't deal with it, and he left, and all he did was leave me a note. He didn't even have the guts to say it to my face. He left me to handle everything myself. He's a coward. I never want to see him or talk to him again. Ever!"

Even a year later, her anger was never far away. It was buried below the surface, but not so deep that it couldn't escape.

Laurel was patient and let Lisa's anger soften before she went on. "I'm not excusing what Noah did by leaving. Not at all. But people deal with loss in different ways. Not always healthy ways. Sometimes it's just too much for one person to handle, and they snap. All I'm saying is, you may want to give him another chance. He might surprise you this time. He's still your twin brother. And he was Danny's best friend. I think you should tell him what's going on with you."

Lisa heard a roaring in her head again, as if she might faint. She didn't want to have this conversation about her brother. Not now. Not when she was worried about Purdue. She got up and went to the sink and poured a glass of cold water for herself, and then she stared out the window at the empty darkness. "There's nothing Noah can do for me."

Her friend sighed with resignation. "Okay."

"I'm sorry, Laurel. That's how I feel."

"I know, and I don't blame you for that. I'm just trying to help."

"Thank you."

Laurel got up from the table. "Look, it'll be daylight soon. I'll make a few phone calls and see if I can figure out the best way to deal with this situation. In the meantime, why don't you lay low until I call, okay? The best thing to do is just stay home and stay out of sight."

Lisa came away from the window and gave her friend another long hug. She could feel Laurel hesitate about hugging her back. Her friend didn't deal well with expressions of emotion. "I don't know what I'd do without you," Lisa said.

Laurel separated herself and responded with a tentative smile. "I'll talk to you soon."

"Okay." Lisa took Laurel's arm and held her back before she could leave. "Hey, one more thing."

"What is it?"

"If you're asking questions about Purdue, be careful," Lisa told her. "Don't say too much to anyone else about what's going on. I know you may think I'm crazy, but I really don't know who we can trust."

7

When Lisa went upstairs again, she discovered that Purdue wasn't in bed.

The blankets were rumpled, and his clothes were gone. She checked the bathroom and closet, but there was no sign of him anywhere. She realized that the boy must have slipped downstairs while she and Laurel were talking in the kitchen, and he was so light of foot that they hadn't heard a thing. He was an escape artist who'd escaped again.

Lisa ran back to the first floor. In the foyer, she felt the slightest draft in the hallway that led to the rear of the house. The cool air led her to the back door, which opened onto the empty land stretching for miles behind her property. The door was closed, but the lock was undone, and she could feel a breath of wind through the frame. She opened the door and went outside, trembling in the chill. The breeze swirled her brown hair.

All she could see around her were the barren fields and the craggy trees dotting the landscape like soldiers. Somewhere back there were rivers and roads, parks and railroad tracks, leading as far as Canada. Purdue could be anywhere. There were no footprints this time to give her a clue about where he'd gone. She shouted for him over and over, but got no answer. He'd run away.

In a fog, Lisa went back inside the house. She returned to the kitchen with a heavy heart and made more tea, but she still didn't turn the lights on. There was an emptiness around her now that she hated, and it felt as if it would never go away.

Part of it was losing the boy. Part of it was Laurel's mention of Noah.

Her twin, born six minutes after her. Her brother who, like Purdue, had run away from home and left her behind.

She fished her wallet out of her pocket and took out the handwritten note that was folded inside. She still kept it there. She'd read it a thousand times, and every time it made her angry. She went back and forth between screaming and crying whenever she saw it again.

> *I'm sorry, Lis. It's too much for me. Too much death. Too much grief. I can't deal with the Dark Star anymore. I hate to leave you, but I have to get away from this place. If I don't, I think I'll lose myself completely. Don't hate me, okay?*
> *Noah*

Her brother. A selfish man-child who made everything about him. Not a thought to what it meant to her to go through it all alone. No, she never wanted to hear Noah's voice again. Her family was gone.

"Hey, Lisa."

Her head snapped up. She saw a small figure standing among the shadows in the kitchen doorway. It was Purdue. He was back. She felt a warm rush of emotion, like sunshine pushing away the white clouds.

"Oh my God!" She hurried to him and swept him into her arms. Then she knelt on the floor in front of him and took his hands. "Where were you? Where did you go? I was so worried about you!"

"I hid. I'm sorry."

"I looked everywhere and couldn't find you!"

"I went into that little cottage outside with all the books. I waited there until I saw the other lady leave."

"But why did you hide?"

"She scared me," Purdue said.

"Scared you? No, no, Laurel's my friend. You can trust her. She's one of the good guys."

He frowned. "I was awake when she came upstairs. I pretended to be asleep. I didn't like the way she looked at me."

"How did she look at you?"

"Like she knew who I was."

Lisa's brow furrowed with the tiniest pang of worry. "No, that's impossible. There's no way that Laurel could know who you are. And if she recognized you, she would have told me."

"She knew me, Lisa," Purdue repeated. "I could tell."

"Did she talk to you? Did she say anything?"

"No."

"Well, did you know *her*? Did she look familiar to you at all?"

"No."

Lisa shook her head. "Then believe me—you don't have any reason to be scared of Laurel. She's always trying to figure people out, and that may be why you felt the way you did. That's just how she is. The fact is, she would do anything to help me, and there aren't many people like that in the world. She wants to help you, too."

"She wants to take me away from you. I heard her. She thinks you should give me to the police. I told you, the police want to kill me."

"Yes, I know what you said. Don't worry, I'll stay with you until we get to the bottom of this. The main thing is to keep you safe. We need to find out what happened to you, and then we need to figure out where you come from and get you back to your family."

"I don't have a family," the boy announced.

He said it so simply and quietly that it broke her heart.

"Why do you say that?" she asked.

"Because it's true."

"Did you remember something about who you are?"

"No, I'm just pretty sure my family is gone. That's why I left."

"Left where?"

"Wherever I was."

He was talking in riddles, and Lisa couldn't understand him. But that didn't matter to her. He was back, which was the only thing that was important. She picked up the boy—he felt light as a feather—and put him down in one of the kitchen chairs. Outside the windows, the pink of dawn had begun to wake up the world. She could hear the morning chorus of the birds, all squawking their greetings to the day.

"Do you want some breakfast?" she asked.

"I'm not very hungry."

"Well, I'm going to make bacon and eggs, and I'll bet you get hungry when you smell them."

Lisa puttered in the kitchen, humming as she put breakfast together. Purdue sat in the chair and watched her with the same quiet seriousness he always did. He had his hands folded neatly together in front of him. He didn't say anything at all until the sizzle of bacon had already filled the room.

"I heard you tell that lady that *you* don't have any family, either," Purdue said.

Lisa kept her voice light. "Yes, that's right."

"Why not?"

She flipped the bacon with tongs and cracked eggs directly into a skillet. "Oh, a lot of things happened. It's a long story."

"Was it sad?"

She broke the yolks with a plastic spoon and stirred around the eggs. "Yes, it was very sad."

He nodded intently, processing this information. Breakfast was ready, and Lisa put the meal onto two plates that she deposited on the table. She sat down in her chair and picked up a fork and knife, but she noticed that Purdue wasn't eating at all. She didn't like the fact that he had no appetite. "My eggs are world famous, Special Agent Purdue.

You better try them. And bacon's best when it's crispy, right? I like my bacon almost black."

The boy made no effort to pick up his fork. "What happened?"

"What do you mean?"

"What happened to your family?"

Lisa took a bite of bacon. She picked up a forkful of eggs and then put it back down. "Do you know what it means when somebody dies?"

"Yes."

"Well, that's what happened. They all died."

"How?"

"Different ways. The how isn't really important. They're gone."

"Does it hurt?"

"Yes, it hurts very much."

"How did they die?" he asked again.

She stared at her plate and found that her own appetite had vanished, too. "This isn't something I talk about, Purdue."

"Please?"

"Why is it important to you?"

"Because I like you."

She mustered a smile, but it was hollow. "I like you, too."

"Was your family big?"

"Pretty big. I had four younger brothers, plus my parents. We were all very close. All of us squeezed into one little house in Thief River Falls." She took a deep breath, feeling the Dark Star arrive like a cloud over the sun. "My mom . . . my mom was killed in a car accident two years ago. That was hard enough on all of us, but it turned out to be just the beginning. My father was so sad without my mother that he couldn't handle it. He couldn't live without her. A month later, he—well, he killed himself. Then my youngest brother died in his sleep. He had what doctors call a stroke, which is like a heart attack in the brain. I'm sure it was caused by the stress of losing both of our parents. And three months after that, my two other brothers were driving home in a thunderstorm, and they tried to make it across a flooded road. Their car was washed away, and they both drowned. That was all in the space of six months. Six months took away my whole family."

She heard herself reciting the facts as if the words were coming from someone else. She felt far away, looking down on the room, detached from her body. Oddly, she felt nothing. She'd cried about it so many times that she'd cried herself out and had nothing left but a numbness that never went away.

"I heard you say you still had a twin brother," Purdue murmured.

"Yes. Noah. He left."

"After everybody died?"

"Yes. I bought this house, because I couldn't live in Thief River Falls anymore. Noah lived here with me for a while, but it became too much for him. I think seeing me every day was too much of a reminder of the Dark Star."

"What's that?"

"Oh, that's what he and I called that year. The Dark Star. You know what an eclipse is, when a shadow blocks out the sun? That year was like an eclipse that erased our entire family."

Purdue sat at the table with a little crinkle in his forehead. He seemed to think about everything she said. "So I guess you're lost, too, huh? Like me."

"I guess so."

"I don't like it. Being lost, I mean. I feel like I've forgotten everything important."

"I don't like it, either. The difference is, you won't always be lost, Purdue. You and me, we're going to figure out who you are and where you're supposed to be."

"I don't have any place to be," the boy said.

"You do. Trust me. We all do."

"If we're both lost, Lisa, why can't I just stay here with you? You don't have a family; I don't have a family. I could live here."

He said it earnestly, as if it were the most natural solution in the world. They both needed someone, and they'd found each other. End of problem. Lisa didn't know how to answer him.

"Well, first let's find out who you really are. Right now, you've forgotten everything, but when you remember, you'll probably discover that you have a family who misses you and is going crazy trying to find you."

Purdue shook his head firmly. "No, I think it'll be worse if I remember things. I'm better off forgetting."

"Why do you say that?"

The boy didn't answer. He chewed a fingernail and looked scared.

"Purdue? Did you remember something?"

His blue eyes opened wide, and then he nodded.

"What is it?" she asked. "What do you remember?"

"Voices."

"What did they say?"

Purdue closed his eyes. He put his hands over his ears, as if he were trying to block out the noise from somewhere. *"You saw what he did to her. Make him scream."*

Lisa shivered. "Who were they talking about?"

"I don't know." He opened his eyes again, and his gaze pleaded with her to help him.

Lisa reached into her pocket and removed the spent cartridge she'd found in the boy's jeans. She put it on the table where he could see it. "This was in your pocket. It came from a gun. It came from somebody firing a bullet. Do you remember where you got this?"

He stared at the brass, and she could feel the fear rising in his body. *"No."*

"Is that really true? Or are you just too scared to tell me?"

He was silent, biting his lip.

"These voices you heard," she went on. "Did you see the men who were talking? Do you know who they were?"

"Police."

"Did they have guns?"

"Yes."

"What else do you remember about them? Did any of them fire their guns?"

He was quiet again. Lisa got up from the chair and came around to the other side of the table and sat next to him. "It may be scary, but you're going to have to trust me. We can figure out the truth together, but I need your help. Tell me what else you remember."

He tried to talk, but he choked up, as if he was about to cry. Then he sniffled and wiped his face.

"Fingers," he said in a low voice.

She stared at him in confusion. "Fingers? I don't understand."

"Somebody's fingers were lying on the ground," he told her. "The men cut them off."

8

Laurel had told her to stay home, but Lisa couldn't do that, not after what she'd just heard from Purdue. She wasn't going to stay in the dark, and she wasn't going to wait in the house until the police officers from the previous night appeared on her front porch again. She needed to know what was going on.

"You and I are going to get some answers," she told the boy. "Are you up for that?"

"I think so."

"Okay then. The first puzzle we need to solve is exactly how you got here last night. We're going to work our way backward. That means taking a little drive around the area and seeing if you remember anything. Got it?"

"Got it."

They left the house together and headed across the driveway to her garage. Lisa unlocked the garage door and threw it open on its metal rails. Her pickup was inside, still wet from the previous day's downpour. She undid the flatbed door to let the standing water drain. Inside were bags of sand, a dirty shovel, road salt, a handful of sodden two-by-fours, and an emergency roadside kit in a red plastic shell. In rural Minnesota, you always had to be prepared for the possibility of getting stranded on the back roads far from any help.

Lisa relocked the truck bed and opened the passenger door. "Hop in," she told Purdue.

The boy climbed inside, and Lisa shut the door behind him. She wore her white down vest, and she patted the pocket to make sure her Ruger was safely zipped inside. Then she got behind the wheel and backed the truck out of the garage.

When she reached the highway, she could see for miles. It was just after daybreak on a misty morning, and there was nothingness in every direction. Out here, the earth was flat all the way to the horizon, where the gray land met the gray sky. Railroad tracks paralleled the highway, but there were no trains coming. Telephone wires stretched between an endless series of poles that lined the road like crucifixion crosses. The scrub brush shook in the fields as the wind blew, making a dull kaleidoscope of gold, rust, and washed-out green. She could see small stands of trees huddled together in the far distance. Turning right, the highway led to the border not even half an hour away on the road to Winnipeg. Turning left took her south through places like Strandquist and Newfolden on the way back to Thief River Falls.

The nearest town to her was Lake Bronson, one of those roadside towns that was over almost before it began. It was still several miles north. A river squiggled through the town streets and widened into a lake in the state park two miles east. She'd lived in this area for over a year, but she still didn't know the town well. It wasn't home to her. No place was home anymore.

Lisa pointed toward the railroad tracks. "Do you remember coming this way? Across the train tracks?"

The boy shook his head. "No."

"What about the highway? Did you hike along the highway at all?"

"No, I told you, I came through the fields behind the house."

"All right. There aren't any roads that head directly that way. I'll find the next crossroad and come around on the other side. If anything looks familiar to you, you let me know, okay?"

"Okay."

Lisa headed north. She drove for a mile, seeing no farms or other vehicles coming or going. The clouds spat on the windshield, enough that she had to run the wipers occasionally. Unlike Laurel, she didn't like the noise of the radio distracting her. She preferred silence when she drove. The only sounds were the hum of her tires and the shudder of the wind speeding out of the northern plains.

When she spotted a driveway leading across the railroad tracks to a mobile home sheltered inside a grove of birches, she slowed the truck so the boy could take a look. "What about there? Do you remember that place?"

"No, I don't think so."

"When the truck stopped, were you near a house? Or was it a trailer like that one?"

"A house, I think. It was dark and rainy, and I couldn't really see. I don't remember very well."

"That's all right. We'll keep going."

Lisa accelerated again. The telephone poles sped by beside them. A solitary truck carrying a load of timber passed going the opposite way. Not long after, she reached an intersection at a single-lane dirt road. There were no structures and no traffic nearby, just two empty roads cutting across each other. She turned right, traveling past farm fields that had already been plowed over for the winter season. Fall colors painted the trees that grew along the ribbon of a creek.

"So you write books?" Purdue asked, breaking the silence.

"Yes, I do."

"What kind of books?"

"Thrillers."

"You mean like where people get killed and stuff?"

Lisa smiled. "Sometimes."

"Is it hard to write a book?"

"It's very hard."

"So why do you do it?"

She found herself slowing the pickup, watching the furrows of black dirt in the fields. "Well, I don't really have a choice. That's how my brain is wired."

"What do you mean?"

Lisa pointed out the window. "What do you see out there?"

"Nothing."

She pulled the truck onto the shoulder. Her wheels splashed through the puddles as she drifted to a stop. "No, seriously. Tell me exactly what you see."

Purdue folded his arms together as if he were working on a school assignment. "I see tire ruts, like from a tractor. Mud, because it's been raining. Bits of old cornstalks. Evergreens way far down on the other end of the field. A little bit of smoke going up in the sky, like somebody has a fire. Is that right?"

"Yes, that's right, but that's not what I see."

The boy frowned. "What do you see?"

"I see something pretty scary. Maybe too scary for you."

"No, tell me."

"I see a dead body in the field. A woman. She's wearing a red blouse that makes a splash of color against the black soil. I don't know who she is yet, but I'm wondering who was cruel enough to leave her in this remote place. I see a sheriff's car coming down the highway toward us at high speed. I can see its red lights from a mile away. There's a man inside. He's a good man, a handsome man, but he's afraid, because this woman isn't the first victim, and he knows what he's going to find when he examines her body. An arrow, black, with white feathers, stuck in the woman's mouth and going through the back of her neck into the mud. There's a single word painted on the shaft of the arrow in tiny ancient script like you'd find in an old Bible. The word is *Demon*."

Purdue's mouth hung open. "Seriously? That's what you see?"

"Yup. Scary, right?"

"Yeah, but scary stories are fun. I like them. What does it all mean?"

"I don't know. I won't know until I write the book. But all my life, those are the things I've seen wherever I go. I don't look at the world the way other people do. I live somewhere else. To me, every place turns into stories and crimes and characters and mysteries."

"That sounds pretty cool."

"It is. Although honestly, there are days when I wish I could see nothing but tractor ruts, just like you."

She gave Purdue a grin. With a scrape of rock under her tires, she guided the pickup back onto the dirt road and headed east. Another mile passed. She could see the boy staring through the window, deep in thought, as if he was trying to see the things that she saw. Thriller things. Mystery things. And maybe he could. Children had the gift, the second sight, the sixth sense. Sometimes she wondered if most writers were really just children who'd never grown up.

At the next dirt road, she turned again.

That was when Purdue shouted, "There! That's it!"

Lisa tapped the brakes. She leaned across the pickup, her stare following the direction where the boy was pointing. A quarter mile away, she saw a cluster of farm buildings on the border of an old cornfield. The property had seen better days, the white paint on the house flaking away, an old snowmobile rusting in the unmowed grass. She drove on until she reached the dented mailbox near the road, which bore the name LANCASTER.

In the driveway near the house was a dirty black Volkswagen panel van.

"That's the truck I was in," Purdue said.

"You're sure?"

"Yes, that's it. It was black, just like that. I remember now, the back door was open, so I snuck inside. There was a blanket bunched up in the back, and I hid under it. Then somebody came and slammed the door, and the truck drove away. This is where I got out. Right here."

Lisa studied the farm field, and she could see trees marking the horizon line under the dark clouds a couple of miles away. There were no roads between here and there. She knew what you would find if you took off across the field and kept going through the trees.

Her house.

"Stay here," she told Purdue.

The farm felt deserted, almost abandoned. She turned into the driveway and parked behind the van, and when she got out of the pickup, a fierce wind pushed at her back. A few stray drops of rain landed on her face. She walked toward the house and realized that the quietness of the property was an illusion. Getting closer, she heard wind chimes, and she smelled fresh bread. A dog barked, and then a white Lab bounded across the overgrown grass to greet her. She bent down, letting it get to know her, and the two of them climbed up the porch steps together.

Lisa rapped her knuckles on the frame. A few seconds later, a middle-aged woman pushed open the screen door, letting the dog inside. She stepped outside onto the porch with Lisa. She had graying hair and a pleasant face, and she wore a cream-colored dress with a bright white apron tied around her waist. With the door open, the smell of baking bread got stronger.

The woman smiled. "Can I help you?"

"Are you Mrs. Lancaster?" Lisa asked, remembering the name on the mailbox.

"Yes."

"My name's Lisa—" she began, but the woman stopped her before she could say anything more.

"Oh, I know who you are, Ms. Power. I was actually at a talk you did at the library a couple of years ago. I have to tell you, I just love your books. It's so exciting to see places I know in a bestseller. Especially when we live out here in the middle of nowhere."

"Well, thank you. That's very kind."

"What can I do for you? Are you working on something new? If you need a crime scene, feel free to use our house. Kill anyone you want."

Lisa laughed. "I appreciate the offer. Actually, this may sound like a strange question, but it's about your truck outside. Do you know if it was out on the roads yesterday evening?"

"Oh, yes, my husband does deliveries all around the area. He didn't get back until pretty late."

"Do you know where he was last night?"

"I'm pretty sure his last stop was at the hospital in Thief River Falls."

"The hospital?"

"That's right. Why, is there a problem?"

"No, no problem." Lisa struggled for a lie to explain herself, and then she realized that the only thing that made sense was the truth. "Actually, it's possible your husband had a little stowaway in his truck without realizing it. A child. A boy showed up at my house last night, and I think he may have hidden in the back of your van. Then he headed off across the fields."

"Oh, my goodness! Is he okay?"

"I think so, but I'm trying to figure out where he belongs."

"Is he a runaway?"

"Something like that."

"Well, I wish I could help, but I'm sure Eldred didn't have a clue that the boy was in his truck. He didn't say anything about it. I can't believe the child came all this way and then just wandered off. How terrible. He could have been seriously hurt. I'm so glad he found you."

"Did your husband mention anything unusual going on at the hospital when he made his delivery?" Lisa asked.

"Unusual? I don't think so. Did the boy run away from there? Was he a patient?"

"I'm not sure yet."

"Well, if I can do anything at all to help, please let me know."

"Thank you. I will. I appreciate your time, Mrs. Lancaster."

"Of course. Don't make us wait too long for that next book!"

"I'll try."

Lisa turned to leave, but before she got off the porch, the woman called after her.

"Oh, wait! I don't know what I was thinking! I must be so flustered meeting a celebrity. You asked about anything unusual going on, and I completely forgot about what happened at the house overnight."

"What happened?" Lisa asked.

"The police! The police showed up. I'm surprised they didn't visit your house, too."

"Local police?"

"No, Pennington County, actually."

"What did they want? Were they looking for a boy?"

Mrs. Lancaster shook her head. "No, no, that's not what they said. They told me they were looking for a man. A dangerous man. A fugitive of some kind, I guess. They said they were searching the entire area. We made sure to lock our doors after they were here, I'll tell you that."

"Did they say who this man was?" Lisa asked.

"No, but it makes me wonder if he's connected to this little boy of yours. You better get him in safe hands soon."

"Why do you say that?"

"Well, this man they were hunting for, apparently he's involved in human trafficking across the border. Children! Taking children from their parents! Can you imagine anyone doing something like that?"

9

Human trafficking.

Lisa thought about the police showing up at her house with their guns out in the middle of the night. And about Purdue, injured, escaping from somewhere, with no memory of the trauma that had brought him to her. Maybe the real danger to the boy was from a stranger in the shadows. A criminal, out to recapture a child who'd escaped from his web.

She hiked down the Lancaster driveway back to her pickup truck. When she glanced in the window, she saw that Purdue had drifted to sleep while waiting for her. She got into the truck quietly, trying not to wake him, and she drove out on the empty roads again. She wondered if she'd made a mistake by not going to the police right away. It occurred to her that the best thing to do was to go back home and wait for the two deputies to return and hand the boy over to them.

And yet. And yet.

Something stopped her. Purdue's panic about the police still gave her pause.

Kill the boy.

She continued north for a couple of miles to the next intersection, and then she turned left toward the main highway. But she needed a place to think. When she spotted a dirt road, she slowed and turned, hidden by the cover of the trees. Even the jostling of the truck on the uneven road didn't wake Purdue. She continued until the trees ended at a small swimming pond that she knew well. The weeds near the shore were crushed where others had parked here before her. Out on the water, rain dimpled the black surface. It was getting colder, and she could see a hint of texture in the rain, as if it was threatening to become snow.

Beside her, Purdue twitched like a puppy. She heard him making noises in his sleep, as if he was caught in a bad dream. She reached over and gently put a hand on his knee, but at the barest touch, he jolted awake, screaming. He lashed out with his tiny fists; his legs kicked; his blue eyes were frozen with fear. When he looked at her, she saw no recognition in his eyes. He grabbed for the door handle and was halfway out of the truck when she threw her arms around him and pulled him back.

"Wait! Purdue, wait, it's me, it's Lisa. Everything's okay."

She held him tightly, trying to calm him. He strained against her, as slippery and hard to hold as a snake. Then, slowly, his nightmare yielded. He looked around, at the truck, at the trees, at the lake, at her. His breathing slowed, and he let her ease him back onto the seat of the pickup. The door still hung ajar, wind and rain blowing inside.

"It was just a dream," she told him.

"Yeah."

"Dreams can feel pretty real, but you're all right."

Purdue scrambled across the seat and hugged her around the neck. It was an unexpected gesture, but she liked how it made her feel. Needed. Wanted. Loved. And more than anything, not alone anymore. The stress of her life somehow evaporated in that moment, as if his heartbeat could somehow slow hers down.

"Tell me about your dream," she said.

He let go of her but stayed very close. "It was really bad."

"Well, talking about a dream usually makes it less scary."

"I was being chased," he said.

"By a man?"

The boy shook his head. "By an alligator! A white alligator. All white, big long white teeth, white body, everything white except for these black eyes staring at me. And it was fast. Really fast. I kept running, but it kept getting closer. Its mouth was snapping up and down. He was going to eat me."

"You're right—that's pretty scary. Was it daytime or nighttime in this dream?"

"It was night, and it was cold."

"Do you remember where you were going? Where were you running to?"

The answer seemed to pop into his head. "Home."

"Where's home?"

"I don't know."

She slipped an arm around his shoulder. "Well, don't worry; you're awake now. No more alligators."

He leaned his head into her shoulder, and they sat there quietly. The door was still open, making the truck cold, but she didn't care. The tiny pond in front of the truck had whitecaps. The trees twisted like dancers. Out in the distance of the field, she saw a deer picking its way through the golden underbrush. It looked young, hardly able to stand on its own. She didn't see a mother deer anywhere around.

Lisa thought about Purdue's dream. Something about it made her sad. She realized that she felt a little forlorn hearing him talk about going home. It was good, it was inevitable, it was what had to happen, but it reminded her that at the end of the day, Purdue had a place to be that wasn't with her.

His name, whatever it was, was not Purdue.

"The woman in the house told me some things," Lisa said.

"What did she say?"

"She said her husband's truck made its last stop at the hospital in Thief River Falls. Is that where you sneaked into the back? Is it possible you were a patient at the hospital? Because if you were, then we should get you back there right away."

Purdue shook his head. "People die in the hospital," he told her, which was the same thing he'd said before.

"Yes, I understand, but is that where you were? Did someone take you there after you got hurt?"

"I already told you. I don't know!"

But this time, he looked like a boy who was keeping secrets from her. A boy who was lying. She wondered how much of his memory loss was an act and whether, for some reason, he was hiding what had really happened to him.

"Mrs. Lancaster also told me that the police were looking for a criminal," Lisa went on. "A man who hurts kids and takes them away from their families. Do you know anyone like that? Is it possible you're here because of a man like that? If you remember, it's okay to tell me. Really. He can't hurt you while you're with me."

"But I don't," he protested. "I don't remember."

Lisa let the silence draw out before she said anything more. Then she spoke quietly. "I need to take you to the police, Purdue. It's time. I should have done it last night."

"No!" The boy looked close to crying again. "No, if you do that, they'll *kill* me. I told you!"

"I won't let that happen."

"Don't let me go, Lisa. Please. Keep me with you. I want to stay with you!"

He hugged her again, even more tightly than before, and she melted at the idea that he didn't want to let go of her. She realized that she didn't want to let go of him, either. Not just yet. For now, they would stick together.

"Well, I'd still like to get some more answers about what's going on. If that takes another couple of hours, so be it. I haven't heard anything from Laurel, but I thought of someone else who may be able to help us. I'm going to call him."

"Who is he?" Purdue asked.

"He works for the FBI in Minneapolis. His name is Will Woolwich. I haven't talked to him in a long time, but I think he'll remember me. Back when I was doing research for my very first book, I met with him, and he helped me a lot. He gave me behind-the-scenes information about how they deal with their cases. I was just a nobody then, a wannabe writer, so I was very grateful."

She didn't add that she'd always suspected that Will was interested in her and that his feelings had contributed to the access he gave her. She'd been a young, pretty twenty-seven-year-old back then, sharp witted and sharp tongued. Will was tall, black, and skinny, a former college basketball player. He was handsome in his perfect suit, the way all the feds were. If she'd been available, she might have thought about dating him, but by the time she met Will, she was already engaged to Danny.

Lisa booted up her phone. She'd kept Will in her contacts all these years, although she'd never reached out to him again. She wondered if his number had changed, but when she dialed him, he answered on the first ring.

"Special Agent Woolwich," he said, his silky voice still familiar, still conjuring the image of him in her mind.

"Agent Woolwich," she said with a slight hesitation. "It's Lisa Power calling."

There was a pregnant pause on the line. When he spoke again, she could hear the same thing she'd heard in his voice all those years ago. Interest. It gave her the tiniest spark of satisfaction to know she could still elicit that reaction.

"Lisa Power," Will replied. "Wow, how long has it been? Ten, eleven years now, right?"

"Something like that."

"You've done well for yourself. I'm proud of you. I remember this twenty-something girl telling me all about how she was going to write thrillers for a living, and I thought to myself, *Yeah, we'll see about that.*"

"Well, you were very nice to that girl. You helped me a lot."

"It was my pleasure. I've followed your career, you know. I've read all your books. They're very good."

"Thank you. I'm honored."

"I hear there's going to be a movie, too."

"Next summer, hopefully. Reese tells me the filming is done. She says she's happy with it, so that has to be a good thing, right? I can't decide whether to see it or not. Writers always tend to be the biggest critics when their work shows up on-screen. I don't want to be that person."

"I'll see it and tell you how it is."

Lisa smiled. "Thanks."

"Anyway, I don't suppose this is a social call. What can I do for you? Are you doing research on a new book?"

"No, not this time. Actually, I don't know whether you can help me or not, but I don't feel comfortable going to the local police about this yet. I wasn't sure who else to talk to, so I called you."

His voice turned instantly serious. "What's going on?"

Lisa glanced across the pickup truck at Purdue. "I was wondering if you'd heard anything about a manhunt underway in Pennington or Kittson Counties involving a human trafficking operation. I was told the police are searching for someone. A fugitive of some kind."

"A manhunt? I don't know anything about that off the top of my head, but that wouldn't be my area of focus. I'm mostly in financial crimes these days."

She was disappointed. "Yes, I understand."

"Why can't you talk to the local cops?"

"It's a little hard to explain. The story about the manhunt came from the local police, and I'm just not—I just don't know whether to trust what I've been told."

He didn't push her for details, and she was grateful. "Well, let me look into it, and I'll call you back. It may take me some time to get answers out of the local field office, and depending on what I find, there may well be things I'm not able to share if we're talking about an active investigation. But I'll do what I can."

"I really appreciate it, Will."

"I'll be in touch as soon as I know something more."

"It's very kind of you to help me like this."

"It's no problem."

She waited for him to hang up, but she could hear in his voice that he wasn't done yet.

"One other thing, Lisa," Will added.

"What is it?"

"I know this was a long time ago, and we didn't have a chance to talk back then. I thought about reaching out to you many times, and I'm sorry that I never did."

"I'm not sure I understand."

Will sounded awkward, which wasn't like him at all. "Well, when we met, I remember you said you were engaged. Later, when I got your first book, I saw some of the interviews you did, and I heard about what happened to Danny. About him passing away."

"Oh."

"It sounds like he was quite the hero."

"Yes. He was."

"This is very belated, but I wanted to tell you how sorry I am."

Lisa tried to summon a smile, but it just wasn't there. "Thank you, Will. That's sweet of you. But as you say, Danny died a long time ago."

10

"Who's Danny?" Purdue asked.

Lisa didn't answer right away. Danny's death was part of her past, and there had been so much more loss since then. And yet he was always there with her. Their lives together were like snapshots, photos in her mind of little bits of their history. She saw him wherever she went. Like the pond in front of the pickup where she was now. They'd been here together. When she looked at the water, she still saw herself as a teenager, swimming with Danny and Noah. Drying on towels under the sunshine afterward. Hoping her brother didn't notice that she and Danny were holding hands.

"How about we go down to the little lake?" Lisa said to Purdue.

"Okay."

"Are you warm enough?"

"I'm fine."

They both got out of the truck. She tramped through the weeds, and the boy splashed in the mud the way boys do. Where the pond water slurped around the tall brush, she stopped and put an arm around Purdue's shoulder. He felt small and vulnerable with those skinny bones of his. The wind whipped his blond hair, and the mist made his face shine. He pointed at an eagle overhead, making high circles above the fields. They both followed its progress as the circles got bigger and wider, until the bird was just a tiny dot lost in the clouds.

"I met Danny in high school," Lisa told him, when she was finally able to talk about it. "He was a year older than me, but I knew who he was. All the girls did. My brother Noah went out for the baseball team, and Danny was a pitcher. He and Noah became friends, and so Danny and I became friends, too. The three of us started doing everything together. Every evening, every weekend, we'd be hanging out. I don't really remember when Danny and I started to become more than friends. But at some point, we knew we were in love. We had lots of plans. Get married. Have kids."

"Did you?" Purdue asked.

"Well, life is a little more complicated than that. We went to different colleges after high school, and we broke up. We didn't see each other for several years."

"Why?"

Lisa shrugged at the bad memories. "Danny's father had big plans of his own for Danny. College, law school, politics. Danny was supposed to be going places, maybe even Congress or governor someday. He didn't want any of that, but you don't say no to Danny's father. I told Danny he had to make a choice, either me or The Plan. He chose The Plan, at least for a while. He went to law school, got a job as a lobbyist at a big firm in Minneapolis. He was on his way. I became a nurse at the hospital in Thief River Falls. I lived with my parents and wrote books. I didn't sell any of them, but I kept writing."

"So what happened?"

"On my twenty-seventh birthday, Danny showed up at our door," Lisa said. "He'd quit his job and moved back to Thief River Falls. He'd begun training to be a firefighter, which was what he'd really wanted to do since we were in high school. A few months later, we were engaged. We rented a house next to my parents, and we moved in there. I don't suppose I'll ever be that happy again."

Purdue had a child's gift for picking up on emotions. "Don't be sad, Lisa."

"Oh, I'm okay."

"Danny's father must have been mad."

"Yes, he was," Lisa agreed. "He was unhappy with Danny, but mostly he was angry at me. As far as he was concerned, *I* was the one who screwed up his plan. The fact that Danny never wanted it didn't matter to him. Danny came back here for me, so that meant it was my fault. Everything that happened afterward was my fault, too. He blamed me when Danny died. In his mind, I'm the one who killed his son."

"Why would he think that?"

She closed her eyes, feeling haunted. "Because I let Danny go."

"Go where?"

Lisa smiled. If she didn't smile, she would cry again, even after ten years in between. She could still picture that last morning with Danny so clearly, in the little bedroom in the house next door to her parents, with the sunlight making a dusty stream through the window. They'd made love in the middle of the night, with their bodies moist from the sticky August air and the crickets keeping time with their rhythm. She remembered him getting out of bed. He'd let his golden hair grow long, and she liked it that way. She could see the definition of his muscles, the ripples in his chest, the flex in his arms and legs. He was in the best shape of his life. Strong. Ready for anything.

"There was a fire in California," Lisa explained. "Danny volunteered to help."

"Was it dangerous?"

"Very."

"Were you scared?"

"I was terrified," Lisa said.

She thought about the video of the fires outside Bakersfield. The towering flames as tall as dragons. Ash falling over a thousand miles. The scorched trees, the wreckage of homes, the blackened hillsides. Fire was a wily, malevolent enemy. The love of her life was getting ready to strap on his gear and head into an inferno.

"If you were so scared, why did you let him go?" Purdue asked.

It was such a simple question. Why?

She'd asked herself that same question a thousand times. It would have been so easy to make him stay. Two words, that was all she'd needed. Two words, and he would never have left her side. She'd been so close to telling him: *Don't go.* But he was determined, he was excited, and she wasn't going to stand in his way.

"I was scared, but Danny wasn't scared at all," she said. "He told me not to worry. He said the time would fly by. I'd be busy with the plans for the wedding. We were getting married two months later. He was sure I'd be busy with publishers, too. My first book was out with an agent, and he was convinced I'd get a deal soon. He was so supportive of my dreams. He believed in me even when I didn't believe in myself. So I had to do the same for him. I couldn't take him away from something he really wanted to do."

"He left? He went to fight the fire?"

"Yes, he did."

She saw their last moments together in her head. She remembered him coming back to bed and sitting next to her on the rumpled sheets. Lacing his fingers tightly with hers. Kissing her, a soft kiss that became long and passionate. They'd both smiled, but their smiles were fake. And then he'd walked away from her. Letting go of him was the hardest thing she'd ever done.

Two words. She should have made him stay.

"What happened to him?" Purdue asked.

"Danny was in California for a month. He could have gone home, but he volunteered to stay when a new fire broke out. People said it was growing like a monster. It was bearing down on this neighborhood in the hills, and he stayed in the area longer than he should have to make sure that everyone got out. Everyone did, because of him. But not Danny. The fire jumped ahead of him and trapped him."

Purdue frowned. "I'm really sorry, Lisa."

"Yeah. Me too." She felt her eyes fill with tears again; she couldn't hold them back. "Danny's father barely spoke to me after that. He blamed me for losing him. He said I could have stopped him from going, and he's right. I let him go."

"It wasn't your fault."

"No. But there's a lot I would have done differently if I had the chance. While he was gone, my agent called. Danny was right. She'd sold my first book. And I didn't tell him. I didn't want to give him the news over the phone. I wanted us to be together. I had so much to tell him when he was back, and I wanted to make it a big surprise. So I waited. That's what I have to live with. I waited, and I never got to tell him about anything."

11

As soon as Lisa turned off the highway onto the main street in Lake Bronson, she felt eyes watching her from every direction. There were no secrets and no strangers in a small town. Two older women at the doors of the Covenant Church leaned in and whispered to each other as they spotted her pickup. A farmer standing outside the town's grain elevators took a cigarette out of his mouth and twisted his whole body to follow her as she drove by. Across the street, a man pumping gas at the Cenex station tapped his baseball cap with a nod of recognition. She didn't know any of them, but they knew her.

That's Lisa Power.

It wasn't just because of her books. People knew her because of the Dark Star, too. She was a local celebrity stalked by tragedy.

"I need to get some cash," Lisa told Purdue. "I'll pick up drinks and sandwiches for us at the market. Do me a favor, and stretch across the seat while I'm inside, okay? I don't want anyone to see you."

"Okay."

Her truck bumped across two sets of railroad tracks. She saw the sign for the town grocery ahead of her, just a small building with the word MARKET hung over the door. She'd visited the store once before on a last-minute quest to buy Betty Crocker mix for a chocolate birthday cake. Four cars were parked on the street outside, practically an overflow crowd for the tiny market. She pulled past the building and parked near an open patch of land adjacent to an auto repair shop.

She whispered to Purdue. "Remember what I said. Stay out of sight."

Lisa climbed out of the pickup into the cool late-morning air. She shivered a little in the wind and brushed her brown hair away from her face. She blinked nervously as she peered at the quiet neighborhood. In the doorway of the auto garage, a teenager in grease-smeared overalls looked up from the engine of a Ford Explorer. He gave her a salute with the business end of a wrench.

"Hello. You're Miss Power, aren't you? The writer woman?"

Another stranger who knew who she was.

She hoped her smile didn't look as awkward as it felt. "Yes, hello."

Lisa hurried away, uncomfortable with being under a spotlight. She stole glances around her as she walked, but didn't see more spies. A young woman unloading packages in front of the post office didn't notice Lisa. The local bar down the cross street was deserted except for an empty white Chevy Malibu parked outside. She saw two old men near the American Legion building, but they were in the midst of a loud argument and didn't look in her direction.

She ducked inside the small market, where the jingle of a bell on the door drew everyone's attention. Her arrival shut down the conversations at the cash register. The heavyset, bearded man behind the counter, who wore a blue-checked apron over his sweater and khakis, stopped as he was scanning the price on a can of soup. His customers stared at her with uncomfortable looks of surprise. Lisa felt a flush rise in her face.

"You're Ms. Power, aren't you?" the cashier asked, smoothing his thick beard. "Anything I can help you with?"

"I just need a few things. Do you have an ATM?"

"It's at the back of the store," he told her.

"Thank you."

"It's nice to see you here, Ms. Power," one of the women in the checkout line added. She carried a two-year-old toddler in her arms, who squirmed to get free and run around the store. "I'm sure you hear this a lot, but I'm waiting impatiently for your next book."

"So's my publisher," Lisa said, bending her lips into another tentative smile and disappearing down an aisle stocked with cereal boxes and bags of tortilla chips and pretzels.

Behind her, the silence erupted into whispers. The talk was all under their breath, but Lisa pricked up her ears and could hear fragments of words near the counter.

The police were here.

Did you hear about the boy?

Maybe she needs help.

She was shocked to realize that they knew what was going on, and then she remembered that it was her own fault. She'd told Mrs. Lancaster about Purdue, which was enough to start rumors racing around town like a 5G wireless signal. They were all good people with good intentions, but Lisa knew where good intentions typically led. Soon the whole town would know exactly where she was, and she didn't like that.

Lisa stopped in front of the ATM machine. She reached into her pocket for her wallet, but as she took it out, she found that her hands were trembling so badly she could hardly function. It took her several tries to pry the bank card from the slot in her wallet, and when she finally got it out, the card slipped from her fingers and fell to the floor. She picked it up, inserted the card into the machine, and then managed to key in the wrong security PIN and had to start over. When the machine spat the card out, she dropped it again, and she felt like a fool, as if everyone were watching her go to pieces.

Eventually, she managed to take out two hundred dollars and shove it into her wallet. With the transaction done, she exhaled with relief and embarrassment. Then she turned around, and a little cry shot from her mouth. She jumped back in fear.

She wasn't alone.

A man stood behind her, way too close.

Lisa heard words tumbling out of her mouth, but she wasn't really sure what she was saying. "Oh! Oh, I'm so sorry, are you waiting for the machine? I was taking forever. You must think I'm an idiot. Anyway, I'm done, it's all yours—sorry about that."

The man had fire-red hair, and his hard face was devoid of expression. Lisa realized that she was still blocking the ATM.

"I guess it would help if I moved!" she exclaimed, as she shoved her wallet back in her pocket and headed for the next grocery aisle. The man had his bank card ready in his hand, and he pushed it into the machine slot without another glance at her.

Lisa lingered in an aisle stocked with canned vegetables, and she cast a discreet eye at the man at the ATM. He was medium height and strongly built, probably in his thirties. He had pale skin that was almost ivory white and wore his blazing red hair cut very short, with matching stubble on his chin and upper lip. Tiny circular sunglasses with auburn lenses hid his eyes. She could see an array of odd scars on his forearms, like cuts made by a razor blade. Despite the chill of the day, he wore jeans and nothing but a tight-fitting white T-shirt.

He never looked over at her. Not once. And yet his presence enveloped her like a cloud of menace.

Lisa rushed to gather up what she needed. She chose a couple of prepackaged sandwiches from the refrigerated deli area and a bag of spicy chips and two cans of Coke. Balancing all of it in her hands, she ducked back to the end of the aisle again for another quick glance. The man at the ATM was gone. She checked the next aisle, and the next aisle after that, but she didn't see him anywhere. He'd disappeared, but she hadn't heard the jingle of the market door.

Where was he?

Out of instinct, as the hair on the back of her neck stood up, Lisa spun around. There he was, not even six feet away, staring at her from behind his sunglasses. As soon as he saw her turn, he switched his gaze to the shelves, focusing on diapers and baby formula. But he didn't strike her as a man with a baby. No, he was watching her, and now he knew that she was watching him, too.

Lisa brought her items to the cash register. The people who had been there when she came into the store hadn't moved, and their conversation died away again as they saw her. They cleared a path for her to check out, and as the cashier scanned her items, she glanced over her shoulder to see if the man in the auburn sunglasses was following her. She didn't see him, but she knew he hadn't left the store. She paid in cash and waited impatiently as the bearded cashier bagged what she'd purchased.

"Here you are, Ms. Power," he said. And then, as he watched her look toward the back of the store for the tenth time, he asked, "I don't mean to pry, but is everything okay?"

"What? Oh, yes."

"Are you sure? I mean, we heard that—"

"Everything's fine!" she said lightly, interrupting him, because she didn't want any mention of Purdue with the ginger-haired man hovering within earshot. "It's just one of those days where I feel like I've forgotten something. I don't want to have to make another trip back here later. Anyway, this is a very nice store. I'm sorry I haven't been in here more before now."

"Well, we'd love to see you anytime."

"Thank you!"

Lisa bunched the plastic bag in her fist, smiled pleasantly at the other customers, and pushed through the door with another clang of the bell. She ducked her head into her chest and walked quickly down the sidewalk toward her pickup. She was almost at the truck when she heard the bell jingling again, but she didn't look behind her. She knew who it was. She knew it was him. She practically ran for her door, climbed inside, and fumbled with the key to start the engine.

Next to her, Purdue began to get up, but she hissed at him. "No, not yet, stay down, stay down!"

She swung the wheel and pulled away from the curb. As she did, she stole a glance into the truck's rearview mirror. She could see the ginger man in front of the market door, following her truck as she drove away. He had something in his hand. A phone. She didn't want to seem in a hurry, but as soon as the road curved and the market disappeared from sight, she accelerated hard. At the next intersection, she made a sharp right turn.

"What's going on?" Purdue asked from the floor of the truck.

"Stay down; I'll tell you in a minute."

She turned into the first driveway on the cross street and steered the truck behind a green farmhouse, where it was invisible from the road. She got out of the truck and ran back to the corner of the house, giving her a view toward the road through a band of trees. She didn't have to wait long. A few seconds later, a white Malibu sped into view. It slowed at the intersection, and from where she was, she was able to recognize the man with the auburn sunglasses at the wheel. He paused, studying the cross street, and she ducked out of sight until she heard his engine gun. When she looked back, she saw the sedan disappearing eastward at high speed.

Lisa jogged back to the pickup. She headed the other way in the truck, back toward the main north-south highway.

"Okay, come on up," she told Purdue.

The boy clambered into the seat again. "What happened? Why did I have to hide?"

"There was a man in the market. I didn't want him to see you, and I was worried that he might be following me."

"Was he?"

"Maybe. I'm not sure. If he was, hopefully I lost him." She stared across the truck at Purdue. "If I describe him to you, can you tell me if he sounds familiar to you? Like you know him from somewhere?"

"Okay."

"A muscular man, not too tall. Very pale skin, short red hair, red beard. Scars on his forearms."

Purdue said nothing, but the color vanished from his face.

"Purdue?" Lisa asked urgently. "Are you okay?"

"He was one of the men. He was there."

"You know him? Who is he?"

"The other men called him Liam. He looked just like you said."

"There were other men? What do you remember about them?"

The boy's brow furrowed as he tried to puzzle it out. "There were four of them. Two policemen. They had uniforms and badges. And an old man. He was the boss. But the man with the red hair was there, too."

"Where?" Lisa asked. "Where did this happen? Where were you?"

"By the water," Purdue replied. "I remember we were all by the water. That's where they killed the man."

12

Lisa leaned over the bridge railing above the torrent surging through the Lake Bronson Dam. The current erupted into white foam as it squeezed into the narrow channel of the river. The noise was as loud as thunder. She held Purdue's hand and watched his face, which looked awestruck at the tumbling water. That was the strange balance of being a child. One minute you could be remembering something terrible, and the next you could be staring at a river without a care in the world.

They wandered to the south end of the bridge. The reservoir on the other side of the dam was calm and gray. The cold rain from the clouds had begun hardening into sleet. Her pickup was parked not far away in one of the campgrounds of the state park.

"What do we do now?" Purdue asked as they crossed the road.

"We'll hang out here until Will calls me back," Lisa replied. "Depending on what he says, we can decide what to do next."

"Are you scared?"

"Scared? No, why should I be scared when I've got a big strong man like you to protect me?"

Purdue giggled.

She led him past an empty fishing dock that jutted into the quiet water, and then they followed a path into the trees, which were a palette of reds and yellows. The rain was lighter in the woods, but the shadows around them made the afternoon in the park feel like night.

As they walked, she tried to wrest more details out of Purdue's memory.

"So you saw someone's fingers being cut off," she said.

"Yes."

"And now you remember someone being killed near the water. Was it the same person?"

"I think so."

"Man or woman?"

"Man."

"Do you know who he was?"

Purdue shook his head.

"Did you see his face? Do you know what he looked like?"

"Well, it was dark. He was pretty big, like a football player."

"So this happened at night?"

"Yes."

"Was it last night? The night you came to me?"

"I think so."

"And did you actually see this man being killed?"

"Yes."

"That must have been terrible. Can you tell me what happened?"

Purdue nodded. His face was serious, as it usually was. He related the events in a detached, emotionless voice, which made what he said even more horrifying.

"They stuffed something in the man's mouth so he couldn't scream," he told her. "Then I watched them cut off his fingers one at a time. All of them. The man with the red hair did that. Liam. He had a big pair of clippers, and one of them would put each finger between the blades and hold it there. The man tied to the tree kept trying to get free, but he couldn't. There was all this blood."

Lisa tried to hold back the nausea she felt. "The man was tied to a tree?"

Purdue nodded. "Uh-huh."

"Where?"

"By the water."

"A lake? A river?"

"I don't know. I'm sorry, I just see bits and pieces. I was hiding by the water."

"That's okay. What happened next?"

"They killed him."

"How did they do that?"

"The white alligator shot him in the head."

"The alligator? Like in your dream?"

"Yes."

"I don't understand, Purdue."

"It was a man who did it, but when I see him in my head, I don't see a person. All I see is the alligator. A white alligator."

"Okay," Lisa said, although she didn't know exactly what the boy meant. "Tell me more. What happened after that?"

"The old man came down to the water. He saw me there. He called for the others, and they dragged me back to the tree. They sat me down on the ground, and that was where I found the bullet. I just held on to it."

"But you don't know where you were?"

Purdue shook his head. "No."

"How did you get there? How did you find these men?"

"I don't know that, either. I was just there. I don't know where I came from."

"And then what happened?"

"Kill the boy."

"Who said that? The red-haired man? Liam?"

"No. The old man."

Lisa briefly closed her eyes. "Did they hurt you?"

"I think they hit me with something. That's when I stopped remembering things. It's like I fell asleep and didn't wake up. Not until I was in the back of the truck." He gave her another serious stare. "I don't want to go back there, Lisa."

"You won't."

They reached the end of the wooded trail. Her pickup was waiting for them in the middle of a grassy camping area studded with fire pits and picnic benches. Glimpses of the lake came and went behind the trees. No one else was around, just birds flitting through the branches and a few squirrels playing a game of chase. She and Purdue had already eaten lunch, and there was nothing to do now but wait. Wait for Will to call. Wait for someone who could lead them out of this nightmare.

A torture scene in the woods. A murder.

And a boy who could only remember fragments of what he'd seen.

She opened the door of the pickup, and Purdue climbed inside. Before she closed the door, she told him, "Stay here. I have to use the bathroom. I'll be right back."

"Okay, Lisa."

She shut the door with the boy inside. She checked the area again to make sure they were alone, and then she headed across the campground to a primitive toilet fifty yards away. It was just a portable plastic unit that gave off a foul smell when she opened the door. She wasn't inside long. Not even a couple of minutes. She heard nothing while she was there, just the tap of rain on the roof of the toilet drowning out all the other sounds around her. When she came out, her gaze automatically went straight to her pickup, and her heart skipped a beat.

The passenger door hung open. The seat was empty.

"Purdue!"

Lisa sprinted for the truck. She skidded to a stop on the wet grass and dove inside to see if the boy was hiding in the pickup. She checked the rear seat and then the flatbed, but he wasn't there. Frantic, she got out and surveyed the campground. She eyed a bare patch of dirt near the truck that was mostly mud. There, she saw two sets of footprints, both running away toward the path that led to the lake. One set was small. A boy's tracks. The other was larger and obviously belonged to a man.

Purdue was being chased.

Lisa unzipped the pocket of her white vest. She took out her Ruger and then loaded it with the clip. She kept the gun in her hand as she ran toward the lake, following the footprints. They led her to a dense patch of forest where the trees grew thick and dark and overgrown brush encroached on the trail. The mud turned to brown grass, and the tracks that were guiding her disappeared. As the wind blew, colored leaves floated in the air. She slowed, shifting her gaze to peer into the woods on both sides. Her breathing came fast, but she tried to hold it in to listen. She walked slowly now, step by step. The sweat on her hand made the butt of the gun slippery.

The trail broke from the woods near a sheltered section of the lake, a little inlet where a field of cattails grew out of the water. She saw a dead tree along the shore, its bare branches haunted by a dozen crows squawking an alarm. It was as if they were beckoning her, telling her to go that way. The grassy trail followed the waterline, and she hugged the lake for at least a hundred yards, cold rain landing on her face. The water was on her right, and a wall of elderberry bushes was on her left. She murmured Purdue's name under her breath every few steps, hoping he was hiding nearby, hoping he could hear her.

But she was alone.

Ahead of her, the trail forked. One direction stayed with the water; one turned away from the lake and disappeared into the shadows of the forest, as if it were the mouth of a cave. She headed into the woods. She had no idea if she was going the right way. She wished she could hear something, some clue, that would tell her where he was. Anything.

Then her wish came true in the worst way.

The crack of a gunshot rocked the park, echoing in the trees. The crows flew airborne with startled cries. Lisa's heart sank with despair, and at the same time, murderous rage bloomed in her chest. If anyone had harmed her boy, if she'd lost him forever, if she'd failed him—

Suddenly, footsteps stampeded from the forest ahead of her. She could hear branches breaking, weeds trampling, the panic of someone getting closer and closer. She froze with indecision, the gun poised in her right hand. She wiped rain from her eyes to help her see better. Something moved, a flash of color. And then the boy was right in front of her. Where the trail curved, Purdue sprinted toward her, his hair flying, his face screwed up with terror.

He ran right into her open arms. She scooped him up and held him, but there was no time for desperate relief. More footsteps were coming fast. Heavy footsteps. She pushed through the wall of elderberries beside her, with her arms still wrapped around the boy. The branches scratched her face and made a deep, painful cut across her collarbone. She buried herself in the foliage and sank to her knees, hoping the camouflage of the brush made them invisible. She clapped a hand over Purdue's mouth and put a finger to her lips to silence him. She could feel his hot breath on her palm and feel his chest going in and out as she held him tightly. The blood pulsed on her shoulder.

She put her mouth to his ear and murmured, "Shhhh . . ."

The footsteps slowed as they got closer. Purdue shook with fear, and she was afraid he would rattle the branches and give them away. Through the dense elderberries, she could see a sliver of the man's face and body. It was the ginger man, the man from the market, the torturer who had cut off someone's fingers. Liam. His hand held a fierce black pistol, and she could smell smoke leaching from the barrel. He stopped directly in front of them on the trail, almost close enough to touch if she reached through the branches. She was conscious of the stark whiteness of her vest, but the leaves were packed thickly together, hiding them. He was in the light, and they were in the darkness.

Purdue had his eyes closed. His face was pressed against her chest.

Lisa watched and waited. The man could feel their presence, because he didn't move. His gun was level at his hip, ready to fire. The slightest sound would betray them, and she didn't know how long the boy could stay still.

Then, from deep in the woods, something rescued them. A bird. A rabbit. A deer. An animal of some kind rustled the brush, and the man heard it and ran back the way he'd come. When he was gone, Lisa bolted from cover. There was no hiding the sound as she broke free of the elderberries, but she hoped the man was too busy running to hear them. She picked up Purdue, and he clung to her neck and wrapped his bony legs around her waist, and she ran. The boy wasn't heavy, but she couldn't go fast, and she couldn't even look behind her to see if the man was laying chase. She stumbled along the trail, past the dead tree and the crows, past the lakeshore and the cattails, through the mud and into the clearing where her pickup was parked.

The passenger door was still open. She piled Purdue inside and dashed to the opposite door to get in. She cast one last look behind her, and there was the red-haired man breaking from the muddy trail. She turned on the engine and jammed down the accelerator, making the tires scream and the chassis swerve as they shot away from him. He ran after them, then stopped to raise his gun and aim it at the back of the truck. She cried out and grabbed Purdue's shoulder and pulled the boy down, but the gunshot went wild.

She sped through a curve on the access road, leaving the man behind her. Not even half a mile later, she swerved out of the park at high speed. The man's white Malibu was parked on the opposite shoulder of the road near the dam. She hit the brakes hard and screeched to a stop right next to the car. She rolled down her window. Trying to keep her arm steady, she pulled back the slide on her Ruger and pointed the gun out the window, aiming at the left front tire of the Malibu.

She squeezed off a shot.

And missed.

And then another shot. This time, the tire exploded, and the car jolted downward, its rim clanging against the asphalt. She eyed the mirror one last time. The man was behind her again, running. He sprinted for them down the middle of the park road, but he was too far away to fire, and he wasn't going anywhere in his sedan now.

Lisa rolled up the window. The interior of the pickup smelled burnt from the gunfire. She floored the accelerator, and they took off down the highway into the freezing rain.

13

Five miles passed in a haze before Lisa's emotions got the better of her and she broke down. She felt utterly unprepared for what was happening to her, but she couldn't allow herself to feel that way for long. She had to let it out and move on. She pulled off the dirt road, cupped both hands over her face, and sobbed. Her shoulders shook as fear and relief poured out of her. Her neck stung with pain, and when she looked down, she realized that the cut across her collarbone was still bleeding and had made a crimson stain as it soaked through her shirt and into her white vest. Seeing the blood brought a wave of nausea.

She felt like a different person. A changed person. Hiding in the elderberries, watching that man hunting for Purdue, she'd realized something frightening about herself. She was capable of violence. She was capable of killing, just like the people she wrote about in her books. If that man had come for the boy, she would have pulled the trigger. She was prepared to defend this child with her life if she had to. And she would take the life of anyone who got in her way.

"I'm sorry."

Next to her, Purdue's voice was full of misery.

Lisa wiped her face and tried to get hold of herself. She looked across the car and could hardly see Purdue through her tears. He was a boy made up of watercolors, the paint running in the rain. "You? You don't have anything to feel sorry about."

"This is all my fault."

"No. Don't say things like that. I don't know whose fault it is, but it's not yours."

Her words didn't seem to give him any comfort. She understood. The worst things in the world could happen to a child, and they would take it all on themselves. It didn't matter where the evil came from. A bad man. A terrible accident. A cruel disease. A child could be on his deathbed and still apologize for the pain in someone else's face. *Don't be sad . . .*

"You need to send me away," he told her. "I should go."

"No. Absolutely not."

"All I'm doing is causing you trouble."

Lisa cupped his chin with her hand and spoke slowly to try to get him to hear her. "That's not true. I don't want you feeling that way."

He shook his head. "Why are you helping me?"

The thought sprang into her mind: *Because I need to be saved every bit as much as you.*

But she didn't say that.

"Because you need help," Lisa replied. "That's what my mother taught me. If someone needs help, you drop everything, and you help them. Just like you hope they would do for you."

"But what are we going to do?" the boy asked. "They're trying to kill me. That means they'll kill you, too. I don't want that."

Lisa stared through the sleet at the miles of empty fields. This remote region, so bitter and harsh, had always been home to her, but at this moment, it felt like foreign ground.

"We're leaving," she said.

"For where?"

"I'm not sure yet, but it's not safe to stay here anymore. We need to get out of this place. I need a couple of minutes at home to get a bandage on my neck and change clothes, and then we'll hit the road. How does that sound?"

A smile crept onto the boy's face. "That sounds good."

"Okay, then."

Lisa checked her mirror, then steered from the shoulder onto the lonely dirt road. They didn't have far to go. Two more miles led them back to the highway that went past her house. She turned into the teeth of the precipitation that streaked from the sky. It was getting colder, and the pavement already felt slippery under her tires. She drove south with the railroad tracks and the telephone poles keeping her company.

When she was a quarter mile from her house, she drifted to a stop in the middle of the highway lane. There was no traffic in either direction to be concerned about. She leaned forward, trying to see her house, wanting to make sure no one was waiting for them. If the police had come back, they'd already been there and left again. The land was empty. Her house looked sterile and abandoned.

"I think the coast is clear," she told Purdue. "This won't take me long."

She turned into the driveway and drove until the truck was immediately outside her front porch. She turned off the engine. "Do you need to use the bathroom?" she asked the boy.

"No."

"You're sure?" she said with a smile.

Purdue nodded.

"Okay, well, we'll need to stop for gas along the way. I'll be right back."

Lisa got out of the pickup. The sleet nipped at her face like a pack of mosquitoes. She climbed the porch steps, and then she removed her keys from her pocket as she walked to the front door. Before she could put the key in the lock, she noticed that the door wasn't latched.

It was open an inch, rattling in the wind.

Had she left it that way? She didn't always remember to lock her front door, but she was certain she had done so this time.

"Hello?" she called, slowly pushing the door inward. "Is anyone there?"

There was no point in being coy. If someone had broken in, they'd already seen her arrive. But no one answered. The house was cool and quiet, just the way she'd left it. Even so, there was a smell inside that wasn't right. A hint of body odor. Someone had been there while she was gone. When she studied the hardwood floor, she could see that wetness had been tracked inside by someone's shoes, and the puddles hadn't had time to dry.

Lisa debated turning around and leaving immediately, but if her intruder had already come and gone, she decided she had time to deal with her wound. She ran upstairs to her bathroom and peeled off her vest and top. The blood from the cut on her neck had made a sticky mess from her collarbone all the way across her right breast, and she used a damp towel to clean herself. Quickly, she disinfected and dressed the cut itself. In her bedroom, she put on a new bra and a flannel shirt and deposited a few necessities from her dresser in a travel bag. The whole process took barely five minutes. She went to the kitchen, grabbed a box of power bars and some cheese sticks from the refrigerator, and then found a red leather jacket in her hall closet to replace the vest. She slipped her gun inside the pocket and went back outside. She made sure to lock the door behind her.

She hurried down the porch steps and across the gravel to the pickup, where she threw the bag behind her seat. Then she got in quickly and started the engine again. Her anxiety was on her face, and she knew Purdue could see it, but she didn't say anything about what had happened. She put the truck in reverse and backed into a three-point turn, but as she did, she heard a low warning from the boy next to her.

"Lisa, *look*."

She glanced out the driver's window.

A police car was turning off the highway.

Her fear spiked as she recognized the vehicle. It was the same black SUV she'd seen overnight, from the Pennington County Sheriff's Department. They were trapped, with no way to escape.

"Get down," she instructed Purdue. "Don't let them see you."

"What are you going to do?"

"I don't know, but I won't let them hurt you. Now stay out of sight."

Lisa got out of the truck before the police SUV got close to her. She walked toward the narrow ribbon of her driveway. She was conscious of the weight of the Ruger in her jacket, and when she shoved her hands in the pockets, she slipped her palm around the butt of the gun. The black SUV stopped in front of her, blocking the way. She could see the deputies through the windshield.

Two men got out. They wore chocolate-brown uniforms from the sheriff's department and flat-brimmed hats. She hadn't been able to make out the faces of the cops who'd visited her house overnight, but she was sure that these were the same men. They had the right look.

One of the cops approached her, and one stayed by the door of the SUV. They looked about the same age—midtwenties—but the driver, who was heading her way, was clearly the one in charge. He took off his hat; his big head was bald. He was bulky, with the thick-necked build of a wrestler. He was clean shaven, and he had jutting ears and narrow, squinting eyes. His mouth didn't smile; instead, his lips pushed together into a thin line.

"Ms. Power?" the man said in a voice that had no inflection. "I'm Deputy Garrett. My partner over there is Deputy Stoll."

His partner, standing next to the SUV, was shorter and doughier. He had curly brown hair and long sideburns. He was working hard to offer a friendly face, but the warmth looked false.

Lisa thought about Purdue's story. *Two of them were policemen.*

She shivered. Cold rain dripped down her back.

"I don't know who you are, Deputy Garrett," she snapped. "I don't know Deputy Stoll, either, which is odd, because I'm pretty familiar with all of the police officers in Pennington County."

"Well, Deputy Stoll and I are both new, ma'am. Transfers from Warroad. We've only been on the job here in the county for the past couple of months."

"I see. And did the two of you pay a visit to my house in the middle of the night?"

The deputy rubbed his chin with a thick fist. She'd surprised him by knowing that. "Yes, actually, we did. We didn't think you were home. We knocked, but there was no answer."

"You had your weapons out while you were on my property," Lisa said. "Why is that?"

"No, ma'am. I assure you we didn't."

"I saw your guns very clearly in the moonlight, Deputy."

"I'm sorry, but you're mistaken."

Lisa frowned. She didn't think she'd made a mistake, but his certainty was making her doubt herself. "You also checked to see if my front door was locked. Am I mistaken about that, too?"

Deputy Garrett grimaced as a wave of sleet slashed across his face. He looked uncomfortable now. "Ms. Power, if you would let me explain. You must know why we're—"

Lisa interrupted him. "I got home a few minutes ago, and my front door was open, Deputy. I know I locked it before I left this morning. Did you break into my house? Do you have a warrant that would let you do that?"

"Ms. Power, please. I understand that you're upset. We mean you no harm at all. Truly. Our only concern right now is the missing boy. We know he's with you, and I'm sure that you feel protective of him, but it would be better for all of us if you let us take him with us."

Lisa stiffened. He'd said it out loud. *The boy.*

He knew about the boy; he knew Purdue had come to her house. Then she realized: of course he knew. The word was all over town by now. They were looking for a boy, and she'd found a boy.

She tried to read the stolid faces of the police officers, but their expressions gave nothing away. She didn't know what to believe anymore. If they were telling the truth, then the safest place for Purdue was to go with them. Maybe this whole nightmare was exactly what it looked like: a boy who'd escaped from a human trafficking ring; a ginger-haired killer who was trying to get him back; and the police officers hunting for both of them. These men, Deputy Garrett and Deputy Stoll, were the good guys.

But that wasn't the story Purdue had told her. The boy had said that two of the killers he'd seen were cops. And yet he'd also admitted that it was night and he couldn't see clearly. His emotions were running high. He'd witnessed a shocking crime. He'd been injured and his memory shattered into broken pieces. There was no way to know how his young brain had dealt with all that trauma.

What if he was wrong? In that case, the longer Purdue stayed with her, the more she was putting him at risk.

But what if he was right?

Then she would be delivering him into the hands of the people who wanted him dead.

She glanced at the windows of her pickup truck. The boy was hiding, just as she'd told him to do. She found herself frozen with indecision, like a high-wire artist in the wind, unable to go forward or backward. But standing still wasn't an option, either.

"If I let you take him with you, I want to go, too," Lisa said softly. "He trusts me. If you separate us, he'll just run away again."

Deputy Garrett exchanged a glance with his partner. Something odd flickered across his face that made Lisa uneasy with her decision. "Yes, of course," he told her. "That's not a problem. You can come with us."

"Good."

"You're doing the right thing, Ms. Power."

Lisa still felt anxious. "I hope so."

"Where is he?" Garrett asked.

She hesitated before answering. She could picture Purdue's face in her mind. That mop of blond hair; that smart, serious, quizzical expression as he analyzed everything. That fear and panic when she first saw him through her bedroom window. He was definitely running. Running from death. Running from murderers.

Running from the police.

Lisa thought, *What if the boy is right?*

"Ms. Power?" Deputy Garrett said again. "Please. Where is he?"

She opened her mouth to tell him. It was the only thing she could do. Then her phone started to ring in her pocket, making a loud, jarring noise in the still air. She took a step backward, away from the two deputies.

"I have to get this," she said.

"Ms. Power, the boy."

"It'll just be a minute, I promise."

She grabbed her phone and answered it. "Hello?"

"Lisa, it's Will Woolwich with the FBI."

"Oh, hi," she said, not taking her eyes off the police officers in front of her. "Thanks for calling me back."

"I wanted to let you know that I've investigated this story you told me about human trafficking. I talked to our field office in Grand Forks. Believe me—if something was going on, they'd be on top of this. This would be a major interdepartmental operation."

"What did you find out?"

"Well, I don't know who told you about this manhunt, but nothing like that is happening up there."

Lisa didn't answer right away. She breathed the cold air in and out, and she felt the icy rain landing in wet drops on her face. She watched

Deputy Garrett and Deputy Stoll, whose faces were darkening with concern. She tried to hide her reaction, because she didn't want to give them any hint that she'd found them out.

"Lisa?" Will went on when she was silent. "Are you there? Are you okay?"

"Yes. I'm here. Are you absolutely sure? There's no possibility of a mistake?"

"There's no mistake," he told her. "Whatever is going on in your area, it has nothing to do with human trafficking."

14

Lisa had five seconds to decide what to do. She smiled at the two deputies. She shoved down her fear and summoned complete calm to her face. If she exposed the truth, Will would send help, but help was miles away. There was no FBI to rescue her in this place. Meanwhile, these two men would kill her and kill the boy. Life or death was going to happen in the next few moments, and a voice on the phone couldn't save her. She had to act alone. She didn't care about herself, but she wasn't going to let them harm Purdue.

"Thank you for the information, Will," she said in the calmest voice she could muster. "I really appreciate it." Then she hung up the phone and said to the two men, "Sorry about that."

"Is there a problem?" Deputy Garrett asked her.

"Oh, no, it was a work call. That was my agent in New York. We've been going back and forth on one of the clauses in my latest contract."

"The boy, Ms. Power," the deputy reminded her. "Please."

"Yes, of course."

"Where is he?"

Lisa's mind raced as she tried to decide what to do next. She was cornered, with nowhere to run and no way to grab Purdue and escape. They wouldn't believe her if she lied and told them that he was somewhere else. They also outnumbered and outsized her, and they both had guns.

"Ms. Power?"

She gestured over his shoulder. "He's in that little shed behind the garage."

Deputy Garrett's gaze flicked to the large aluminum shed and its latched door. He flagged the other deputy to accompany him, and then he stepped forward to Lisa and extended his hand to be shaken. She was nervous about taking it, but she let him crush her own hand with a fist that looked like a bear's paw.

"I know this was hard for you, Ms. Power, but you're doing the right thing. We'll take good care of him."

She forced a smile onto her face. *Liar.* "Remember your promise, Deputy. I'm coming with you. I don't want the boy to be alone."

"Yes, of course."

Then she glanced down at Deputy Garrett's hand, where something bright white drew her eyes. When she saw it, she struggled to hide her reaction. He had a tattoo emblazoned on the back of his hand, starting at the bumps of his knuckles and winding onto his wrist.

It was an alligator.

A snow-white, albino alligator, its mouth open, showing long teeth, its eyes black and beady, full of violence. When the deputy dropped Lisa's hand and flexed his fingers, the jaws of the alligator snapped open and shut. As his wrist moved, the tail seemed to swish, as if it were pushing the reptile forward to its next helpless prey.

She heard Purdue's voice. *The white alligator shot him in the head.*

"Is everything okay?" Garrett asked, watching her face.

"Yes. Everything's fine."

"Deputy Stoll and I will go get the boy."

"Of course. I'll come with you."

She tried to make her legs move to follow them, but her limbs felt like rubber. She had to act right now. She had to do something. If she and Purdue got in the SUV with the two men, their next stop would be a grave site. The remote lands offered plenty of places to hide bodies that would never be found. Evil men dug up the ground all the time in her books.

Deputy Garrett headed across the gravel toward the shed, with his partner following just behind him. With horror, Lisa realized that they were going to walk right by the driver's door of her pickup, and she held her breath to see if they would glance inside and spot Purdue hiding below the passenger seat.

They didn't.

They were focused on the aluminum shed.

Lisa rushed to catch up with them, but she let them walk ahead of her. Deputy Garrett got to the metal door and undid the latch, and as he pulled the door open, the hinges squealed. Even with the door open, the shed was dark and deep. There was no light. The rusty machines sat on the floor like dead animals, and the smell of dust and fertilizer seeped into the fresh air.

Garrett filled the doorway with his bulky frame. "I don't see him."

"He must be hiding at the back."

The deputy glanced over his shoulder at her with a vague suspicion, as if trying to gauge whether she was lying to him. He squeezed inside, and a few seconds later, she saw the bright glow of a flashlight he'd taken from his belt. It wouldn't take him long to realize that Purdue wasn't in the shed.

His partner, Deputy Stoll, hovered near the doorway. His back was to her, but he was still at least two steps outside the shed, and he showed no sign of following his partner inside. He was a big man. If she pushed him, even from behind and with the element of surprise, she didn't know if she could jar him off his feet.

She was running out of time.

"Ms. Power," Deputy Garrett called, and she could hear the change in the tone of his voice. It was low and angry now. "He's not here."

"Are you sure? Did you check everywhere?"

"He's *not* here."

"Well, maybe he sneaked off. He does that."

"You're playing games with us, Ms. Power. That's really not a good idea. You have to tell us where you're hiding the boy."

Lisa watched Deputy Stoll begin to turn around to face her, and she could see the beam of Deputy Garrett's flashlight as he retraced his steps toward the front of the shed. She realized she had no choice. There was nothing else to do. She took her right hand out of her pocket, with her fingers clutching the grip of the Ruger and her index finger hovering under the trigger guard.

"Stop!" Lisa barked at the second cop. "Stay where you are, and don't move."

Stoll froze and shouted to his partner. "Garrett, *she's got a gun.*"

Lisa heard the clang of Deputy Garrett's boots on the metal floor. His face appeared in the shadows of the shed behind his partner. "Ms. Power, what the hell are you doing? Put away that gun. Put it on the ground, and back away from it right now. Don't make things worse for yourself."

"Get in the shed!" Lisa shouted. "Both of you! Put your hands up!"

"Listen to me. We're not going to hurt you."

His voice was as smooth and sweet as honey. She didn't believe him for a minute.

"No, you're not. You're not going to touch me, and you're not going to touch the boy. Keep your hands in the air! Back up!"

The two deputies showed her their hands, and they took several steps back into the shadows of the shed. She was conscious of the guns on their belts. And their radios. She thought about having them strip off their gear and toss it out, but she didn't want to give them any chance to trick her.

"All the way back," she told them coldly. "Against the rear wall."

"Ms. Power, don't do this. There's no way this ends well. Let's talk, okay? All we want to do is talk. Put down the gun, and tell us where the boy is."

"He's safe. And he's going to stay that way."

She clutched the gun tightly in her right hand, and she grabbed the padlock off the nail where she always kept it. She felt clumsy and terrified, and she tried to keep her fingers from trembling. She thought about how to do it all in one smooth motion. Keep the gun on them. Latch the door. Lock it. All before they could charge her, crash through the door, and topple her backward.

"I don't know who the two of you are," she said. She kept talking, because she wanted them listening to the sound of her voice. She didn't want them thinking about their guns or about rushing the door.

"I don't know if you're dirty cops," she went on, "or whether you're even cops at all, but you're not getting anywhere near that boy. I know what you did. You and your red-haired friend, Liam. I know about the bullet in the man's head. The *fingers*. It's all coming out. Whatever this is about, believe me, it's all coming out."

Neither of the men said a word. Their faces were dark in the shadows.

Lisa moved fast. The lock was ready in her left hand. She used her other hand, the hand that still held the gun, to grab the aluminum door. She fought the strong wind to close the door, but her hand struggled to do two things at once, and the gun slipped out of her grasp and fell to the gravel.

They saw it. They heard it. She heard them shout and heard the stomp of their boots as they ran toward her.

She slammed the door shut and closed the steel latch around the bar. She fumbled with the shackle as she threaded it through the hole in the latch, and at the very instant the lock snapped shut, the entire structure shuddered as the combined weight of the two men landed heavily against the door. Lisa screamed and jumped backward. The hinges groaned.

The door held, but it wouldn't hold for long. It was an old shed, and the metal was rusted and weak. As she stood outside, she heard the two cops back up and charge the door again. Again the door refused to open, but she could hear the awful screech of metal tearing away from metal.

Soon they would be free. She needed to get away *now*.

Lisa scooped her gun from the ground and ran for the pickup truck. She ran for Purdue.

15

As Lisa drove, the rain finally took a break. So did the wind. The air grew still.

She didn't know where to go, and she didn't trust the main highway. People would be looking for her. So she took the back roads to Laurel March's farm. Laurel and her husband, Curtis, owned a hobby farm on a large plot of land northeast of the town of Halma. Curtis grew soybeans, and Laurel ran her medical practice from a home office and made calls at clinics around the northern counties. They lived in a rambler that had belonged to his parents, and they grew their own vegetables and rode horses, and Curtis flew a little Cessna around the northland when he and his workers weren't in the fields. Lisa had always thought of them as having the perfect life, but nothing was perfect. She knew that Laurel and Curtis had tried unsuccessfully for years to have a child of their own, and they still carried that disappointment with them.

She parked her pickup near the field where Laurel's two horses, Ziggy and Carl, grazed in the green grass. The horses knew Lisa well. On summer Saturdays, she and Laurel had been known to ride for hours, almost to the Canadian border. If things had been different right now, she would have saddled up Ziggy and let Purdue ride behind her with his hands holding on to her waist, and they would have galloped across the meadow. That sounded like paradise. The cold air in her face and her hair blowing crazily. The slap of the horse's hooves in the mud and the snort of his breath. The boy's skinny arms clinging to her hips.

"I like horses," Purdue said, as if reading her mind.

"Me too."

"I think my mom liked horses."

Lisa glanced down at the boy. His serious face was even more serious than usual. "Your mom?"

"Yeah."

"Do you remember her?"

"No, but I think she liked horses."

Lisa said nothing. She felt a tightness in her throat, because Purdue was using the past tense about his mother without even realizing it. It was also the first time he'd talked about having a mother at all, the first time he'd opened that door for her a little bit. When he'd said he didn't remember anything at all about his mother or his family, she hadn't believed him, but she knew from her own experience that opening doors could be a scary thing.

She took Purdue by the hand and led him away toward Laurel's house. In the garden outside, there was a gazebo that Curtis had built by hand, fully enclosed to keep out the summer bugs, with a conical roof and a fairy weathervane on top. Lisa knew that Laurel kept toys and games there for when children came to visit. She took Purdue to the gazebo, and inside they found a one thousand–piece jigsaw puzzle, barely started, with the pieces spread across an oak table. The picture on the puzzle box showed a collage of cats. Something about the unfinished puzzle made Lisa sad, as if she knew no one was ever going to put the pieces together.

"Do you want to work on the puzzle while I talk to Laurel?" Lisa asked.

"Okay."

"Start with the corners."

"I know."

"Don't go anywhere. If you see anyone or if anyone turns off the road, you come running inside and find me. Got it?"

"Got it."

Lisa turned away, but Purdue called after her. "Hey, Lisa?"

"Yes?"

"I still don't like her."

"Laurel? You should give her another chance. She wants to help."

The boy shrugged. "If you say so."

Lisa left Purdue with the puzzle and headed for Laurel's door. The house wasn't large, and it was painted bright yellow, like a beam of sunshine. Laurel always wanted her house to be a buffer against the gray northern days. Beyond the house, she saw farm equipment sitting unused, because the ground was too wet to let Curtis and his men in the fields. On the border of the farmland was a narrow strip of grass that Curtis used as a runway, and his restored Cessna Skylark sat at the end, as if hungry for the sky. Laurel herself never went up in the plane with her husband. She hated flying. But Lisa had flown with Curtis many times. For her, the thrill was worth the fear.

She noticed that Laurel's red Ford Bronco wasn't parked near the house, and she wondered if her friend was out. When she knocked on the door, Curtis was the one who answered. He looked surprised to see her.

"Oh. Lisa."

"Hi, Curtis. Is Laurel home?"

"No. She had an appointment, but I expect her back soon. Do you want to wait?"

"Sure."

Curtis waved her inside. They stood awkwardly together in the foyer, and then Curtis gave her a hug, which was even more awkward. He wasn't an expressive man, but Lisa suspected that Laurel had told him what was going on. Curtis took off his Enestvedt Seed baseball cap and smoothed his sweaty, graying hair. He was older than Laurel, almost sixty, and he had the lean frame and slightly crooked physique of a man who'd done hard physical work every day of his life. He wore a pale-blue button-down shirt with the sleeves rolled up and dark jeans.

Lisa knew him to be knowledgeable about everything from mechanical engineering to the Chinese economy. He had a curious streak and read voraciously. Like most northern farmers, he also had a graveness of manner that strangers would consider aloof. He rarely smiled or laughed. He drank one beer every Sunday after church. Life was serious business, and Curtis was a serious man.

"You want to wait in Laurel's office?" he asked.

"Okay."

"Can I get you anything? Coffee, milk?"

"No. Thank you."

"Well, you know the way."

Curtis left her alone. Lisa didn't feel offended by his abruptness, because that was who he was. She did know the way to Laurel's office, because she'd been here many times. Sometimes by herself, sometimes with Noah. She followed a hallway painted in warm goldenrod and decorated with photographs of sunflowers to a brightly lit room at the corner of the house. Laurel kept a rolltop desk and a locked filing cabinet in one corner, but the rest of the office furniture was plush and comfortable. A worn leather sofa loaded with pillows. An overstuffed chair. An area rug with bell-shaped designs in red and blue. A Tiffany floor lamp. It was a place where Lisa had always felt comfortable.

She sat down on the sofa and let her body sink into the cushions. Piano music played softly from hidden speakers, something classical and relaxing. In front of her was a claw-foot antique coffee table that held a stuffed cat, a box of tissues in a floral holder, and a mason jar of potpourri that gave the room an aroma of patchouli. There was one other item on the table, too. It was her own novel. *Thief River Falls.* Her fourth thriller, her award winner, the book that would be a movie soon, the book that had changed her life.

She picked up the hardcover copy and opened it to the title page. It was inscribed to Laurel in Lisa's own handwriting with a quote from Carl Sandburg about a wild girl holding on to her dreams. Lisa remembered writing that inscription and remembered the little nod of Laurel's head as she read it. Then she opened the book to the prologue and read the first sentence, which she knew by heart, the first sentence she'd written and rewritten a hundred times:

> Down, down, down comes the rain of black dirt, landing in showers on the boy's small body and slowly burying him in the ground.

Lisa closed the book and put it back on the antique table without flipping through any of the other pages. The story was too much for her now. Everything was too much.

She heard a noise in the hallway and saw Laurel heading past the sunflower photos. Her friend never walked fast. Laurel stopped along the way to straighten one of the picture frames, and she took a step back to make sure it was level. Then she came into the office and closed the door behind her. She reached down and squeezed Lisa's hand.

"I'm so sorry I wasn't here when you arrived," she said.

"I haven't been waiting long," Lisa replied.

"Good."

Laurel took a seat in the overstuffed chair. Her eyes noticed everything. Lisa could see her take note of the position of *Thief River Falls* on the table, as if she recognized that it had moved from where it was before. She also noted the empty cushion on the sofa next to Lisa, who was sitting in the middle. When Noah had come with her, he'd sat on the end. A year had passed, and Lisa still found herself leaving a space for him.

"Did you find out anything?" Lisa asked. "You said you were going to make some calls. I hope you were careful about who you talked to."

"I did make some calls. That's how I've spent most of my day."

"And?"

As always, Laurel chose her words carefully. "I wish I had answers for you. I don't."

Lisa frowned. "So either no one knows what's going on, or they won't say a word. That's the problem. I don't know who to trust."

"You can trust me," Laurel replied.

That was true, but Lisa found it an odd thing for her friend to say.

"I told you to stay home," Laurel added. "I said you should lay low while I looked into this."

"I know, but I couldn't sit there and do nothing. I had to get out and ask questions. I managed to kick a hornet's nest while I was doing it."

"What do you mean?"

Lisa explained. She needed to unburden herself about what was going on, so she related everything that had happened in the past few hours. She told Laurel about her visit to Mrs. Lancaster, about her conversation with Will Woolwich at the FBI, about the desperate escape from the ginger man in the state park, and finally about her confrontation with the police officers outside her shed. That story brought a look of horror to her friend's face.

"You *pulled a gun* on two police officers?" Laurel exclaimed. "My God, Lisa, you're lucky they didn't shoot you. You could have been killed."

"They would have killed me anyway if I'd gone with them. And Purdue, too. At least I got away."

"For now, but what happens when they find you again? The police are going to consider you *dangerous*."

"That's why I need to get out of town."

"And go where?" Laurel asked.

"Anywhere. I don't care. But I can't use any of the main roads. They'll be looking for me and my truck. I just need to get far away from Thief River Falls."

"Why does that matter? TRF is already an hour away."

Lisa got off the sofa. She found herself pacing again. Restless. "Because this all goes back to Thief River Falls! Those two cops—if they're even cops at all—they're from Pennington County. The truck where Purdue stowed away made its last stop at the hospital in Thief River Falls. Don't you see? That's where this all started."

"Then we should go back there and get some answers," Laurel said. "Together."

Lisa shook her head. "And put Purdue in danger? No. I won't do that."

"So the boy is still with you?"

"He's in your gazebo." Lisa took a seat on the sofa again, going back to the middle seat by habit. She picked up her novel from the coffee table again, caressed it, and put it back. She took the mason jar and inhaled the scent. Then she gave her friend a little smile. "He doesn't like you, by the way."

"You mean Purdue? He doesn't like me?"

"No."

"Why not?"

"He thinks you know more than you're telling me. That you know who he is." She tried to read the expression on her friend's face, but Laurel was inscrutable. "I mean, that's wrong, isn't it? You don't know anything about Purdue, do you? About why people are hunting for him?"

"No, I don't."

"Well, good," Lisa replied.

"If you want to get away from here, you need to figure out where you're going," Laurel said.

"I told you it doesn't matter where I go. Somewhere else, where we'll be safe, where I can find people I can trust."

"I can think of one place," Laurel said.

"Where?"

Her friend pursed her lips, as if debating whether to say anything more. "Fargo."

"Why there?"

"I've known something for a long time, Lisa. I haven't told you before now, but I know where Noah is. I've known all along."

"*Noah?* You've talked to him?"

"Not in some time. But I know he's in Fargo. That's not even three hours away by car, Laurel. If you need to get away from here, if you need to find someone you can trust, why not your brother?"

"Because I *can't* trust him," Lisa snapped. "Noah made that very clear. I can't rely on him to be there when I need him."

"Maybe it's time to try."

"And have him run away from me again? No, thanks."

"Then what do you want to do?"

Lisa stared through the window at the fields stretching behind Laurel's house. From where she was, she could see the red Cessna on the grassy runway. She made a decision. "I need a favor."

"What is it?"

"I need Curtis," Lisa said. "I need his help. I want him to fly me to Minneapolis."

"Why there?"

"It's far away. It's a city. This is a small town, Laurel. Everybody knows everybody else around here. Not in Minneapolis. Purdue and I can disappear, blend in. I can go talk to Will at the FBI, and they can figure out who the boy is and why he's in trouble."

Laurel took a long time to answer. "Don't you think it would be easier to stay here with me?"

"If I do that, they'll find me. You know that. How long will it be before they show up here? People know we're friends. And I'm not going to put you and Curtis at risk, too."

Laurel got out of the chair. Her lips were pursed, and this time, she was the one who paced. "I'll talk to Curtis," she said. "But if he agrees, I also have one condition."

"What is it?"

Laurel stopped in front of the sofa and held out her hand, palm upward. "No gun."

"Excuse me?"

"You know how I feel about guns, Lisa. I don't want you or anyone else getting hurt. Give me your gun. Otherwise, that plane isn't going anywhere."

Lisa debated with herself. She didn't like the idea of being unarmed and defenseless. Part of her wanted to say no, to walk away, but if she did that, she was truly on her own.

"Okay," she agreed. "Whatever you say. No gun."

She reached into her jacket pocket and handed the Ruger to Laurel.

16

Lisa made sure her safety belt was buckled, and then she twisted around to check on Purdue in the back seat of the four-seater Cessna. The boy looked ready to head off on a grand adventure. His wavy blond hair flopped in front of his big eyes, which took in everything about the plane and its instruments. She gave him a thumbs-up, and he returned the gesture with an excited grin. He didn't look scared at all. He had faith that she would protect him from whatever was out there, that she would find a way to fix everything. She wasn't so sure. She studied the wet, grassy runway ahead of her, and the charcoal sky looming to the southeast, and she hoped that the boy's faith in her wasn't misplaced.

She waited for Curtis, who stood in the field with Laurel fifty yards away. From their demeanor, it was obvious that they were arguing. Laurel did most of the talking, and Curtis shook his head in firm opposition to whatever she was saying. He planted his feet in the ground and braced his hands on his hips. Lisa wished she could hear what they were saying. She knew they were both smart, stubborn people, and she'd seen them bump heads in the past, but this looked worse than usual.

Before she could climb out of the plane and talk to them, the fight ended. Laurel took both of Curtis's hands, kissed him, and whispered something in his ear. Curtis shrugged her off and headed for the plane without looking back at his wife. Lisa wasn't sure which of them had won, but if history was any indication, she thought that Curtis had finally surrendered to whatever Laurel wanted.

Curtis performed his final safety checks on the plane's exterior. Then he got into the pilot's seat without acknowledging his passengers. He ran through his cockpit checks, not saying a word to Lisa as he did, and he squinted at the clouds.

"Everything okay?" she asked him finally.

"Fine." His voice was clipped, but that wasn't unusual. Curtis never used two words when one was enough.

"What was that about?" she asked.

"Nothing. Don't worry about it."

But Lisa was worried anyway. She was certain they'd been arguing about her. And Purdue.

"Thank you for doing this," she said.

"I do what I'm told," he replied, which did nothing to ease Lisa's concerns.

He put on a headset and started the engine. A second headset hung on a hook in front of her, but she left it where it was. She welcomed the white noise, no matter how loud. In front of her, the propeller accelerated, making fluttery half moons in front of the windshield. Lisa felt the plane rock and heard the whine of the motor grow louder as they inched forward. The ground beneath them was uneven, and she could feel every bump. Spray rose from pools of standing water as they plowed through it. The plane hardly seemed to move at all, even as they went faster, but in no time, the nose tilted up and the Cessna floated off the ground, as if it couldn't wait to fly. The wings waggled, and the plane dipped. They took a few seconds to steady.

Lisa looked back through the window, watching Laurel grow smaller. They could see each other, but her friend didn't wave. She wasn't the sentimental type. Even so, she could see Laurel following them as Curtis increased altitude and then bent into a turn that took them back over the house. Lisa leaned with the plane. The sharp angle always made her feel untethered, as if she would spill through the door and fall. She wondered if it made Purdue afraid, but when she looked over her shoulder, she saw the boy staring out the window, mesmerized by the flat earth stretching out below them.

As they climbed higher, the ground became a checkerboard of roads and farm fields, occasionally interrupted by an uneven plot of woodland. There weren't many lakes in this part of the land of ten thousand lakes. Curtis was using Highway 59 as a guidepost to lead them southeast, and she recognized the familiar landmarks, the places she knew. She could see the thin black line of a freight train on the railroad tracks, heading toward Canada. A cluster of roads met like threads leading into the nucleus of a cell, which was the town of Karlstad. The houses and streets below them came and went, and the emptiness of the earth took over again.

It was a rocky flight, the worst she'd ever been on with Curtis. The clouds were a low shroud, so low she felt as if she could raise her hand and skim her fingers through them. As they flew, rain began to spit across the windshield. The unsettled air threw the plane around like a drunk dancer, lifting her off the seat with each rise and fall. The unexpected jolts made her want to scream, but she held it in, biting her tongue so hard she was sure it would bleed.

Curtis touched her shoulder and gestured at the headset. She slipped it over her ears, and he spoke into the microphone.

"We need to keep an eye on this," he said, his voice crackling into her ears. "Weather's getting worse."

Lisa nodded without a word. She left the headset on. Curtis's face was calm, but that didn't make her any less nervous. Her fingers were clutched around the leather grip on the door, but it was hard to hold on through the pockets of turbulence. They'd only been airborne for a few minutes, and the flight already felt long. Minneapolis seemed a world away. She looked back at Purdue, but he rode the waves like a kid on a roller coaster. She envied him that innocence.

Her eyes followed the squares of green fields, as dark as emeralds under the grim sky. The highway shot south like an arrow, but they were too high to see any cars on the road. A strange sense of foreboding clouded her mind, a feeling of danger and despair that she was flying into a nightmare. Through the window, between the raindrops, she could see a black snake on the ground, slithery and poisonous, coiling in tight swirls, and she knew what that snake was. It was the Thief River. And she knew why her stomach felt hollow, why she could hardly breathe, why tears had begun to leak from her eyes.

They were closing in on the town of Thief River Falls.

She could see it all from up here, every building she knew, every cross street, every park that had been part of her childhood. Thief River Falls, where the Thief River and the Red Lake River met in a kind of psychedelic Y. This was the town where she'd been born. Until recently, it was a town she'd loved and had never dreamed of leaving. Anyone who lived in this place had to embrace its fierceness and remoteness, because this was not a soft part of the world. It was a town that stared north at the bitter Canadian plains and pounded in tent stakes against the winter winds. It was a town dropped down in the middle of nothingness, where every mile looked like every other mile.

She loved the drama of its name, the way each word rolled off her tongue like a thriller with a twist ending. *Thief. River. Falls.* It was made to be the title of a book, the title of *her* book. When you saw the name on a highway sign, you knew you were coming to a place that had stories to tell, a place the Indians had made their own centuries ago, a place where pioneers had lived and died, a place of farmers and loggers. It didn't matter how many years passed. Nothing changed. Drive a mile in any direction, and you went back in time, and the stories weren't far away.

Thief River Falls. Population nine thousand. And they all knew their hometown girl, Lisa Power.

She knew it was wrong to blame the town for everything that had happened to her, but she did. Every house, shop, trail, and intersection was a reminder of what she'd lost. The thing about living where she'd been born was that all her memories made a chain, linked together, like pencil marks scratched on a wall as she got taller. There was a time when Greenwood Cemetery had reminded her of midnight adventures at homecoming. Now it was where Danny was buried. There was a time when passing the Arctic Cat headquarters had reminded her of snowmobiling with her brothers on Christmas Eve. Now it was a reminder that her brothers had both worked on the factory floor before they died in the flood.

She couldn't X out her memories with a black marker. All she could do was run away from them, and that was what she'd been trying to do. When they started coming back, she ran even faster.

Slowly, the plane crossed over the town and left it behind. Lisa closed her eyes and breathed a sigh of relief. But her relief was short lived. It was as if the town refused to let her go. As they headed south, the rain got worse, pouring in sheets across the windows and sticking with a kind of glaze. The plane yawed as it fought the wind, bucking like a mechanical bull. It felt like something was wrong. She saw Curtis twist his shoulders to look back and check the left wing. Whatever he saw made him bend his lips into a frown.

Then he took the radio and said one word. "Ice."

Ice on the windows. Ice on the wings.

She mouthed back at him. "What do we do?"

"Land."

She didn't bother saying no. It wouldn't do any good. She felt the plane descending; she leaned as it swung around. They weren't going back north to the grassy runway they'd left. Underneath the clouds, barely a mile to the east, she could see the long ribbon of pavement at the Thief River Falls airport. That was where Curtis was taking her. She'd flown into one storm, and now she was flying into an entirely different storm. No matter how hard she tried to get away, the town clung to her like a hawk with prey.

The plane sank lower, struggling against the current that wanted to keep them airborne. The ground grew larger, coming up fast. The buildings of the small airport took shape ahead of them. She squeezed her hands into fists and closed her eyes, and she felt the plane bounce as the wheels hit the runway. When she opened them again, she saw the drab fields around them. Their speed slowed; the whine of the engine got softer.

Whether she liked it or not, she was inside the dark heart of the mystery.

She was home.

17

The IPA in Noah Power's hand was cold and cloudy, and when he drank it, he could taste a bite of citrus in the back of his mouth. That was how he liked his ales. It was strong, too, with a kick that left a mellow haze in his head, particularly on his third pint. He sat on a stool near the taproom windows, looking out at the rush hour traffic on First Avenue in downtown Fargo.

Down, down, down came the rain.

Whenever it poured, he thought of it like that. Those were Lisa's words from the prologue of her fourth book, *Thief River Falls*. He could still hear the words in Lisa's voice. She'd read the book to the whole family after it was done. They'd spent an entire February weekend that way, with beers in hand and a fire roaring in the fireplace, all of them gathered around her. It was the last time he could remember the family being together like that. She'd spent ten hours reading the manuscript to them on Friday and Saturday evenings, from the first sentence to the last. Noah remembered how proud he'd been of his twin sister and how he'd known that book was going to change her entire life.

As he sat in the taproom, his mind sent her a message: *Talk to me, Lis.*

That had been their little game when they were kids. They would lie in their beds in the darkness and try to hear what the other was thinking. People said that only identical twins experienced a kind of telepathy between them, but Noah knew that wasn't true. He and Lisa had it, too. Throughout his life, there had been moments where he was all alone and he would hear Lisa say something, as vividly as if she'd been standing next to him. There were other times when he didn't hear words but simply felt a torrid rush of emotion, whether it was joy, or anger, or grief, or fear. And he knew in those moments that something was happening to his sister.

He'd never even told Lisa that it was the telepathy that had finally driven him away. It was one thing to live with his own grief, but he'd had to deal with hers, too. When she felt the pain, so did he. When she cried, so did he. The combination had been too much, like a weight on his chest so heavy that he couldn't even breathe. He needed to find a way not to share it all with her. Yes, he'd been a coward. Yes, he'd run away. But the alternative would have been to take his life, like their father, and when he'd gone so far as to put a gun in his mouth, he knew he had to run. It was that or pull the trigger.

But he wasn't a fool. In running, he'd severed the bond between him and his sister. He'd felt a rush of fury in his head like a lightning bolt while he was on the road, and he knew—*he knew*—that Lisa was reading the note he'd left for her. Since that moment, there had been nothing. No voice in his mind. No emotion. They'd become two separate people for the first time in their lives.

Until last night.

Last night, he'd felt her come back.

Noah drank his beer and stared with empty eyes at the busy street. Darkness hadn't fallen yet, but the rain and cloud cover made the city look like night. The lights of the cars were on. Inside the crowded taproom, the noise and laughter of dozens of drinkers made it possible to stay in his own bubble somewhere far away. He sat and listened, waiting for Lisa to talk to him again. He could feel her reaching out from wherever she was, and he wondered if she could feel him reaching back.

I'm here, Lis.

Right now, what he felt from his sister was an emotion deeper than anything that had ever passed between them, like an eruption from the sun. He had trouble even defining what it was, and the closest word he could find was despair.

"Knock knock. Anyone home?"

Noah started, as if awakening from a bad dream. He was back in the real world in Fargo, and he wasn't actually alone in the taproom. His fiancée, Janie, was with him.

"Sorry," he told her.

"Seventeen minutes."

"What?"

"Seventeen minutes," Janie said. "That's how long since you said anything."

"I didn't realize."

She stroked his cheek with a hand tipped with lavender fingernails. She had long, straight brunette hair and green eyes that made him think of an Egyptian Isis. She was very tall—taller than him—and skinny as a rail.

"I don't mind you being gone," she said. "I like staring at your face. But I don't like seeing you so troubled."

"I know."

"I have to ask. Is it us? Are you rethinking things?"

"No, definitely not. I'm not rethinking anything."

And he wasn't. He'd only known Janie for six months, but after a lifetime assuming there was no such thing as a soul mate, he'd found his. Janie was to him what Danny had been to Lisa. They were the same age, almost forty. They'd met in the unlikeliest of places, a car dealership, when Janie had sold him a used Ford Explorer. She was Janie Swetland, car salesperson by day, hospice volunteer and cat lover by night. She was also a reader and knew his sister's books, which was the first thing they'd had in common. After dating for only a week, he'd confessed his biggest sin to her, about running away from Lisa when she needed him.

He'd assumed that would be the end of his relationship with Janie. No one could ever love anyone who was as selfish as he'd been. Instead, Janie had kissed him and told him that he was going to have to forgive himself someday for being human, even if his sister never did.

"You want to talk about what's going on?" Janie asked him.

"I do, but I'm not sure I'm ready yet."

"That's okay. Keep drinking. IPAs are like truth serum. Sooner or later, it's going to come out."

"After three beers, I know what has to come out," Noah said.

He got off the stool, feeling wobbly. He made his way through the crowd to the men's room, which was empty, and he got rid of as much beer as he could. When he was washing his hands, he found himself staring into the mirror, getting lost again. It wasn't his own face he saw staring back at him. It was Lisa's. For fraternal twins, they looked a lot alike. The same deep-brown hair, with a slight curl to it. The same prominent nose, a little more prominent than either of them liked. And the same wide, curious eyes that were like a polygraph, giving everything away. No one looking at them would have missed that they were brother and sister.

He felt emotion from Lisa again, the same as the previous night. That sense of despair as white-hot as the sun.

And then he heard her voice. Harsh, bitter, unmistakable.

Go away, Noah.

He left the bathroom and returned to the table near the window. Janie was waiting for him, and she read his eyes, the ones that always told the truth.

"You ready to talk?" she said.

He drained the last of the beer in the glass. "Yes, but this will sound strange."

"Okay."

"Something terrible is happening to my sister."

Janie took his hand with concern. "How do you know? Have you spoken to her?"

"No."

She stared at him with only the briefest moment of confusion. Then she read his eyes again, and somehow she understood what he was saying. He didn't need to explain how he knew. They were twins, and that was enough.

"Then you should go to her," Janie said.

Noah stared out at the rain. Somewhere out there, Lisa had gone silent, building a wall around herself and keeping him out. "Well, there's a problem with that. I'm pretty sure I'm the last person on earth that my sister wants to see."

Will Woolwich grabbed his raincoat from the hook on his cubicle wall. He could see through the building window that the rain was still coming down. He had more work to do, but he could do it at home. His apartment was only a few blocks from the FBI main office in the Minneapolis suburb of Brooklyn Center. He opened his briefcase, grabbed several file folders from his desk, and then closed and locked it. He was about to leave when he noticed the yellow pad near his phone.

That was where he'd made his notes about the query from Lisa Power.

It had brought up old feelings to talk to her again. Crushes like that never really went away, no matter how much time had passed. He could still picture her face when he thought about her, although that wasn't fair, because he'd seen it on book jackets over the years. A lot of water had gone under the bridge in the ten years since they'd met, but even so, he remembered how much he'd liked her.

He decided to call her back. Just a routine follow-up. Just to see if she was really okay. There had been something odd in her voice as she'd hung up the phone. She'd sounded upset, maybe even scared. And the whole nature of her call, about a police manhunt that wasn't taking place at all, didn't make sense to him.

With his coat still on, Will sat back down at his desk. Before he could even reach for the phone, it began to ring, and he scooped up the receiver.

"Special Agent Woolwich."

He heard a man's voice on the other end, a little squeaky and young. "Special Agent Woolwich, this is Matthew Baines. I'm an assistant county attorney in Pennington County. You called our office earlier today. I'm very sorry for the delay in getting back to you. The county attorney would have called you himself, but he's had a death in the family, and he's out for a few days."

"I'm sorry to hear it. I appreciate the callback, Mr. Baines. I was able to get my questions answered, but in fact, I was just about to do some additional follow-up. Maybe you can help me."

"I'm happy to. What is this about?"

"I received a civilian report that law enforcement in your area were mounting special activities today regarding human trafficking operations. It involved some kind of fugitive manhunt."

"A manhunt?" the attorney replied with surprise. "No, I don't know anything about that. I'm sure we'd be in the loop if it was happening."

"Yes, it looks like there was nothing to it," Will said, "but I know the source personally, so I said I would check it out. I already let her know that there appeared to be no substance to the rumors."

"Do you mind if I ask who your source was?"

"I don't think there's anything confidential about it at this point. I imagine she's sort of a celebrity up there. It was the writer, Lisa Power."

"Ah." Something in the man's voice changed. "Yes, we all know Lisa."

"Well, her call was a little strange. I just want to make sure she's okay."

"That's kind of you, but I don't think you've got any reason to be concerned."

"Oh?"

"Yes, I don't know anything about these manhunt rumors, but I do know the police already talked to Lisa this afternoon. The county attorney actually knows her quite well, and he sent two sheriff's deputies to follow up with her. If there were any kind of problem, I'd have heard about it. As you say, she's pretty well known in these parts."

"Well, that's good to hear," Will replied. "I'm glad the locals have things under control. If I can help from my end, don't hesitate to get me involved."

"I'll pass that along to my boss."

"Thank you," Will said. "By the way, I hate to admit this, but could you remind me who the county attorney in Pennington County actually is? I don't remember the name off the top of my head."

Will heard a smile in the voice on the other end. Rural counties probably got that query all the time.

"He's been the county attorney here for almost thirty years," the man replied. "That makes him kind of a legend in Thief River Falls. His name is Denis Farrell."

18

Lisa stood under the overhang outside the terminal building at the Thief River Falls airport. In front of her, rain poured off the flat roof like a waterfall. Purdue sat on a bench next to her, his legs crossed, peering at the sky. There were a handful of cars in the parking lot opposite the building, mostly airport employees. Almost no one came and went in the evening October storm, but Lisa looked down and let her hair fall across her face, hoping not to be recognized.

Being here, so close to her past, she felt her stress level increase a hundred times over.

Curtis emerged from inside the terminal with his backpack over his shoulder. He shook his head and scowled at the rain, as if his fickle friend Mother Nature were playing another trick on him. According to the weather forecast, the rain wouldn't be stopping anytime soon. Overnight, as the temperatures fell, it would turn to ice and then finally to snow.

"I can hangar the plane here until morning," he told Lisa. "We can try to get out then."

"Okay."

But it wasn't okay. Twelve hours until morning felt like a lifetime away, and anything could happen between now and then. Wherever she went in this area, people would know her, and word would spread. It was impossible for Lisa to hide in Thief River Falls.

"You can go back home tonight if you want," Lisa told Curtis. "I'll pay to get you a rental car."

"What about you?"

"I don't think it's safe for me to be at your house." She stared into the rain, which blew across the asphalt like an invading army. "I'm not sure it's safe to be anywhere."

"Well, wherever you go, I go. Laurel made it very clear I wasn't to leave you alone. Not for a second."

Lisa smiled, because she could hear those words coming out of her friend's mouth. "Thank you, Curtis."

"What would you like to do? Get a couple of motel rooms? There are places not too far from the airport. If it would make you feel better, I can go inside and get the rooms myself. Nobody has to see you. I can bring back some takeout for us, too."

Lisa thought about it. "That might work."

"I see a cab over there," Curtis said, pointing across the parking lot. "Let me check if it's waiting for somebody or whether we can hop in."

She watched Curtis walk into the rain, not even flinching as the downpour soaked him. Most people would cover their heads or hunch over and shove their hands in their pockets. Not a farmer like Curtis. He trudged across the parking lot in his work boots as if the sun were shining and tapped on the driver's window of the taxi.

It wasn't really much of a taxi. The car was a 1990s-era Caprice Classic, painted burgundy, with patches of orange rust on the trunk and a bumper that was attached to the rest of the car with duct tape. A big handwritten sign in the corner of the rear window said, "TAXI." Next to the sign was an oversize photograph of a Roswell alien taped to the glass, along with bumper stickers about ghosts, cats, marijuana, and guns.

Curtis waved at her from the car. He opened the back door and waited, and Lisa headed for the taxi, with Purdue trailing behind her. She let the boy slide inside first, and Curtis followed them and shut the door. He had to try it three times to get the door latch to click.

The interior of the cab matched the exterior. Foam spilled out of tears in the two-tone seat cushions, and cigarette smoke lingered in the shut-up space. The backs of the front seats were taped over with Halloween decorations. A plastic skeleton in a noose dangled from the rearview mirror.

Lisa saw the driver's face in profile. She was young, not even thirty, with spiky blond hair that was streaked with purple and sat up like a bristle brush on her head. Two Celtic knots had been carefully shaved into the side of her skull. She was attractive, with high cheekbones, a ski-slope nose adorned with three rhinestone studs, and a slightly jutting chin. Her top was made of black mesh, and she had a long neck. When their eyes met in the car's mirror, Lisa saw that the woman had black eye shadow painted above glimmering blue eyes.

As soon as the driver saw Lisa, she exclaimed in a breathy voice, "Oh! Oh my God, it's you! I can't believe it!"

The woman threw open the driver's door and raced around the front of the Caprice. With rain drenching her, she yanked open the back door, thrust her body across Purdue as if the boy wasn't even there at all, and gathered up Lisa into a bear hug that practically lifted her out of the seat.

"It's me, Lisa! It's Shyla. Shyla Dunn."

Lisa had met thousands of readers over the past decade, and after a while, the names and faces began to blur. And yet as she stared at Shyla's distinctive punk/New Age look, she recognized something familiar in her features from years ago, long before she became an author. She knew this woman, but it had nothing to do with her books. Their relationship went back to when Lisa was a nurse and Shyla was no more than eighteen years old.

"The hospital," Lisa murmured. "You were a patient."

"Yes! You stood up for me when I was just a kid. My boyfriend assaulted me, and the police didn't care. They acted like it was my fault. You shamed them into doing something, and they put the son of a bitch in prison. That was all you, Lisa. The county attorney wouldn't listen to me, but he listened to you."

"Well, I didn't give him much of a choice. That's the only reason he got involved. Believe me, Denis Farrell has never been a fan of mine."

Shyla hugged her again. "I'm just so happy to run into you! I moved away after all that shit went down, and I only came back to town a few months ago. So I never had a chance to thank you properly. What you did was such a big thing to me."

Lisa found herself tearing up at Shyla's gratitude. She was proud of being a writer, but sometimes she wondered if writing books was just her way of keeping reality at bay. She could sit in her little room and make up stories, and that meant she didn't have to go out and face the world anymore. It had been different when she was a nurse and had to deal with reality every day.

The young woman gave Lisa another smile, with an innocence that belied the toughness of her physical appearance. Soaking wet, she returned to the driver's seat of the cab and twisted around to stare at Lisa in the back seat. "Look at me going on and taking up all your time when you have somewhere to be. Where do you want to go? Free ride, anywhere you want."

Lisa eyed Curtis. "What do you think? The Quality Inn?"

"Fine with me."

Shyla shook her head in confusion. "A hotel? You're looking for a hotel? Don't you still live around here?"

"Well, it's hard to explain, Shyla. I'm actually looking to lay low while I'm here. I'd rather no one knew I was in town."

Lisa didn't say anything more than that, but she saw an immediate shift in Shyla's expression. The young woman's face grew serious, as if she'd decided that fate had given her a chance to pay it forward.

"I won't tell a soul," Shyla said. "As far as I'm concerned, you're not here. But you're not going to a hotel. You're staying with me. I've got a little house on Columbia right across the river from Hartz Park. It's quiet, and as long as you're not allergic to cats, there's plenty of room. No one will know you're there, and you can stay as long as you need to."

"Oh, Shyla, that's very generous, but we don't want to intrude."

"You're not. You protected me, so I'll protect you."

"I didn't say I needed protection."

Shyla shook her head. "You didn't need to. It's written all over your face. Now come on. I've got beef barley soup in the Crock-Pot."

Lisa glanced at Curtis, who shrugged his acceptance. "Okay," she said. "Let's go."

Shyla steered the strange Caprice cab out the airport road onto Highway 17 and headed north. The heavy rain and the growing darkness made Lisa feel safely anonymous as she looked out the window, confident that no one could see her. The highway was a straight shot into town, heading past miles of open soybean fields before houses and spruce trees began to pop up on both sides of the road. With each mile closer to town, her heartbeat accelerated. They passed the elementary school that she'd attended as a child. They passed the forested border of Greenwood Park. She knew what was coming next—the cemetery— and she couldn't even look at the sprawling meadow of headstones that went on for blocks. Everyone she loved was buried there. She just stared down at her lap until they'd left it behind.

Shyla turned left at Parkview Street and drove through a quiet neighborhood to the cross street that ran parallel to the Red Lake River. Her house was on the corner, near the footbridge that led across the water to Hartz Park. It was a small blue bungalow that needed fresh paint, with a grassy driveway and detached garage. The shallow backyard was nestled with tall evergreens, and the lawn was mostly made up of dandelion weeds. The mailbox, like the Caprice, was covered in rust.

"Home sweet home," Shyla said. "I know it's not much. My uncle died and left it to me. That's why I came back to TRF."

Lisa sighed with relief. "It's perfect."

"Well, good."

They all climbed out of the cab into the driving rain. Lisa noticed one wet, unhappy cat wandering across the lawn to nuzzle at Shyla's leg. Then another joined the first, and another after that, and another after that. Shyla squatted to stroke all of them, and then she picked up three of the wet cats and headed for the garage.

"They know it's dinnertime when I get home," she said. "I keep their food in the garage."

Lisa smiled. "How many do you have?"

"Well, officially ten, but word gets around in the neighborhood. I think there's a sign along the riverbank that points stray cats to my house. Anyway, once I feed them, I can get you guys set up in my spare bedrooms and get some bowls of soup on the table. I baked some crusty bread this morning, too. I use a machine, but it's still pretty good."

"Thank you, Shyla."

The young woman let the cats jump from her arms, and then she retrieved a key to unlock the detached garage. She opened the door and found a light switch.

As bright light lit up the small space, Curtis whistled at what was inside. "Ho-lee crap."

There was a 1990s-era Camaro parked inside, blue with black racing stripes down the hood and spotlessly clean. It was in perfect condition, and it was enough to make any car collector salivate. But that wasn't what Curtis was whistling at. He was staring at the rear wall of the garage. Shyla had an arsenal stored there, enough guns to start a small revolution. Pistols. Revolvers. Hunting rifles. Shotguns. Nearly every brand was represented, from Glock, Ruger, and Smith & Wesson to Winchester, Bushmaster, and Armalite. Some were antiques; others were gleaming, black, and new. Lisa counted four AR-15s.

"Come on, sweeties, dinnertime," Shyla called, as she began scooping out Science Diet for at least a dozen cats who crowded around her legs and pushed and shoved at the bowls.

"Wow," Lisa said.

"Yeah, I'm a crazy cat lady—what can I say?"

"That's not what I meant."

"What, the car? I know; it's a beaut. My uncle was a collector. He left me the Camaro, too. Honestly, I don't use it much myself. I'm not really into cars."

Curtis interjected. "The car's cool, but did he also leave you the guns?"

Shyla looked over her shoulder at the wall and then shrugged, as if she'd forgotten the guns were there. "Oh, that. No, those babies are all mine. I guess I have enough, but I keep buying more. After what I went through, I'm not taking any chances. My parents think it's overkill, but let me tell you, if anyone ever comes after me again, they are in for one big-ass surprise."

19

Hours later, as the night crept closer to morning, Lisa lay in bed in the perfect darkness. There wasn't a light anywhere inside or outside. It was disorienting to be in a strange house and a strange bed and not be able to see anything at all. The rain had begun to freeze after midnight, tapping on the window glass like the fingernails of someone wanting to come inside. And yet despite all that, she was at peace for a brief moment. She felt secure here, at least for a little while, where no one could find them. Her stomach was full; Shyla's soup had been hearty and delicious, and the soup had been followed by homemade peach pie. She could feel the warmth of at least three cats sharing the bed near her feet.

Next to her, Purdue whispered in a tiny little voice. "Are you awake, Lisa?"

"Yes."

"Me too."

"You should try to get more sleep. We have a long day ahead."

"I tried. I can't."

"Is everything okay? Did you remember something more?"

"No. It's not that."

"Then what is it?" Lisa asked.

"We shouldn't be here," Purdue said.

"Where? Here in this house?"

"No, not the house. I like Shyla. But I don't like this place. There's something about the whole town. We're not safe here, Lisa. This is where the bad things happened. I can't remember all of it, but I'm sure it happened right here."

Lisa was quiet for a while. "Well, don't worry—we'll get out of here as soon as we can. We'll go somewhere else that's safe. Once it's light, we'll get on the plane, and we'll leave Thief River Falls behind."

"I don't think so. I think you're wrong."

"What do you mean?"

"It's just a feeling I have," the boy said. "I don't think I'll ever leave Thief River Falls."

Lisa chewed on her lip to keep away the sadness. It wasn't right, hearing those words from a boy so young. She wanted to say something to comfort him, but she realized that she was the one who needed comfort. Purdue didn't sound upset or afraid of what he was saying. He was a serious boy thinking about serious things. She was the one who was terrified by what was out there for him.

She reached over and stroked his hair. "You know what I think?"

"What?"

"I think we should have more pie."

She heard Purdue giggle in the darkness.

Lisa got out of bed. The hardwood floor was cold. She hunted for her shoes and then slipped her feet into them. She found her clothes, which had dried on the radiator during the night, and she put them on. She felt her way in the darkness across the small bedroom to the closed door and then let herself out into the hallway. The house wasn't big. There was another bedroom adjacent to this one for Curtis and then Shyla's bedroom in the corner. That was all.

She headed for the kitchen, stepping carefully to avoid several cats sleeping in her path. She could hear the rumble of snores and purrs. A streetlight near the river cast enough light to help her make out the furniture around her. A clock glowed on the microwave; it was just past five in the morning. She went to the refrigerator, but before she opened the door, she stopped.

Through the rear door in the kitchen, she saw a pinprick light in the backyard. She squinted to see it better. The light danced like a firefly, appearing and disappearing near the trees, and she realized it was the glow of a cell phone screen. Someone was outside, pacing back and forth in the cold.

She couldn't see who it was.

Lisa backed away from the door. Instinctively, she looked around the kitchen for something she could use to defend herself, and she found a heavy stone pestle from a mortar and pestle set, like a miniature baton. She clutched it in her hand and then retraced her steps through the house to the bedroom where Curtis was sleeping. If she was going outside, she wanted backup.

She drummed her fingers lightly on the door. "Curtis?"

There was no answer, and she knocked again with the same result. With a slight hesitation, she twisted the knob and opened the bedroom door. Inside, she called his name again, louder, but still got no answer. She felt around the wall for the light switch and turned it on, and she was temporarily blinded by the brightness. When she could see again, she spotted empty, rumpled sheets on the twin bed.

Curtis was gone.

Lisa didn't understand. Where was he? Then she relaxed a little as she thought, *It's him. He's the one outside. He's talking to Laurel.*

She went back to the house's rear door, which she opened quietly. Cold air whistled through the crack. Outside, there was no moon, no stars, just clouds, so she couldn't be seen. When she took one careful step, she felt a sheet of ice under her feet. The porch was slick from a wave of freezing rain. She held on to the railing and took it an inch at a time as she made her way down to the back lawn.

Ice had formed there, too, and it broke like glass as she walked on it. She went slowly to avoid making noise, at least until she was absolutely sure it was Curtis in the yard. She still had the stone pestle in her hand. Not far away, the light of the cell phone moved back and forth near the trees, and a man's voice rose above the icy patter of the rain. His tone was hushed and agitated. She recognized the voice and felt a wave of relief.

It *was* Curtis.

Then her relief evaporated as she got close enough to hear what he was saying.

"No! No, you can't send anyone over here. This woman has a damned armory in her garage. I'm sure there are guns inside the house, too. It's way too risky. Lisa's obsessed with this boy, and she's determined to rescue him. If you confront her about it directly, this thing could turn into a firefight, and nobody wants that. You have to be patient."

Lisa stood motionless as the rain froze on her clothes. The longer she stood there, listening, the more she became a pillar of ice. She wanted to move, but she couldn't. Horror bled through her mind and sank like a weight into her stomach. Curtis was one of them. She'd been set up. The forced landing in the plane was fake; it had all been done to keep her here in Thief River Falls, to make sure she didn't escape with Purdue. And that meant something even worse.

Laurel.

Laurel was part of it, too.

She couldn't trust her best friend. Everything Laurel had told her had been a lie. She should have listened to Purdue's suspicions about her. The betrayal tasted bitter in her mouth.

Curtis kept talking. "Look, the plan is to go back to the airport in the morning. Wait until then. This woman Shyla drops us off, and then she's out of the picture. You can have Garrett and Stoll waiting in the hangar near the plane. At that point, we're done."

Lisa knew she was alone. Truly alone. She shouldn't have been surprised, because her life had been leading here for the past two years, taking away everyone she loved, one by one.

"All right, I'll text you when we're heading to the airport. Don't worry, I'll make sure nothing goes wrong."

Curtis hung up.

Lisa wasn't sure what to do, whether she should run, or hide, or pretend she hadn't heard everything she'd just heard. If she could get back to the house without Curtis knowing she'd been outside, she could slip away with Purdue and be gone before it was light.

But she ran out of time.

Curtis had shoved his phone into his pocket and was now headed straight for her. His footsteps crunched through the layer of ice. He practically collided with her before he even realized she was there. When he saw her blocking his way, he stopped, and she heard a curse under his breath. They were both little more than dark silhouettes in the yard, but he knew it was her, and he knew the game was up.

"You bastard," she hissed.

"Lisa, calm down. Let me explain. This isn't what you think it is."

"No? Because it sounds like you're setting me up, Curtis. It sounds like *both* of you have been part of this from the beginning. You and Laurel."

She turned for the house, but she knew he wouldn't let her go. Not now. Not when she knew the truth. She tried to run, but she took only two slippery steps before her feet spilled out beneath her, and she crashed to the wet ground on her stomach, knocking the air out of her chest. She rolled over, gasping for breath. Curtis loomed over her body, reaching for her. She skidded out of his grasp, but he closed the gap between them with a few steps.

"Lisa, *wait*. Listen to me. Don't make this hard on yourself. All they want is the boy."

All they want is the boy.

Hearing that made something break inside her. She crossed a line. A line that the heroes in her books had to cross, when violence was the only answer. She could just make out the shine of Curtis's eyes, and when he was directly above her, she swung the little stone pestle like a billy club, hearing it rush through the air and connect on Curtis's skull with a mean crack. He fell hard, his knees giving way. He collapsed on top of her, and she had to shove with both hands to dislodge his body and squeeze out from beneath him. She was still struggling to breathe, laboring to swell her lungs again. Next to her, Curtis wasn't moving.

"Lisa?"

A small scared voice came from behind her. It was Purdue. He'd followed her into the yard.

She managed to get to her feet. He ran to her and threw his hands around her waist and hung on for life. She held him, too, but she knew they didn't have much time. Curtis would be conscious again soon, and when he was, they needed to be long gone.

"Come on," she croaked, trying to get the words out.

"What's going on?"

"I'll tell you later. Right now, we need to go."

She didn't go back inside the house. She took Purdue's hand, and they made careful tracks across the icy grass, moving in and out of the shelter of the evergreens. A black cat sped across their path, like a bad omen, and three other cats scampered for cover as they ran closer. They passed Shyla's detached garage and found themselves in the muddy driveway next to her Caprice.

Lisa realized she had no idea what to do next. They had nowhere to go and no way to get there. They could run. They could take the bridge and cross the river into the park, but it wouldn't take long for them to be caught out on foot once daylight broke over the town.

Then she heard a woman's voice from the front of the house.

"Stop! Who's out there? Turn around slowly, and keep those hands where I can see them!"

Lisa made sure Purdue was protected and invisible behind her. She turned around slowly, her arms in the air. A bright light erupted in her face, a flashlight pinning her like an escaped prisoner. This time, when the voice spoke again, she realized it was Shyla. The woman's tone immediately relaxed.

"Lisa! Is that you? Are you okay? I heard a noise outside, and I don't mess around when that happens."

The porch light clicked on with a yellow glow. Lisa saw Shyla at the top of the steps with an AR-15 cradled in her arms, and she had no doubt that the rifle was loaded and ready to fire. Shyla was already fully dressed in camouflage and had hunting boots on her feet. She came down from the porch and marched across the driveway with the cool readiness of a soldier.

"You're leaving already?" Shyla asked. "Now?"

"Yes. Sorry. Thank you so much for everything, but we have to get out of here."

"What about your friend? The old guy?"

"It turns out he's not really a friend."

"Where is he?"

"In the backyard. Unconscious for now. I don't want him to know where I'm going."

"Well, where *are* you going?"

"Honestly, I'm not sure," Lisa said. "Somewhere far away."

Shyla looked as if she was trying to make sense of the expression on Lisa's face. "You still haven't told me what's going on."

"If I knew, Shyla, I'd tell you. I don't. I just know I need to get away from Thief River Falls as fast as I can."

"You won't get far on foot," Shyla said. "You need wheels."

She hiked past Lisa to the door of the garage, unlocked it, and threw it open. The light came on, illuminating the blue sports car inside. Shyla dug in her pants for a set of keys and tossed them to Lisa, who caught them on the fly.

"Take the Camaro," Shyla said. "It's free, and it's fast."

"Are you sure?"

Shyla shrugged. "I never drive it. Get it back to me when you can. Or keep it. I don't care."

"You're a lifesaver, Shyla."

"Hey, I owe you," she replied. Then she put a hand on Lisa's shoulder. "Be straight with me—are you in some kind of trouble? You've got the look of someone who isn't safe. I know that look, because I've been there myself."

"You're right. I don't think I'm safe."

"Then let's make sure you can fight back."

Shyla opened the driver's door of the Camaro and leaned inside to pop the trunk. She went over to the arsenal on her back wall and took down two weapons, a semiautomatic pistol and an AR-15, which she put in the trunk without a word. Then she unlocked a large cabinet in the corner of the garage and gathered up several magazines of ammunition for both guns. She loaded those in the trunk, too, and slammed it shut.

"You know how to use these?" Shyla asked.

"Yes."

"Okay, good. I hope you don't have to."

"Thank you, Shyla. I don't even know what to say."

"You don't have to say anything. Just stay alive, and stay safe. Now go."

20

Curtis cupped the back of his head. His fingers came away with a cold, sticky mess of blood. His entire skull throbbed, pulsing with each heartbeat like a hammer rapping against bone.

He supported himself against a tree as he tried to stay standing, and he watched the taillights of the Camaro as Lisa drove away. The woman, Shyla, locked the garage door. He could see her in the glow of the porch light. She stared right back at him, although he wasn't sure if she could actually see him where he stood in the darkness. Shyla had an AR-15 in her arms, level and ready to fire, and Curtis had no interest in waiting around to see what she did with it. He backed up into the yard and then staggered toward the cross street. When he got there, he sank to his knees and threw up. Then he limped away down the icy street, leaving Shyla Dunn and her guns behind him.

He was alone on the road and still a long hike from Pennington Avenue. The houses on either side were dark. No one was awake.

Curtis retrieved his phone from his pocket and dialed.

"It's me," he said. "Change of plans."

"What do you mean, change of plans? I just talked to you. What the hell is going on?"

County Attorney Denis Farrell had the raspy, impatient voice of someone who hadn't slept all night and wasn't in the mood for unpleasant surprises. Curtis had known Farrell for years. He didn't like him much, but Farrell also wasn't the kind of man he wanted to cross.

"Lisa's gone," Curtis told him.

"Gone? You were supposed to watch her! You were supposed to keep her under control!"

"I know, but she heard me talking to you. She heard what we were planning at the airport. She hit me and took off. You need to get someone out here to pick me up. My head hurts like hell."

"All right, all right, quit whining. I'll have someone out there in a few minutes. How did Lisa get away? On foot?"

"No. The woman gave her a car. It's a blue Camaro with black racing stripes. I don't remember the license plate, but the thing shouldn't be too hard to spot."

"Where do you think she'll go?"

"She wanted to leave town to protect the boy, so I assume that's still what she'll try to do. She'll probably head to the Cities."

"All right, I'll talk to the sheriff and get patrols out to watch the roads," Farrell replied. "We'll find her before she's out of the county."

"You better hang on, Denis. This thing is a lot more complicated now. Your men need to take it easy."

"Why?"

"I'm pretty sure Lisa is armed. I told you, this Shyla woman is a walking billboard for the NRA. I think she loaded Lisa up with weapons before she left. Your people need to be prepared."

"What kind of weapons are we talking about?" Farrell asked.

"Shyla had everything. Pistols. Shotguns. Assault rifles. Heavy-duty stuff."

Farrell was silent for a long time. "I cannot believe this."

"Well, believe it," Curtis told him. "You can't just pull her off the road and expect this to go well. I listened to how Lisa talks about that boy. As far as she's concerned, she'll die to keep him safe and away from us. She isn't giving up without a fight."

Denis Farrell put down the phone. He missed corded phones, which you could slam into their cradle.

He pushed back the chair from behind his desk and labored to stand up. His walking stick leaned against the bookshelves, and he grabbed it for support. Over his head, beams groaned in the old house as his wife, Gillian, paced back and forth in their bedroom. Neither one of them had slept. Gillian probably had a drink in her hand, the way she'd had for the last twenty-four hours.

For a man whose whole life was about control, the current situation for Denis was intolerable. He needed someone to blame, someone to be the target of his wrath and rage. Now he had it. Everything that had gone wrong in the past day was the fault of Lisa Power.

"That was your husband," Farrell told Laurel March. "He screwed up."

Laurel sat in a wooden chair on the other side of the desk, with the yellow glow of a brass lamp lighting her up. Otherwise, the office was gloomy, filled with long shadows. Her face bloomed with concern, and she leaned forward in the chair.

"What do you mean by that?" she asked.

"Lisa hit him and ran."

"She *hit* him?" Laurel asked sharply. "Is Curtis okay?"

Denis dismissed her concerns with a wave of his walking stick. "Oh, please. He's a farmer. Farmers are indestructible. The man could stick his face in a thresher and not even need a bandage. He'll be fine."

"I need to go to him."

"Don't bother. We're busy here, and you and I have work to do. I'll text Garrett to pick up Curtis and bring him back here." Denis ran a hand along the many hardcovers on his bookshelves, which rose all the way to the ceiling. He'd collected them for most of his life, and there wasn't a speck of dust on any of them. His interests were wide ranging. Novels. Histories. Biographies. Political theory. Among the shelves were Lisa Power's four books, including the one that had made her a legend in town. *Thief River Falls.*

The book in which she'd humiliated him.

"According to Curtis, Lisa is armed now," Denis went on. "Apparently this taxi driver passed along some of her guns to her."

Laurel closed her eyes. "Oh, no."

"Dr. March, do you have any idea how dangerous this situation has become? Do you understand the risks if this goes bad?"

"I do," Laurel said. "Of course I do."

"This is a disaster. Why do you think I told you to come down here? You said you could *prevent* this from happening. You told me the best thing to do was *play along* and pretend to be on her side. You told me you could get the boy back and make this whole thing with Lisa go away. Instead, now I have her out there somewhere in town with an assault rifle!"

"I'm sorry. You're absolutely right; this was my mistake. Curtis didn't want to be part of the plan. I forced him, and I shouldn't have done that. I just thought it would be easier to get Lisa to do what we wanted if she was dealing with a familiar face."

"You were wrong. Instead, the two of you managed to make it worse."

"We had no way of anticipating what would happen with Shyla Dunn," Laurel protested.

"That's no excuse. In my business, you have to learn to expect the unexpected. Anyway, how big a threat are we talking about here? Does Lisa even know how to use these weapons?"

"Sure, she does. She grew up with guns."

Denis shook his head. "Well, that's just great."

Laurel got out of the chair and made her way across the office. Her face was expressionless. For someone who had driven down here in the middle of the night, she looked clean and put together, which was annoying to Denis. She had this unshakable evenness of temper about her that always got on his nerves. He didn't trust people who weren't emotionally invested in the outcome of a problem.

"Look, I know how difficult this situation is," Laurel said, "but don't do anything simply because you're angry, Denis. You need to listen to me. I know you. We go back a long way. We've worked together for years."

"I realize that," Denis replied, "and I'm sure you know I'm grateful for your help. By the way, does Lisa know about our relationship? Did you tell her?"

"Of course not."

"All right. So what's your point?"

"My point is, you and Lisa have history, but that has nothing to do with what's happening right now. You have to put that aside."

"This is not about me having a grudge against Lisa Power," Denis snapped.

"Are you sure?"

"Yes, I'm sure. This woman is putting everyone at risk. I know she's a friend of yours, and I know the whole town loves her, but right now, I can't afford to think about any of that. She's a threat, and with every hour that passes, she's becoming more of a threat. She is armed and dangerous. I'm going to do what needs to be done to take care of this situation before it gets worse."

"What does that mean?" Laurel asked.

"Exactly what I said."

"What are you going to do? *Shoot* her? Do you think that's the answer?"

"I hope it doesn't come to that, but that's up to her."

"Lisa won't turn to violence," Laurel insisted. "Trust me. That's not who she is."

"Your word doesn't count for much right now," Denis replied. "And I believe your husband would tell you that she's already violent. She attacked him, remember?"

Laurel said nothing.

"Meanwhile, what do we do about the boy?" Denis asked. "That's where this all started, and we're still no closer to getting him back."

Laurel grimaced and stared through the office windows at the first glimmers of morning over the river. "I promise you, Denis, we will find Harlan. I told you that from the beginning. Sooner or later, we'll convince Lisa to give him to us. But right now, that may be the least of our worries."

21

Before dawn broke, the temperature fell, and the freezing rain turned to snow. As Lisa drove, the whole world became white around her. Snow poured through her headlights and swept across her windshield. She had to go slowly. The Camaro was unfamiliar to her, and the car's tires fought for traction on the ice.

She wanted to go south toward Minneapolis, but she assumed that was what they expected her to do. So she headed north through town, making multiple turns, staying on the side streets while she figured out their next move. The darkness and the snow gave her cover, which she needed, because she knew the word would be out soon. Everyone would be looking for a blue Camaro.

On Atlantic Avenue, she passed one of the local diners. Despite the early hour, the neon sign told her that the restaurant was open. She could get food and coffee and make a plan. She pulled into the diner's unpaved parking lot and drove to the far back, where the Camaro couldn't be seen from the street. There were only four or five other cars in the lot.

"I'll be right back," she told Purdue. "I won't be long. Do you want something? Maybe pancakes?"

"French toast."

Lisa smiled. "Okay. That's my favorite, too."

She climbed out of the sports car into the snow, which whipped into her face. She wore a flannel shirt under her leather jacket, but she was still cold. She trudged through the long parking lot to the diner entrance, and she peered through the window before going inside. The interior was long and narrow, with laminate booths. It wasn't even six in the morning, and only a couple of the booths were filled. She slipped through the door and took the first empty booth near the front window, where she could keep an eye on the street.

Her desire to remain anonymous lasted all of five seconds.

"Lisa Power!"

The excited voice of the waitress boomed through the mostly empty restaurant like a foghorn. In an instant, everyone in the diner was looking at her. Some obviously knew who she was; some were simply curious. As Lisa forced a smile on her face, the waitress hurried over. She slipped into the booth and leaned across the table to grab Lisa's hands.

"Lisa, I am so thrilled to meet you!"

Her name tag read MISSY. She was slim and in her fifties, with sandy-brown hair in a messy pile on her head and a long face dotted with a few age spots and wrinkles. She wore a homemade crocheted blue top and jeans, with an apron tied around her waist. She had the throaty voice of a smoker and brought a whiff of cigarettes with her.

"I'm sorry—do you mind if I call you Lisa?" the waitress went on. "I feel like I know you. I am a big, big, big fan. Me and my sister and my mother, we all love your books. They are not going to believe it when I tell them you came into the diner. Can we take a selfie together?"

"Well, I'm in a little bit of a hurry, Missy."

"Oh, this won't take long!"

The waitress already had her phone in her hand. She rushed around to the other side of the booth, squeezed next to Lisa, and slung an arm around her shoulder. She extended her other arm with the camera and beamed at the lens. Lisa did her best selfie smile as Missy squeezed off several photos.

The woman clambered out of the booth again, looking pleased. "Thank you *so* much. This is amazing. I'm going to post these to Facebook right now."

"*No*," Lisa interrupted, too loudly. "Actually, would you mind waiting until I leave?"

"Oh, sure, sure, whatever you like. I bet we'd have people rushing over here as soon as they saw it. I get it—you want to have your breakfast in peace. I totally understand."

"Thank you. Actually, could I get my order to go?"

"Absolutely. Anything you want, hon."

Lisa didn't bother looking at the menu. Every diner had the same things. She ordered french toast times two, plus coffee and hash browns and a side of bacon. Missy wrote it all down and headed to the kitchen counter to pass along the order. Lisa stared down at her hands rather than look around the diner, because she could feel the eyes of the other people sneaking glances at her.

Nervously, Lisa kept an eye on the diner window. The snow fell like a cloud over the world, but little had accumulated on the ground so far. Instead, the streets shone with a frozen glaze. As she sat there, she saw a Pennington County sheriff's vehicle roll past the restaurant, and she held her breath, wondering if the SUV would turn in to the parking lot. But it didn't. It continued down Atlantic Avenue out of sight.

"You know, I read *Thief River Falls* in one day."

Missy was back, and she took a seat opposite Lisa again, as if they were old friends. She put a mug of coffee in front of her.

"Really?" Lisa said politely.

"Oh, I couldn't put it down. My mom and I had to battle over who got to read it first, but I won. I love that you used real places around here in the book. Every chapter I would go, 'Hey! I know right where that is!'"

"Yes, readers like that."

"We sure do! And of course, I thought it was hysterical that you used your own house as the scene of the murder. That was so wild."

Lisa smiled blankly again. That was another downside of celebrity in a small town. Everyone knew where she lived. Or where she used to live. She and Noah still owned their parents' house, where they'd all grown up, but neither of them had visited the place for nearly a year. In the aftermath of the Dark Star that had stolen away their whole family, they'd never taken the time to sell it or rent it. So it sat there, empty, furnished, gathering dust like a museum no one visited.

Missy was still talking.

"Are you doing research for a new book? Is there going to be a sequel?"

"I don't know yet. And no, I'm not doing research right now. I'm not going to be in town long."

"Too bad. You know, if you're looking for a crime scene in your next book, feel free to use my house. We have a little place just three blocks away from here. In fact, if you need a name for a victim and you want to kill off my sister, she'd get a kick out of that. Her name is Millicent. Milly and Missy, that's us."

"I'll keep that in mind," Lisa said. She gestured at the kitchen counter behind Missy, where the cook had placed two foam take-out containers. "Is that my order, by any chance?"

The waitress looked over her shoulder. "It sure is. Let me grab that for you."

She got out of the booth, but then leaned over the table again. She spoke softly, and her face turned serious. "I'm so sorry, Lisa. You know, I was so caught up with seeing you that I didn't even think. I feel like a fool. I should have asked before now. How are you?"

"Excuse me?"

"Well, how are you? Are you all right? Everybody knows what you've been through."

Lisa hesitated. "Do they?"

"Oh, sure. You know TRF. People talk. So are you okay?"

"Yes, I'm okay."

"Really?"

"Really."

"Well, if you need anything at all, you come back here. I mean it. Nobody's a stranger around here, least of all someone like you. People stick together, right? We look after our own. You live here, you're part of the family."

"That's very nice."

"You should know how proud everyone is of you."

"Thank you, Missy."

"I'll get your food," she said.

Lisa knew the waitress meant well, but she couldn't wait to be gone from this place. She peeled a couple of bills from her wallet and put money on the table that included a large tip, and she was already standing up when Missy brought over her take-out order wrapped in a plastic bag. The waitress hugged her, which made Lisa uncomfortable. She backed out of the door and almost dropped her food, because the footing was treacherous.

On the street, another police vehicle passed at high speed. This time, its lights swirled, responding to a call, and Lisa covered her face with the bag of food. She retreated, slipping and sliding, to the rear of the parking lot and got into the Camaro next to Purdue. Despite the falling snow, the car was absurdly visible, and she knew she needed to get out of town before it was daylight. She had the feeling that if she could only find a way out of Thief River Falls, they would both be free.

"We'll take the back roads," she told Purdue.

They were close to Highway 1, which headed east out of town. From there, she could eventually hook up with a southbound highway and make her way toward Minneapolis. She turned right in the snow, still driving slowly. There were almost no other cars nearby in the early morning, but she felt nervous and exposed. The road led her across a bridge at the crown of the Y, where the town's two rivers met. In the old days, this area at the confluence of the rivers had been the site of the falls that gave the town its name. But since the dam had been built downstream, the waters here were calm.

153

As she inched forward, her windshield wipers pushed away the snow. She passed the community college, and not long after, the houses and apartments thinned as she neared the border of the town. There were miles of open land ahead of her, and once she was there, she could lose herself in the web of minor roads, like playing a game of *Tetris*. She began to relax a little, thinking they'd made it out of town before the alarm spread, but then she realized she was wrong.

Through the pouring snow, she saw the taillights of a vehicle down the highway, parked on the shoulder. She squinted at the road ahead of her and tapped the brakes, feeling the Camaro skid. Her heart sank. She knew what it was. It was a sheriff's cruiser, and its location was no accident.

They were waiting for her. Blocking the route out of town.

If they were watching the eastbound highway, they were watching all the roads. They had her trapped in a box.

"We have to go back," she murmured.

She steered off the highway and swung into a U-turn. She kept an eye on the mirror as she headed back toward town, to make sure the police car didn't make any efforts to follow her. Soon they were in the heart of Thief River Falls again, zigzagging through the empty side streets. It was like she was caught up in a small-town version of "Hotel California." Thief River Falls welcomed her back but refused to let her leave. Every time she tried to escape, she wound up in the same place, forced into a cage.

"I told you," Purdue murmured.

"What?"

"I'll never get out of here."

Lisa didn't know what to say. The boy was right. She couldn't take him away. "If we can't escape this town, there's only one thing to do," she told him. "There's only one way to make this right."

"What's that?"

"We figure out who you really are," she said. "And why people are trying to kill you."

22

Lisa assumed that the police would be watching her family house, but she had the advantage of knowing every square inch of that neighborhood. She knew how to get around undetected. She'd played spy and detective with Noah for years when they were kids, and she'd always been able to sneak up behind him with her cap gun before he knew she was there.

She didn't park the Camaro anywhere close to their house. There was a better place. One of Lisa's old grammar school teachers lived at the far end of Conley Avenue, and she was retired and housebound, with a side yard full of mature trees whose branches hung practically to the ground. Lisa stored the sports car there, mostly out of sight, and then she and Purdue walked two blocks through the front yards toward her old house. The snow flurries and trees gave them cover.

Darkness was giving way to dawn, slowly lighting up homes she knew from her childhood and filling her with memories and sadness. The houses were small and dated back to before World War II. Over the decades, the trees had grown leafy and tall, sheltering the homes. There were no fences. Neighbors didn't need fences here. The driveways were unpaved. In the summer, the open green lawns were dotted with clover, but now it looked like winter and Christmas. The road was directly across the street from the north-south railroad tracks, and Lisa could remember their whole house shaking whenever a train rumbled by.

She was so caught up in her past that she didn't immediately notice that Purdue kept glancing over at the railroad tracks, too. His face looked absorbed in memories of his own. She asked him about it, but he shrugged and said nothing.

Her old house waited for her. Two houses, actually. Her parents' two-story house was on the corner, and next to it was the matchbox rental house where she'd lived for a decade, right up to the moment she bought the place near Lake Bronson. Her entire life sat there side by side. The rental house had new tenants; from where she was, she could see a light inside. But the house of Madeleine and Jerry Power was unoccupied. A time capsule. The key was in her pocket, the way it always was.

If the police were waiting for her, she didn't see them. The streets looked deserted. Even so, she took the precaution of veering into the rear yards of the neighboring houses and taking Purdue around to the back door. Then she let them inside the cold house.

The ghosts of her family welcomed her.

Nothing had changed since she'd been back, other than a thicker layer of dust on the furniture. No matter how much time had gone by, it smelled the same, as if Madeleine were still trailing violet perfume through the rooms. She could hear her mother singing French nursery rhymes in her head. She could hear the excited shouts of her brothers playing football in the yard. When she went to the kitchen window and looked across the driveway at the rental house next door, she saw a young woman moving back and forth behind the curtains, then bending down to talk to a child. It could have been her.

The past felt so vivid it was difficult to believe it was really the past.

"You lived here?" Purdue asked.

"I was born here."

She went upstairs, and Purdue followed her. Her own bedroom, which she'd shared with Noah, was nothing special. It was so small that it was a place to sleep, not a place to play. The one thing she remembered from that room was all the time that she and Noah had spent in the darkness, trying to read each other's thoughts. Noah had always believed in the special power of twins. She wasn't so sure. Yes, there were times when words and emotions would pop into her head out of nowhere, and sometimes she wondered if that was her twin brother. Or maybe it was just her imagination. She'd felt that odd presence a lot lately, and whenever she did, she found herself thinking, *Go away, Noah.*

She didn't want to go into her parents' bedroom, but the place drew her there anyway. Everything was exactly as it had been when they were alive, so it looked as if Madeleine should be sitting at the mirror and humming as she did her makeup, and her father should be in the bathroom, in his white T-shirt, pulling a razor across his face. Their queen bed was neatly made, with its burgundy comforter and pillowcases decorated with a geometric design. The closet door was closed. She always kept it closed.

She'd been the one to open the door and find her father hanging from the rod by the loop of his belt.

The note in his pocket read, *There's no life without Madeleine.*

"You're crying," Purdue said.

"Am I?" She touched her cheek and realized that he was right. "I'm sorry. I haven't been here in a while."

Lisa sat down on the end of the bed, and Purdue sat next to her, pedaling his legs.

"Why are we here?" he asked.

"Because I need a place where you can be safe. Where no one can find you. I have to go out and get some answers, and I don't know how long that will take me. So you can wait here. I'm going to show you a hiding place down in the basement. Noah and I used to go there when we didn't want anyone to find us. If someone comes to the door, I want you to hide there."

"Why can't I come with you?"

"I wish you could. The trouble is, everyone's looking for you. For me, too, but mostly for you. I don't know why, but I do know that it's important that nobody find you until we understand who you are and what happened to you two nights ago. So I want you to stay here while I look for some people who might be able to help us."

The boy's face bent into a frown. "What if you don't come back?"

"I will come back. I promise."

"You're all I have now. I don't want to lose you."

"You're not going to lose me. I'll always protect you."

He nodded, but she didn't think he believed her. He was a smart boy. Promises were empty things. She was trying to be strong for him, and he was trying to be strong for her, but neither of them knew the future.

"How are you going to figure out who I am?" he asked her.

"Well, I need your help with that."

"What do you mean?"

"I know someone hurt you. I know you don't remember everything. But I also think you remember more than you've told me. I wasn't going to push you while we were trying to get out of town, but things are different now. You can't hide the truth from me anymore."

"I don't remember anything," he protested, but he had that nervous look again, the look of a boy who was keeping secrets.

"I think you do remember. At least you remember some things. I think that whatever it is, it's really hard for you, but at some point, we have to figure out how to face hard things. Even memories that are awful and painful for us. Sometimes we really, really don't want to do that, and our brains come up with ways to avoid thinking about them, but sooner or later you have to deal with the pain. You have to stare it down and let it out. That's the only way you can begin to live with it. Does that make any sense?"

He didn't answer. She could see him biting his lip, holding back tears.

"There are a lot of things in this house that I'd rather forget," she told him, shivering as she stared at the closet door. "I haven't been back in more than a year because it was so hard. But here I am. That's the first step."

She waited, hoping Purdue would open up to her. They sat in silence for a long time. The ghosts who were here must have been waiting, too, wondering if she'd meant what she said about facing down the hard things in life. Because she was a hypocrite. She couldn't deal with the Dark Star that had taken her family. She was just like Noah, running away to Lake Bronson when the going got tough.

The house began to shake.

Literally. The floor trembled under her feet, and the windows rattled, and a whistle that was more like a scream split the air. Purdue's eyes widened with wonder.

"What's that?" he asked.

"A train. They go by right in front of the house. Want to see?"

"Yeah!"

They went to the bedroom windows, and Purdue pressed his nose against the glass. Across the street, the engine of a freight train rumbled through the crossing, dragging car after car, some stacked one on top of the other. The freight cars were a kaleidoscope of peeling paint, rust, and wild graffiti, and they went on forever. By instinct, Lisa counted the cars, and she got to seventy-one before the caboose brought up the rear and the earthquake eased under the ground.

Purdue stayed at the window, watching until the train had completely disappeared. Even then, he didn't move; he just stared at the tracks the way he had when the two of them were creeping down the street toward the house. There was always something about boys and trains, but this was more than that.

"Purdue?" she murmured.

He said nothing, but she could tell that the rattling of the train had jarred something loose in his head.

"Purdue, talk to me."

He looked up at her, and suddenly he was calm.

"That's how I got here," he said. "I came on a train. I was running away."

23

"Running away?" Lisa said. "What were you running from?"

"I was in the hospital."

Lisa took his hand. The two of them were still in her parents' bedroom, looking down from the window at the train tracks. He recited the story with that odd detachment he often had in his voice, as if the events had happened to someone else. Maybe that was the only way he could face it, like a character in a novel.

"Why were you in the hospital?" she asked. "Were you sick? Or hurt?"

He shook his head and then wiped his nose with his sleeve. "It wasn't me."

Lisa didn't understand at first. And then she did. She made a guess. "Was it your mother?"

Purdue nodded.

"Do you remember where you were?"

"No. We had to go somewhere because of what was wrong with her. I didn't know where it was. We drove for a long time."

"And where's home? Do you remember that?"

"We didn't really have a home," he said. "We moved around a lot. My mom had friends in different places, and we'd go there and stay with them for a while. But we always kept moving. I don't remember us staying anywhere for a long time. Sometimes we'd just sleep in her car if it wasn't too cold. We kept all of our stuff with us there."

Lisa thought of the key she'd found in his pocket. Not a house key. A car key.

"It was just the two of you?" Lisa asked.

"Yes."

"What about your father?"

The boy shrugged. "I never met him. Mom never talked about him."

Lisa realized that she really was dealing with a lost boy in Purdue. Homeless. The child of a single mother. She'd hoped there would be a better explanation for his missing past, something that gave him a family and a place to go. Instead, here he was. Alone. With her.

"Purdue, what happened to your mom?"

The boy took a long time to say anything more. "Months ago, she started having headaches. Really bad ones. We were staying with one of her friends, and she said Mom should go see a doctor, but Mom didn't want to do that. Doctors cost a lot of money, and we didn't have any. She said it was nothing. She said the headaches would go away, but they didn't. They got worse. A lot worse. There was one night where Mom woke up in the middle of the night, and she was screaming because it hurt so bad."

"That must have been very scary," Lisa murmured.

He nodded. "I made her go to the doctor. She didn't want to, but I said she had to. The doctor put her in a big tube where they could see inside her, and after that, he said she needed to go to a hospital right away."

"Did the doctor say what was wrong with her?"

"Well, he said they were going to take out her brain."

Lisa wanted to smile, but she knew what he meant. "A brain tumor? They were going to remove a brain tumor?"

"I guess so."

"So you went to a hospital?"

"Yes. They shaved my mom's head. I didn't like that. It didn't look like her anymore. I remember sitting in a room and talking with her before they took her away. We talked for a long time. We talked about places we'd been. Stuff we'd done. That was nice. But doctors and nurses kept coming in, and they were whispering to each other. My mom said everything was going to be fine, that I shouldn't be scared or worry about anything. I didn't believe her."

"I understand."

"She talked to me about Canada while we were there, too. She talked about it a lot. She said that's where she grew up. She never told me that before. I don't think her parents were very nice to her. She said her dad did some bad things, and after that, she ran away and never went back. But she said she missed Canada. She talked about how pretty it was in the snow. She wanted me to see it someday."

"It's a beautiful place," Lisa said. "We're pretty close to Canada here, you know."

The boy said nothing.

"What happened next?" she asked.

"They came and took her away. Mom was crying. She was holding my hand and saying how much she loved me and that she would see me soon. Then she was gone. She was gone a long time. Everybody kept coming up and asking how I was, which was really stupid. I was fine. My mom was the one who was sick. They wanted to play games with me, and get stuff for me to eat and drink, and put on videos for me, but I just wanted my mom back."

Lisa had no trouble imagining this calm, serious boy at the center of a whirlwind as all the nurses fussed over him. Nothing was worse in a hospital than a child who was alone.

She didn't want to ask the next question, because she already suspected what the answer was. "Did your mom come back?"

Purdue shook his head. "No. I told you, Lisa: people die in hospitals."

Somehow he managed to fight off his own tears, but Lisa surrendered to hers. She pulled his little body close and hugged him, and she cried silently. It felt strange, as if he were the one comforting her.

"I'm so sorry, Purdue."

"A man and a woman came and told me that Mom died. They said the doctors tried and tried and did everything they could, but Mom's heart stopped in the middle of what they were doing, and it wouldn't start again. They acted like I didn't even know what that meant. Then they started asking me all sorts of questions."

Lisa nodded. "I bet they did."

"They asked about where I lived, and where my dad was, and what family I had, and stuff like that."

"What did you tell them?"

"I lied. I said my dad was on his way, and he'd take me home. I said we lived in a really big house and had lots of money. They didn't believe me. I knew what was going to happen. They were going to take me away and put me with strangers somewhere. That's what they do with kids who don't have anybody."

"What did you do?" Lisa asked.

"I said I was hungry. And I was. So they took me to the cafeteria and got dinner for me, and I put another sandwich and some cookies in my pocket when they weren't looking. Then I said I had to go to the bathroom. But I didn't. I ran down the hallway and out of the hospital."

Lisa shook her head. She thought about this brave, foolish kid, going off on his own in the minutes after his mother had died. She could imagine the panic he'd left behind at the hospital. It wouldn't be hard to find out where this had all happened, but even when she did, she realized she would be sending him back to nothing. He was right. They would give him to strangers. And it still didn't explain how he'd found himself in the middle of a murder scene, with people who wanted him dead.

"Where did you go?"

He pointed out the window. "There were train tracks near the hospital. A train was stopped there, and some guys were hanging out. I asked them where the train was going."

"What did they say?"

"Canada. They said the train was going to Canada. I thought, that's what my mom wanted. She wanted me to see Canada. I figured she was telling me what to do. Like she'd sent the train for me. So I decided to get on."

"What were you planning to do when you got there?"

"I don't know. Mom made it sound really pretty, and I just wanted to see it. So I walked next to the train until I found a car that was open, and I climbed inside. The train started up again right after that. As we left, I could see lots of people outside the hospital. Doctors. Nurses. Police. I figured they were looking for me, so I hid, and nobody saw me. I stayed on the train, and it started going faster. It was great. Way better than being in a car."

"How long were you on the train?"

"All day."

"What did you see?"

"Oh, lots of things! Lots of cows and sheep. We went over a lot of rivers, too. We stopped in some towns. Not big towns. Not like a city. We kept going and going, but eventually it got dark, and it started to get colder. And it started raining outside, too. Pouring. Then we stopped again. I kept waiting for the train to start, but it didn't. It just sat there. I figured maybe we were there, you know? I figured we were in Canada. So I got off the train. I saw a couple men hanging around, and I thought about asking them where I was, but I figured they'd start asking me questions, and then they'd send me back. I didn't want that."

"You stayed here?"

"Yes."

"Do you remember what you saw near the train? Do you remember where you were?"

"I saw a plane," Purdue said. "A plane landed right over my head. I thought it was going to land on top of me."

"You were near the airport," Lisa murmured. "There are railroad tracks just east of there. Where did you go then?"

"I walked. I don't know for how long. I started across some fields, and after a while, I got to a river. I couldn't get across, so I walked next to the water. It was still raining, and I was soaked. I was getting pretty cold and tired, and I was scared. And I missed my mom, you know?"

"I know."

"I found a little house," Purdue went on.

"Like a cabin?"

"I guess."

"Where was it?"

"I don't know. I don't know where I was, but I was still right near the water. I thought I could hide in there for a while, but somebody was inside. A man. He must have heard me, because he came outside, so I hid in the weeds on the riverbank."

"What did this man look like?"

"I told you before—he was big, like a football player."

"What did he do?"

"He looked around and then he went back inside. I was going to keep going, but that's when I heard the other men. They were coming through the woods and whispering to each other. I thought they would see me, but they didn't. There were four of them, the man with the red hair and the two policemen. And the old man. They went right up to the door of the little house, and they went inside. I heard a big fight, and then they dragged the other man out. That's when everything happened. They tied him up and gagged him and then they—they started doing things to him."

"Oh, Purdue." She knew so much more now, and yet she also knew nothing at all. "You told me before that the men found you. They hurt you. How did you get away from them? How did you escape and find your way to me?"

The boy shook his head. "I don't remember. Really, Lisa, I'm telling the truth. I don't remember. It's like one minute I was in the woods while they were killing that man, and then the next minute I was hiding in the truck. And then I was looking up and seeing you in the window of your house. In between, it's all just fuzzy."

"That's okay. You've given me a lot, Purdue. This will help me solve the mystery. I just want you to remember one more thing for me."

"What is it?"

She smiled at him. "Your name. What's your name? I'd like to call you by your real name."

The boy was quiet for a while. This was an easy one, compared to everything else he'd told her. She expected to see his face break into a broad grin, like a child reaching out his hand and seeing a butterfly land on it. But it never did. Instead, his head snapped sideways so that he didn't have to look at her.

"I'm sorry. I don't know."

"Really? Are you sure?"

"I don't remember my name," he insisted.

"That's okay. Don't worry. You'll stay Purdue for a little while longer."

Lisa squeezed his shoulder to make him feel better, so that he knew she didn't blame him. And she didn't. The trouble was, it was painfully obvious that he was lying to her. His shame was written all over his face. This was more than just keeping a secret. This was an out-and-out, pants-on-fire lie.

He did know his name, and he didn't want to tell her what it was. Why would he hide something like that?

166

24

Lisa showed Purdue the secret hiding place in the basement. It wasn't much more than a crawl space, a gap above the foundation and underneath the floorboards where Madeleine had stored her handmade Christmas decorations. The boxes were still there, labeled in her mother's spidery handwriting. Behind the boxes, there was just enough room to slither in and hide, which was what Lisa and Noah had done as kids.

"If you see anyone outside, you run downstairs and crawl in here," she told him. "I'll be back real soon."

"Okay."

She felt a twinge of concern at leaving him behind, but she knew he would be safer at home than with her. She grabbed her mother's old winter coat from the hall closet, and she ventured out into a white world. The snow continued to fall, with the wind swirling it into a tornado. The blizzard was blinding, but that helped her stay concealed. If she couldn't see ten feet in front of her, then neither could anyone else. Including the people who were looking for her.

The weather was keeping most of the town inside. She didn't see anyone as she hurried into the wind toward the end of the street, where the Camaro was hidden in her neighbor's yard. Before she took the car out, she wandered across the grass to the railroad tracks and stared as far as she could in both directions, which was like staring into a dense fog. If she followed those tracks for several miles, she would pass east of the airport, which was where Purdue told her he'd gotten off the train.

Under her feet, she could still feel the vibration of the train that had passed a few minutes earlier. Like a restless teenager, she stood in the middle of the tracks and then walked south, all alone in the storm's cocoon. She knew that one of the town's many cemeteries was to her right, but she couldn't see it. On the left were trees and open land, all invisible. It was easy to let her imagination run wild, and that was what it did.

She heard a voice in her head. Noah's voice.

Lis, what happened? Tell me what's wrong.

She almost turned around to see if he was behind her, but she knew he wasn't. He was two hours away in Fargo, if Laurel had been telling her the truth. But it didn't matter where he was. The only reason he was here in her head was because she'd spent the last two hours in the house where they'd grown up together. As far as she was concerned, she didn't have a brother anymore.

Lisa kept walking. She wasn't sure how far she went, not with the snow playing tricks on her eyes. When the wind briefly subsided, she could see a trailer park on the other side of a dirt road, but then swirls of snow rose up again and scrubbed it away. The real world only seemed to exist for a few seconds before she lost track of it again. It was time to go back. She turned around, but she realized she'd lost all sense of direction. She started walking again and stopped. She could feel the railroad ties under her feet; she was still on the tracks. But she had no sense of whether she was going north or south.

White, white, white. Everything was white. It had felt that way in her head for more than a day, but now it was getting worse. Thief River Falls felt like a frozen alien planet. The snow clung to her eyelids and made her blink and squint. Wind howled, throwing an icy mist in her face and cold razor blades through her clothes. A finger of panic crept up her spine.

An unwelcome thought sprang of its own accord into her mind: *Noah, I need help.*

Then she shoved that thought away before it was even fully formed. She didn't need him or anyone. Alone was fine. She could do this alone. As if to prove she was right, the wind offered up a last whistling gust and then took a break. The snow kept on, but she could see the corner of Annie Street not far away and the neighbor's yard where the Camaro was hidden. With a little laugh at herself, she headed that way.

When she reached the Camaro, she didn't get into the car immediately. Instead, she opened the trunk and stared down at Shyla's guns inside. Part of her wanted to remove them. Get rid of them. But she couldn't do that, not now, not yet. She didn't know how any of this would end and what would be required of her before it did.

Staring at the weapons in the Camaro, it occurred to Lisa for the first time that all of this might end badly.

That sometimes in a thriller, the hero died.

She'd written about death, she'd felt the grief of death, but she'd never faced the idea of dying herself. And yet it didn't scare her. If she had to give up her own life to save Purdue, that was a sacrifice she would willingly make. If she and a gun were the only things standing between that boy and safety, then she would do what she had to do to protect him.

Lisa slammed the trunk shut, got in the car, and backed out into the whiteness of the town.

If there was one person in Thief River Falls who had an ear for the town's secrets, it was Judith Reichl. She was the senior librarian, a job she had held for nearly all Lisa's life. Lisa had known her since she was five years old and got her first library card, which to a bookish little girl was like a religious experience. All these years later, she was still Mrs. Reichl to Lisa, never Judith.

The library building was located on the west side of the Red Lake River, which meant Lisa needed to cross one of the handful of town bridges to get there. It was a choke point for traffic that left her feeling exposed in the Camaro, but she didn't spot anyone watching the bridge. She crossed to the other side of town and parked in the library parking lot, and then she got out and walked beside the one-story redbrick building, with an eye on the cars that came and went.

She was in the belly of the beast here, but it couldn't be helped. The headquarters of the county sheriff's department was immediately across the street. If anyone took a close look out the side window, they'd see her.

No one did. She made it inside the library without being spotted.

This place was like a second home to Lisa. She'd done the very first reading from her first book in this library, with Mrs. Reichl beaming proudly from the back of the meeting room. She'd done similar events here with every other book, except for *Thief River Falls*, where the size of the hometown crowd forced them to reserve the auditorium space at the high school. She still remembered the joyful, terrifying experience of speaking to that crowd, with her entire family cheering for her in the front row.

Lisa knew she had no hope of remaining anonymous here at the library. Every person on the staff knew her. Nearly all the patrons did, too. There was a huge display case near the checkout desk dedicated to her and her books, again thanks to Mrs. Reichl. When the people in the library spotted her, they immediately rushed over to greet her. She was never sure how to extricate herself politely, but Mrs. Reichl spotted her from her office and provided a smooth rescue. The librarian steered her away with an arm around her waist. Lisa breathed a little sigh of thanks into her ear.

The two of them went into her modest office. With a single glance at Lisa's face, Mrs. Reichl obviously spotted that something was wrong, and she closed the door to give them privacy. She pulled two chairs together where they could sit next to each other.

"Well, well, Lisa Power. How are you?"

"I'm all right, Mrs. Reichl."

"Are you really? You don't look so good. You don't need to sugarcoat anything with me."

"Let's just say I'm as good as I can be."

"Of course. Can I get you anything? Some coffee?"

Lisa shook her head. "No, thank you."

"How long has it been? A year? I can't remember the last time you've been in here. Your absence has been duly noted. I know you moved to Lake Bronson, and I'm sure writing has been keeping you busy, but it also left me wondering if you were okay. When I don't see one of my favorite people for so long, I get concerned."

Mrs. Reichl had a honey-sweet voice that never let you realize you were being interrogated. She was slim and small, always neatly put together in a dark wool suit, with her gray hair in a stylish bob. She wore glasses (every librarian Lisa had ever met wore glasses), and she purchased a new style of frame every year. It was one of Mrs. Reichl's few vanities. This year, the glasses had a retro cat's-eye look, with a brown tortoiseshell color. Behind her glasses, she had smart, twinkling eyes, with eyebrows that could arch like the gables of a house when she suspected you were fibbing. Teenagers sneaking books into their backpacks didn't last ten seconds before confessing.

"It's just been a busy year for me," Lisa told her. "That's all."

Mrs. Reichl's eyebrows indicated that she'd failed the polygraph. "I see. And what about Noah? He hasn't been in here in a long time, either."

"Actually, Noah left the area. I think he's in Fargo now."

"You think?"

"Well, he and I haven't talked in a while. We had a falling-out."

"I'm very sorry to hear that," Mrs. Reichl said. "I don't think I ever saw closer siblings than you two. I suppose that's the way it is with twins."

"People change."

Mrs. Reichl tugged on the temples of her glasses. "Eyeglasses change, Lisa. You? You are the same girl I knew when you were five years old. Strong willed, smart, an extraordinary imagination. And also stubbornly independent, never needing another soul."

Lisa smiled. "Not true. I've always needed *you*."

"Yes, yes, that's the kind of smooth deflection I'd expect from a writer," the woman replied with another expressive arch of her eyebrows.

"I'm serious," Lisa assured her. Then she went on quickly before the librarian could keep digging into her personal life. "In fact, that's why I'm here. I could use your help about something."

"Oh, really? All right, I can see you're impatient, as usual. What can I do for you?"

"This is sort of an odd request, but something strange may have happened in town two nights ago. I'm trying to find out the details. I know rumors sometimes make their way across your desk, so I wanted to see if you'd heard anything."

"That *is* an odd question," Mrs. Reichl said. "And vaguely mysterious."

"I know. I'm sorry about that."

"Is this for a new book?"

"No, nothing like that."

The librarian's face was quizzical. "I'm afraid I need a little more detail. Rumors about what? Give me a clue."

Lisa hesitated, deciding what she could say. "Has anyone in town gone missing?"

"Missing? Not that I've heard. I have to tell you, Lisa, I don't like the sound of this. Is everything really all right with you? What is this about?"

"Please. Anything at all."

The librarian removed a pencil from her pocket and tapped it against her lips. "I'm sorry, but I can't think of a thing."

"Whatever happened may have taken place near the river," Lisa added. "Maybe someone around here saw or heard something?"

"Hmm." Mrs. Reichl tilted her head, and her eyes focused over Lisa's shoulder. "You say whatever happened was two nights ago?"

"Yes."

The librarian got out of her chair and went to the office window. "I don't know whether this will be of any help to you, but I think the person you should talk to isn't me. It's that girl out there."

Lisa joined Mrs. Reichl at the window. Near the checkout desk, she spied a young girl, probably seventeen or eighteen, with a stack of books she was preparing to scan. The girl was tall and skinny, way too skinny for a healthy teenager. She had stringy black hair and intense green eyes, two little jewels set deep inside a pale face. She wore a long-sleeved gray T-shirt that slipped off one bony shoulder. The shirt was emblazoned with a large picture of Emily Dickinson, and there was a strange symbiosis between Emily's melancholy expression and the expression of the teenager wearing the shirt.

"Who is she?" Lisa asked.

"Her name is Willow Taylor," Mrs. Reichl replied. "Willow's a writer, like you. A poet. She's very talented."

The girl looked up from her books and noticed the women watching her. Her mouth dropped open as she spotted Lisa. Willow stared back the way an astronomer studies the stars, but when Lisa smiled at her, the girl immediately looked down with an embarrassed expression and opened up the first book in her stack.

"She knows me," Lisa said.

"Oh, yes. Actually, the girl idolizes you. She talks about you and your books all the time. You're her—well, who's all the rage with teenagers these days? You're her Ariana Grande, I guess."

"Impressive pop culture reference, Mrs. Reichl," Lisa said.

"I do have grandchildren."

Lisa noticed that Willow refused to look up from the books in front of her, even though it was obvious she was aware that Lisa was watching her. For Lisa, it was impossible to imagine being anyone's idol. It gave her no thrill. Idols were supposed to be perfect, and Lisa felt far from perfect right now.

She turned back to Mrs. Reichl. "Why do you think I should talk to Willow?"

"You were asking about something unusual that happened two nights ago."

"Yes, that's right."

"Well, Willow was in here yesterday morning, and I heard her talking to a friend about something she'd seen the previous night. The two of them clammed up when I came by, the way teenagers do. I don't know what Willow saw, but the poor girl was trembling like a leaf. She was definitely scared of something."

25

Willow Taylor had already left the library by the time Lisa said goodbye to Mrs. Reichl, but when Lisa hurried outside, she found the teenager standing against the wall near the building's back door. The girl was reading one of the books she'd checked out. She wore no coat, and she danced uncomfortably in the cold as lingering flakes of snow blew through the alley. Their eyes met, and as she had before, Willow looked nervously away when Lisa spotted her.

Lisa walked right over to her. "Hi. It's Willow, right?"

The girl's green eyes widened as if a museum statue had suddenly started talking. "Oh my God. Wow. Hi."

"I'm Lisa."

"I know! I know!"

"I hear you're a writer, like me."

"Me? No way. Well, I mean, I want to be. Right now, I'm not very good."

"That's not what Mrs. Reichl tells me. She says you're a talented poet, and she has a good eye. I've always thought it takes extraspecial talent to be a poet. You really have to understand people's hearts. Novelists like me, we have it easy. We just make stuff up."

"Oh, no, I think you're amazing," Willow gushed. "I learn so much from your books. I really get into the characters and their stories."

"I'm glad." She noticed the pink flush on the girl's skin. Below her Emily Dickinson shirt, the girl wore skintight black pants that left her ankles bare. The teenager's green eyes blinked like Morse code.

"Actually, Willow, I wanted to talk to you about something," Lisa went on.

"To me?"

"That's right."

"Well, sure. Anything."

"Great. But let's get out of the snow, okay? You look like you're freezing."

"Yeah, okay."

The two of them wandered across the parking lot, which was a slippery mess of wet snow and ice. Lisa had parked the Camaro between two larger SUVs so that it wasn't visible from the street. She opened the door to let the teenager inside, and then she went around to the driver's door. When she got in, she turned on the engine to warm up the interior.

"Cool car," Willow said.

"It's not mine. I borrowed it. I drive a boring old pickup."

"Really? Me too. My parents let me drive their pickup to school."

"Do you go to Lincoln?" Lisa asked.

"Yeah."

"I did, too. Are you a junior or a senior?"

"Junior," Willow said. She bounced one knee nervously up and down. "You know, you're pretty famous at school. All the kids read your books. I actually did a paper on you in my English class. I wrote about *Thief River Falls* and talked about why you decided to use real places in the book."

"And why is that?" Lisa asked with a grin.

"Because everybody wants to wake up in the middle of a thriller," the girl replied.

"That's very insightful. How'd you do?"

Willow blushed. "I got an A."

"Good for you."

The girl twisted her fingers together like she had a nervous tic. "This is probably a weird question, but is writing painful for you?"

"That's not a weird question at all. And yes, sometimes you have to go to some pretty dark places."

"Yeah. I know what you mean. My poetry is pretty dark, too. There's lots of blood and killing and swearing and sex. It freaks my parents out. And my teachers. They look at me and say they can't figure out where those things come from."

"Well, why do you think you write about those things?"

"I don't know. That's just where I go. That's what comes out. But the way people react, I'm wondering if something is wrong with me."

Lisa could hear the self-doubt in the girl's voice. It didn't matter what their age was; at some point every child was as lost as Purdue. Looking at her, Lisa realized that this girl could have been a doppelganger of her own younger self. Wounded and sensitive and at that age where the world was full of uncertainty, desire, innocence, and despair. Twenty-plus years later, Lisa sometimes felt as if nothing had changed.

"Believe me, when I was your age, I heard the same things from people," Lisa told her.

"Really?"

"Really. I heard more than once that nice girls should write nice things. That wasn't me. Nothing I wrote was very nice, and it still isn't. People die in my books. They kill. They betray the people who trust them. They lose the people they love. It's not pretty. But you know what? That's life. Writing is a mirror. If someone doesn't like what you write, maybe it's because they don't like what they see in the reflection."

Willow stared down at her lap. She pushed her black hair back behind her ears. "I never thought about it like that."

"Well, as far as I'm concerned, you keep doing what you're doing," Lisa said. "Don't worry about what other people think."

"Thanks."

"I said I wanted to talk to you about something, Willow," Lisa continued. "I need to ask you a question."

"Okay."

"Mrs. Reichl said she overheard you talking to a friend about something that happened two nights ago. She didn't know what it was, but she thought you were scared. I was wondering if you could tell me what was going on."

Willow cocked her head in surprise. "Really? That's what you want to know?"

"Yes. Is that a problem?"

"No, it's just that this is so weird."

"What is?"

"That it's *you* asking me about this," Willow said. The girl looked over at Lisa and then looked away. "I mean, what happened that night was sort of about you."

"About me? I don't understand."

Willow sucked her upper lip between her teeth and didn't say anything. Lisa felt the girl's anxiety spreading like a virus, and it infected her, too. It was the same kind of anticipation she'd felt when she put her hand on the closet door in her parents' bedroom and knew that something horrible was waiting for her inside.

"Willow? What's wrong? Tell me what happened."

The teenager whispered, as if she was sharing a terrible secret. "Do you ever worry about someone bringing your books to life?"

Lisa recoiled as if she'd been slapped. The words coming out of the girl's mouth sounded strangely familiar, like déjà vu from a nightmare. Then she remembered. She'd heard them before. Two nights ago, before everything started, she'd done a book club with a group of women in California. And the husband at the party, Mr. Dhawan, had asked her the exact same thing.

Have you ever been afraid that someone will bring your books to life?

"Why would you ask me that, Willow?"

The girl squirmed in the seat, as if she'd made a mistake. "I'm sorry. I shouldn't have said anything about this. Maybe I should go."

"*No.*" Lisa's voice was harsher than she intended. "No, stay, please. Talk to me. What's going on? Where is this coming from?"

Willow hesitated. "I saw something in the cemetery two nights ago."

"The *cemetery*? What did you see?"

"If I tell you, you're going to think I'm weird. Really weird, not writer weird."

"I promise I won't think that."

Willow shook her head. "You will. But I guess that's okay. I *am* weird. See, the thing is, I wrote a poem a couple of years ago. I called it 'Dance of the Dead.' It's my all-time favorite poem. Normally, I don't really like what I write, but I think this one is pretty good. It's about this girl who goes to a cemetery in the pouring rain. She's lonely, and— well—she's thinking about killing herself. But she doesn't know what it's like to be dead, and she wants to find out before she does anything. So she—so she tries to raise the dead. She does this dance in the rain, and she asks the dead to dance with her. And they do."

Lisa shuddered, listening to Willow build a little shop of horrors. As a writer, she realized that the girl was good. The tingles of fear rose up in Lisa's mind like a body floating to the surface of a lake.

And still she wondered, *What does this have to do with me?*

"In my poem, the dead rise up from the ground as the girl dances," Willow went on. "Old ones and young ones. The ones who were sick, the ones who died in their sleep, the ones who were murdered. They dance with the girl, all of them taking turns. It's like she finally has friends, you know? She finally fits in. Except she doesn't, because she's still alive. But the dead know this, and they want to help her. So they have a lottery, and the winner is the one who has to *kill* the girl. He's handsome. He's young. He's the last one to dance with her, and when it's done, he puts his hands around her neck and chokes her. She doesn't struggle. She knows he loves her and wants her to be with him. And at the end, the dead sink back into the earth, and the girl is left there, with the rain pouring over her body."

"Willow," Lisa murmured, feeling out of breath. "What exactly are you trying to tell me?"

"Two nights ago, *I did that*," the girl confided in a hushed tone.

"You did what? What are you saying?"

"It was pouring down rain, remember? I was in my bedroom reading that poem, and I felt like there was no one in the world who would ever understand me. I wanted to be the girl in the poem. I thought, *Maybe I can make it come to life. Maybe if I go to the cemetery and dance for the dead, they'll come get me. They'll bring me home.* It sounds kind of stupid now, but that's what I did. I drove down to Greenwood Cemetery, and I went out among the graves, and I danced. I kept hoping I'd see the dead rise, and I'd see that boy in the black suit who would come and put his hands around my neck. I thought I'd see my poem come to life. But I didn't. I saw something else."

Lisa couldn't strip her gaze away from the girl's face. There was something horrible and hypnotic in those green eyes. "What did you see?"

"I saw *your* book come to life."

"*What?*"

Willow nodded earnestly. "I danced until my legs got tired, and I had to stop. So I sat down against a tree, and I cried. I don't know how long I sat there. The rain just came down, down, down. But after a while, when I was sitting there, I heard something strange from the other side of the cemetery. Near the trees, you know? Near the path to the river? It was like a scrape of metal against rock. I could just barely hear it. I didn't know what it was, but it felt *familiar*. Like something I knew. And then I remembered. It was just like the prologue of your book. It sounded like someone *digging*. So I got up and went toward the sound. When I got close enough, I could barely make out someone. Just a shadow in the rain. I couldn't see who it was, but I saw what they were doing, and I ran. I ran away as fast as I could."

"Tell me," Lisa said. "What were they doing?"

"They were burying a body in the cemetery. It was just like *Thief River Falls*, Lisa. They were *burying a body*."

26

Lisa knew where she had to go. The cemetery.

She crossed the river again and parked the Camaro in an empty lot amid patches of snowdrifts and fallen leaves. Ahead of her, a path led into the woods. The trees and trails of Greenwood Park began here. So did the prologue of *Thief River Falls*.

The sheer weight of memories in this place was suffocating for her, like being buried alive. Whenever she wanted to feel Danny's presence again, she came here. This was where she, Danny, and Noah had all become friends on their weekends in high school. This was where she and Danny had come on a hot June day during their last summer together, two months before the California fire. They'd found a secluded clearing and shared a bottle of wine, and that was where Danny had taken out an oval-cut diamond ring and asked her to marry him. She hadn't hesitated a moment before saying yes. With the heat of the day on their bare backs and the buzz of the birds and the insects in the trees, they'd celebrated their engagement with a wildly erotic and foolishly unsafe coupling on the soft grass.

It felt like long ago.

The trail was wet under her feet. She kept her head down and her hands in her pockets. Soon she reached a familiar cross trail. Going right would take her to the river and the path that was haunted by Indians and murderers, according to local legend. Dead Man's Trail, they called it. Going left would lead her out of the park toward the open land of the cemetery. Part of her wanted to go right and stay in the past, when she was young and Danny was alive. But she went left, following Willow's instructions. She saw the midday light through the trees, and when she broke free of the woods, the dead were waiting quietly for her in neat, parallel rows.

This was where her entire family was buried.

Madeleine Power, her mother. Gerald Power, her father. Anton, Charles, and Samuel, her brothers. They were together, lined up next to each other under matching gray marble stones. Danny was buried here, too, in a more distant place. Everyone she loved was here, waiting for the day when she would join them. She thought about Willow's poem, and for an instant, she was possessed by a strange desire to dance until the dead came to take her away.

But no. She couldn't do that. According to Willow, Lisa's book had come to life here two nights ago, and she needed to understand why. If the teenager was right, someone had visited the cemetery in the rain and buried a body in the soft ground. Two nights ago, Purdue had also showed up at her house. She didn't believe in coincidences. If reality and fiction were blurring, it was because someone had planned it that way.

Someone was playing a game with her, but it didn't feel like a game at all.

Have you ever been afraid that someone will bring your books to life?

Lisa was alone in the graveyard. The huge field was dusted over with wet snow clinging to the grass, untouched by footprints. Even without the sun, she felt blinded by the reflected brilliance of white light. Rows and rows of headstones pushed out of the ground, stretching for hundreds of feet in every direction. A few trees interrupted their neat geometry. Some trees clung to their colored leaves; others blew them across the field.

She walked up and down the rows. The years on the stones went back for decades, but every now and then, she came across the names of people she knew. A couple of times, they were people she didn't even realize had died. The dentist her family had used when she was a girl had passed away two years ago. A nurse who'd retired not long after Lisa joined the hospital had died only recently. The current year was freshly carved on her stone.

Up and down. Back and forth.

Twenty minutes later, with the cold numbing her skin, she still hadn't found the newly dug grave that Willow had told her about. It occurred to her that maybe the girl had imagined the whole thing. Willow was fragile, probably anorexic, and emotionally overwrought; she'd obviously gone to the cemetery with thoughts of suicide on her brain. Lisa had been concerned enough by the teenager's story that she'd given Willow her cell phone number and told her to call anytime, day or night, if she ever felt an impulse to harm herself.

So maybe there had been no person in the shadows. No shovel scraping metal against rock. No reenacted scene from her favorite novel. Willow had seen what she wanted to see, all in her head, driven by exhaustion and depression. *Brief reactive psychosis*, that was what the shrinks called it. Lisa had researched the syndrome for her first novel and built it into the book's plot. In the face of severe trauma, the brain could conjure entire worlds that didn't exist as a way of blocking out reality. Hallucinations of people and places. Delusions that the mind refused to give up.

Lisa was starting to give up hope of finding anything, but she kept following the rows, continuing past grave after grave.

And then there it was.

Not an illusion. Real.

Near the trees in the cemetery's far eastern corner, she saw a brown stone with rough, unpolished edges. It was the last plot in the row, and there was an open space next to it for someone else to be buried at a future date. The ground in front of the stone had recently been overturned and was a blotchy mixture of snow and black dirt. Not green grass like the other graves.

As if a hole had been made and something—someone—had been buried there.

Lisa cast her gaze around the large cemetery. She saw that someone else had joined her in the peaceful ground. A white Oldsmobile was parked on one of the narrow driveways crisscrossing the field, close to the entrance at Greenwood Street. A man made his way down one of the cemetery rows with a large box in his hand, and every now and then, Lisa could see him stop to pluck something off one of the headstones. His clothes—a dark suit and tie, a neat trench coat—made him look like either a minister or an undertaker.

She headed his way, cutting diagonally across the land. As she got closer, she could see that the man was in his seventies, with slightly hunched shoulders. His white hair sprouted from the top of his head and settled on either side like water from a fountain. His dark eyes were cheerful and alert, and he whistled as he went from grave to grave. Lisa watched him bend down at his knees and pick up a flowerpot filled with weathered plastic roses and deposit it in the box he was carrying. He took one of the sad old white roses from the pot and poked it into the buttonhole of his lapel like a boutonniere.

"Excuse me," Lisa called.

The man eyed Lisa from where he was, and his face showed his surprise that he wasn't alone. "Oh, hello."

"Do you work here?"

The man pushed himself up until he was standing again, and Lisa could hear an audible pop in one of his knees and saw a twinge of discomfort cross the man's face. "No, I'm just a volunteer."

"My name is Lisa Power," she said, but her name drew no recognition from him.

"Tom Manno. Father Manno, actually."

"You're a priest?"

"Recently retired. I still do the occasional funeral service for parishioners I've known for a long time. Plus, I help the city keep the cemetery here in good order. People like to leave things behind when they visit. Flowers, trinkets, little memorials for their loved ones. Usually the city comes through before winter and gathers them up and throws them away. I've never liked that. So I get out here before the cemetery workers arrive and save what I can. I keep it all in storage at the church. No one has ever come back to get anything, but that doesn't matter to me. These objects have meaning to someone, so I want them treated with respect."

"That's very nice," Lisa told him.

Father Manno put down the box at his feet. He stared into the wind at the gravestones surrounding them. "Well, to be perfectly honest, these visits are selfish, too. I like spending time here by myself. I have a chance to catch up with old friends. I can reflect on what's ahead for me, too. Not that I'm looking to rush it, but I've seen enough people unprepared that I'd rather get my head around it. People always assume that priests are just fine with death, as if going to a better world means you don't regret leaving the one you know. How silly."

"Well, I don't mean to intrude," Lisa told him.

"Not at all. Is there something you need?"

"I have a question, actually." She pointed to the corner of the cemetery near the trees. "There's a freshly dug grave back there. I assume someone was buried very recently. I was just wondering if you happened to know who it was, or know anything about it."

Father Manno followed the direction of her finger and shook his head. "I'm afraid not. I'm not involved in every burial here, unless the deceased had a connection to my church."

"Of course. I understand."

"I did do a funeral here a few days ago, but the grave was nowhere near where you're pointing. Besides, I'm sure you know about that one."

Lisa cocked her head in confusion. "No, I don't."

"Oh, I'm sorry. I assumed you lived in town."

"I live an hour north," Lisa said. "Plus, I haven't felt like reading the papers in a while."

"Well, the funeral was for a young woman. Her name was Fiona Farrell. It seemed like half the town was here to pay their respects. I suppose that was partly because of how she died and partly because of who her father is."

"Her father," Lisa murmured.

"Yes, Denis Farrell. The county attorney."

Lisa found herself shivering as the wind sprayed snow across her face. "You just buried Denis Farrell's daughter?"

"That's right."

"How did she die?"

"Oh, it was a terrible thing," Father Manno told her. "The family is absolutely devastated. She was stabbed to death. Brutally murdered."

The hospital administrator sat across the desk from Denis Farrell in the county attorney's home office. Wilson Hoke was an annoying little man, one of those sycophants Denis never trusted because they would constantly dance around what they really wanted to say. Denis had no time for pussyfooters. Physically, Hoke was something of a Bill Gates lookalike, always in a wrinkled pin-striped suit, with a meek voice, messy brown hair, black glasses, and a thin little smile.

"I just wanted to say again, Mr. Farrell, how very sorry I am for your loss," Hoke told him. "It's so shocking. It's so tragic."

Denis didn't need any more condolences, especially not from this man. "Yes, it is. Thank you."

"I can't imagine how difficult this time is for you and your wife."

"To be very honest, we've barely had time to think about the reality of it. Grief will come later."

"Oh, I understand," Hoke replied, nodding his head repeatedly.

Denis found himself tapping his finger on the desk in time with Hoke's head. He looked around his office and felt claustrophobic, because everything in here was a reminder. "This is a busy time for me, Hoke. I'm sorry to rush you along, but what do you want?"

"Oh. Well. I just wanted to follow up about the . . . well, the incident. I wanted to assure you that appropriate security measures will be taken."

Denis shook his head. As expected, Hoke was covering his ass. Trying to make sure that none of the consequences fell on his head. "It's a little late for appropriate measures," he snapped at the man.

"Yes, I realize that. I'm sorry."

"Have you contained the situation at the hospital?" Denis asked.

"As best we can. However, Thief River Falls is still a small town. We all know rumors have a way of getting around."

"Then it's your job to stop them before they start," Denis insisted. "I assume we're both clear on the mess that follows if people find out about this. Neither of us wants that, do we?"

"Of course not." Hoke fiddled with the knot on his tie. As usual, he wasn't saying what he wanted to say, which drove Denis mad. "I was wondering, not wanting to pry or anything, whether there had been any new developments."

"No."

"So we haven't . . . located . . . the boy?"

"No."

Hoke nodded uncomfortably. "Dr. March tells me that you think that Harlan is . . . with . . . Lisa Power?"

"We think so, yes."

"And do you know where they are?"

Denis got up from his desk, not hiding his impatience. He ignored his cane and limped to the bookshelves on the wall. He knew exactly which book he wanted.

Thief River Falls.

He took it down and held it in his hands, and then he flipped forward to the dedication, ripping at each page.

For Danny.

And then to the prologue.

Down, down, down . . .

Denis slammed the book shut. The noise was as loud as the crack of a bullet. "No, we don't know where they are, but Lisa came back to Thief River Falls yesterday evening. She's like a moth to a flame, that one. I have people watching the roads, so she can't leave town. Sooner or later, we'll find her. We'll find both of them."

27

Denis Farrell.

When Lisa heard his name, she knew that he was at the center of whatever was going on. She wasn't surprised at all. He was a ruthless, arrogant son of a bitch who treated the town of Thief River Falls like his personal empire. She'd already seen once before how he reacted to loss in his family. If his life had now been touched by the murder of his daughter, he would be the blackest kind of avenging angel.

She and Denis had been antagonists for more than twenty years. He hated her, and she knew it. To this day, he refused to be in the same room with her. Yes, she'd shamed him into taking action against the man who'd assaulted Shyla Dunn when Lisa was only a young nurse, but the bad blood between them went back much further than that. It really had very little to do with Lisa and everything to do with Denis's son.

The golden boy. The inheritor of the legacy. The young man who was going to expand Denis's reach beyond the flatlands in their little corner of the state to the capitol building in Saint Paul. And maybe beyond, to Washington, DC.

Daniel Farrell.

Danny.

Lisa could still remember the first time she'd met Danny's father. She was fifteen years old, and she and Danny had only been dating for a few weeks when the county attorney's assistant called to invite her to dinner. Not the two of them. Just Lisa. Danny had sarcastically told her that his father was a force to be reckoned with, but even that warning hadn't prepared her for what was ahead. She remembered standing in front of Denis's desk in that dark, baroque office of his and trembling as he lectured her in a booming voice about everything that was not going to happen.

You are *not* getting in the way of my plans for that boy.

You are *not* following Danny to college.

You are *not* marrying my son.

You are *not* going to be in his life after high school. Period.

At that point, Lisa did something that she still regretted. His verbal assault had left her feeling small and abused, and she'd fired back at him with two words. *Screw you,* she said. Only she hadn't phrased it so delicately. No one said those words to Denis Farrell. No one, and certainly not a teenage girl. From that moment forward, their relationship had become a cold war. It was no longer just about Danny following The Plan. It was about making sure he never ended up with *that girl.*

She took no satisfaction in the fact that she'd ultimately won the war, because it was a contest in which there were no winners. In the end, Danny chose her over his father, even though it meant living with Denis's near-total rejection. She hated the idea that she'd been the source of a permanent split between father and son. When Danny went off to California to fight the fires, he hadn't spoken to his father in nearly a year. And they never would again.

She blamed herself for that, and she wasn't alone. Denis blamed her, too. He blamed her for everything that had gone wrong. He blamed her for letting Danny go when she could have made him stay. For ten years, ever since Danny's death, there had been almost no direct contact between them. There were days when she wished for a thaw, for a chance to put the past in the past, but that was never going to come.

Not now. Not after she'd taken his name and made him the villain in *Thief River Falls.*

Denis Farrell. County attorney. Murderer.

She'd intended it as a malicious joke, but she was beginning to fear that Denis was the one who was laughing.

Lisa knew where to find Fiona Farrell's house. In many ways, it was a carbon copy of where Lisa had grown up. A corner house with the same floor plan. Two stories. Looking out across the front yard to the lonely railroad tracks.

She did what she'd done at home, parking the Camaro at the end of the block where it wouldn't be seen. She crept through the backyards toward Fiona's house and approached it from the rear. Like her own house, the construction dated back to before the war, but Denis's money had made sure that his daughter lived in a nicer style. The house was neatly painted in bright white, with hardly a speck of dirt on it. Crossbeams on the gable gave it a Tudor look. The roof had the deep-black color of new shingles. The backyard, situated under trees whose leaves were as orange as fire, was manicured, with decorative rocks around a flower garden and a wooden shed painted white to match the house.

What was most noticeable now was police crime scene tape, strung from tree to tree and surrounding the entire yard.

Lisa took note of the neighborhood, but she didn't see anyone watching the property. There were no police vehicles left to guard the house. The crime scene tape itself had pulled away and torn in places, thanks to days of wind and rain. The murder had happened more than a week earlier. There had already been time for an autopsy and for the body to be released and for Denis to bury his daughter.

She darted across the lawn from the shelter of the trees. She ducked under the sagging crime scene tape and made her way to the back door. There had been a lock there, but no longer. Someone had kicked the door in, leaving it broken, barely hanging on its hinges. No one had repaired it yet. More crime scene tape had been adhered in an X across the frame, but she had no trouble squeezing through it into the house.

It was cold inside. She went from the back porch into the kitchen, where the surfaces still showed the fine debris of fingerprint dust. Evidence markers remained in place. The first thing she noticed was that the forensic team had paid a lot of attention to the kitchen counter and particularly to a butcher block of white-handled knives.

One of the slots, the one for the largest knife, was empty.

Lisa continued into the living room. The furniture was modern, more Minneapolis than Thief River Falls, with a young woman's eye for decor. She suspected it was a combination of Fiona's taste and Denis's credit cards. As she surveyed the room, she found her gaze drawn to the mantel over the fireplace. Fiona had kept framed photographs of her family there. Lisa plucked a tissue from a box on one of the end tables and used it to take each frame in her hand to look at the faces.

She recognized Fiona in a photo that had probably been taken in her college days. She had the family hair, sunny and blond, and blue eyes that were pretty but didn't look happy. Life in the Farrell household wasn't a recipe for contentment. Her big smile yearned for her father's approval. She wore a white tennis outfit and held a racket in her hand, and Lisa noticed that a tennis trophy sat on the mantel next to the picture. Whatever tournament she'd been in, she'd won. That was the kind of performance that was expected of the Farrell children.

Next to that picture was another photograph of Fiona, years later. It must have been a recent shot, because she looked to be in her late twenties. There was no smile in this one. It was a professional portrait, obviously taken in a studio to look artsy, but it revealed more about the subject than she might have intended. Her blue eyes looked lost, staring over the camera at something she couldn't find. Her left hand had its index finger over her lips, as if begging for silence. Her shoulders were bare, making her look naked and vulnerable. The intervening years must have been hard ones.

And then there was Denis. The portrait on the mantel showed him with his wife, Gillian, both of them elegantly dressed. He was in a tuxedo; she was in a long navy-blue gown. It was probably a fund-raiser of some kind. Denis wasn't a big man, only three or four inches taller than Lisa, but he exuded toughness in his appearance. Danny had always said that his father prided himself on making the difficult choices that others wouldn't. He never let emotion get in the way of practicality. But the consequences of those decisions were written in the deep lines on his face and in the painful expression as he tried to stand up straight. He'd spent his life like a statue staring down the elements, but sooner or later, even the hardest stone began to wear away.

Gillian had paid the price, too. Her eyes had the glazed look of a woman who wasn't entirely there. Her smile was hollow. There had been a time, almost a year after Danny died, when Gillian had asked to see Lisa. Her late son's fiancée. They'd met for lunch, not in Thief River Falls but forty-five minutes away in Crookston, obviously in the hope that Denis would never find out. It had been an uncomfortable meal. Gillian had drunk way too much. After they went their separate ways, Gillian had never contacted her directly again.

Lisa felt a wave of anger, staring at the two of them. Then she turned over the silver frame and undid the clips that held the photograph in place. She had no business removing anything from the house, but she took the picture of Denis and Gillian Farrell and tucked it into her pocket anyway.

She backed away from the fireplace. There were no other pictures on the mantel and none on any of the walls or on the tables around the living room. What struck her as strange were the pictures she didn't see.

Danny was invisible. He didn't exist in Fiona's house. There was nothing to suggest that Fiona remembered her brother at all. It was like the Farrells were somehow two entirely separate families, the one in Lisa's memory, where Danny had lived and died, and the one in this other universe, where Fiona was an only child.

Someone else was missing, too.

Fiona's husband.

Her left hand, so prominently displayed in the artsy photograph on the mantel, bore a simple gold band. She'd been married. And yet, like Danny, her husband was an invisible presence in the room. Every symbol of him and their married life had been erased. No pictures. No mementos of a wedding. No signs of a man in the house. A single woman lived here now.

A single woman who was dead.

Lisa looked around the room again, absorbing the details. Near a cherrywood end table, something small glistened on the lush carpet, like a diamond. When she went over there and bent down, she saw that it was a tiny shard of glass. There were a couple of other sparkling shards, too, buried in the pile immediately below the table. She noticed that the end table had a drawer, and using the tissue again, she opened the drawer.

There was another picture frame hidden inside. This one was shattered. Glass filled the drawer like sharp popcorn. An eight-by-ten photograph sat amid the glass. It was a classic wedding photo, Fiona in her white dress, her husband next to her in his black tux. He was a tall, muscular man, with very short black hair and a nose that looked as if it had weathered multiple fights. His lips were bent into a smile that didn't come naturally to his face. He had a hawk's eyes, piercing and observant. Lisa knew the type. A lot of women would find this man sexy and irresistible, the he-man, the boxer in the ring. For Lisa, he was the kind of man who would have sent her running for the hills.

Fiona had married him, but now he was a broken picture in her drawer. Lisa took the photograph, folded it up, and secreted it in her pocket along with the picture of the Farrells.

She knew she should leave before anyone discovered her. She'd hoped that the house might show her some kind of connection between Fiona's murder and Purdue's appearance in her life, but there was nothing to be found. It was time to go. But something kept her in this place, something she wanted to walk away from but couldn't. There was an echo of horror in the house. Like a ghost was screaming at her.

She had never been here before, but it was almost as if she could see and hear what had happened in her head.

The stairs to the second floor were on the far side of the living room, and the echoes drew her there. Near the base of the stairs, she found more broken shards, not of glass but of ceramic. The pieces of a vase lay on the floor. Above her, on the fifth step, was an evidence marker. Whatever had been there had been taken away by the police, but she saw an image in her mind of a woman's high-heel pump, sleek and black, lying forlornly between upstairs and downstairs. Lisa felt her heart beating faster.

She could picture the scene. In her imagination, she heard the thunder of running footsteps. A woman shouting. She heard the clatter of the vase tumbling to the floor; she saw Fiona escaping up the stairs and a man chasing her, grabbing her foot, coming away with a shoe.

Lisa went up the stairs slowly. She grimaced at the images flooding her brain.

At the top of the stairs, there was another evidence marker. She knew that was where the other heel had been stripped away in the chase. It pointed her toward a room at the end of the hall. *This way.* She saw a bedroom door, kicked in like the back door of the house, splinters of wood on the carpet. The doorway took her into the master bedroom, which was painted like a snow castle, all white, a king-size bed with a white comforter and white pillows, white curtains on the windows, white carpet. It looked like a winter fairyland, which was what made the other color so shocking.

Red.

There was blood everywhere. Blood on the bed, spatter on the walls and curtains, a vast crimson sea of blood in the middle of the carpet. Even closing her eyes, she could still see it. She could still smell it. Nausea rose in her throat.

He'd caught up with her right here.

Stabbed her.

Killed her.

28

Lisa parked where she could see the building that housed the region's weekly newspaper, the *Thief River Falls Times*. Light snow continued to fall from the gray sky, and as the temperature dropped, it was beginning to stick everywhere. She was glad to have it cover up the Camaro and keep it hidden. Every now and then she ran the wipers to clear a patch on the windshield where she could see. She checked her watch, which she'd already done a dozen times. It was nearly two in the afternoon. She hoped that Tom Doggett was still a creature of habit.

Tom had been the newspaper's editor for fifteen years. He'd had opportunities to go elsewhere to join an urban daily, but he'd chosen to stay in his hometown. As a journalist, he was tough and good. Dogged Doggett was his nickname, and he'd pissed off most of the movers and shakers in the county on various stories during his time with the paper. That was one reason Lisa trusted him. She didn't think he'd go running to the sheriff or the county attorney as soon as he saw her.

As long as she'd known Tom, he'd taken a smoke break every workday at exactly two in the afternoon. He smoked two cigarettes on the street, not caring about rain, snow, or cold, and then he was done with his vice for the day.

Nervously, Lisa checked her watch again. It was exactly two now. As if an alarm had gone off, the glass door at the *Times* swung open, and Tom Doggett emerged into the snow with his pack of Marlboros in his hand. He walked to the street corner with a shuffling gait. He was medium height and a little heavy. He wore a white dress shirt with the sleeves rolled up, wrinkled khakis, and Hush Puppies. He was almost fifty years old, but he wore his wavy dark hair to his shoulders, as if he was still part of a protest movement. Lisa was never sure if he colored his hair or if he really hadn't grayed yet.

Before the editor could light up his first Marlboro, Lisa fired off a text.

Camaro on 4th.

Seconds later, she watched Tom dig into the pocket of his khakis for his phone. When he read the text, his head swiveled curiously. It didn't take him long, despite the snow, to spot the chassis of the sports car halfway down the cross street. She watched his eyes narrow as he studied the car, wondering who was behind the mystery message. He tapped his hand rhythmically on his thigh as he assessed the situation, but she knew his journalistic curiosity would win out.

Tom strolled across Main Avenue. A sheriff's SUV passed behind him, and Lisa tensed, but the police car didn't stop. The editor passed the gas-station-turned-church on the other side of the street and headed straight to the passenger door of the Camaro. He didn't even knock. He simply opened the door and got in.

"Lisa Power."

"Hi, Tom."

"Next time you want to see me, we need some better spy tradecraft. Like a chalk X on the light post alerting me to a secret meeting. I think we need code phrases to recognize each other, too. I'll say, 'Water is wet.' You say, 'Except on Mars.' How does that sound?"

She smiled. "Sorry. I know this is a little cloak-and-dagger."

"A little. Mind if I smoke?"

"Would you care if I did?"

"Hey, you know it's two o'clock."

Tom used the button to lower the side window about a foot. He extracted the cream-colored end of a Marlboro from the pack and lit the top, causing the white tip to smolder. He inhaled, closed his eyes, and then aimed the smoke from his mouth at the open window. Lisa didn't smoke, but she found the sight of the white cigarette strangely hypnotizing.

"So what's up?" Tom asked her. "Are you feeding me a story? It would be nice to have something a little juicier to work on than the soybean futures."

"Actually, you already have the story," Lisa said. "I'd like to find out what you know about it."

"In return for?"

"My eternal gratitude," Lisa replied.

"Uh-huh. I can tell you the futures price on that. What's the story?"

"Fiona Farrell."

Tom whistled. "Oh, yeah, I know all about that one. But why do you care about Fiona?"

"I'd rather not say right now. When I can tell you more, you'll be the first to know. How's that for a quid pro quo?"

"I assume it's the best I'm going to do. I'm not sure what you want, though. Everything I know about the case has already been printed in the paper."

"I'm behind on my reading. Sorry."

Tom gave Lisa a cynical stare from behind his cigarette. "All right. Well, here's the story. You know what Denis Farrell is like. He kept his daughter under his thumb the way he did when she was still a kid. Fiona was looking for a way out. She decided that the fastest way to get free of Daddy was a guy named Nick Loudon."

"Buzzed black hair? Broken nose?"

"That's him. Fiona met Nick at a bar in Bemidji during a summer festival a couple of years ago. He's a good-looking guy if you like that type, but nobody thought it was a good match. Least of all Denis. But you know how it goes. Girl gets emotional abuse from her father, then turns around and finds a man who makes it even worse. That was Nick Loudon."

"But they got married?"

Tom nodded. "Yup. Last winter."

"Then what?"

"The good times didn't last long. Nick was a mean SOB when he was drunk, which was most of the time. He and Fiona started having fights. Bad ones. Neighbors kept calling the cops; cops kept pulling Nick in. Denis wanted Fiona to kick him out, but she wouldn't do that. So the next time Nick got arrested, Denis made sure he cooled his heels in jail for a couple of days. He thought that might wise him up."

"I'm guessing it didn't," Lisa murmured.

"Oh, no. Nick got out, came home, and put Fiona in the emergency room."

Lisa shook her head and swore under her breath. As a nurse, she'd seen that same movie play out over and over at the hospital. What was worse was seeing how many of the women went back to their abusers, because they had nowhere else to go. She pictured Fiona's sweet face in her head from the photographs on her mantel, and she had no trouble imagining how that face had looked after Nick was done with her. She was angry on Fiona's behalf, and for the first time in her life, she actually felt a little sorry for Denis Farrell.

"This time Nick got two months in jail," Tom went on. "Denis wanted Nick behind bars for a lot longer than that, but you know what the courts are like in these situations. Plus, I think the judge didn't want to look like he was handing out a stiffer sentence because Denis was personally involved. Anyway, Nick went away to do his time, and Denis made sure Fiona got a restraining order and a divorce. When Nick got out in the middle of September, Denis had a sheriff's car parked outside Fiona's home day and night in case Nick decided to go after his ex-wife again. Except nothing happened. Nick left town. He got in his car, and according to the credit card receipts, he drove all the way to Florida. Delray. The family was pretty relieved to have him gone, you know? We all figured that was that."

Lisa closed her eyes. "That wasn't that, was it?"

"No," Tom replied. He flicked his first cigarette out the car window. "That was definitely not that."

"What happened?"

"Ten days ago, Nick drove back to Thief River Falls. He parked a couple of blocks from Fiona's place. Denis still had a cop outside—better safe than sorry—but Nick waited until the guy left the car to take a leak and swung a pipe into the cop's skull. Knocked him out cold. Then he went after Fiona. She never even had time to call 911. He kicked in the back door, grabbed a butcher knife, and went after her. Neighbors heard screaming and called the cops, but by the time they got there, Nick was gone, and Fiona was dead in the bedroom. Seventy-plus stab wounds. I mean, he just went after her in a frenzy. Worst crime around here in decades. Maybe ever."

Lisa could see the blood on the carpet. The screams reverberated in her head. She could picture Fiona on her back, could see Nick over her with his arm flying up and down, blood spraying everywhere. It was as if she'd been there to witness the whole thing. She felt sick again.

"They're sure it was Nick who did it?" she said.

"Oh, yeah. Prints everywhere. On the knife. On the pipe where the cop was hit. Neighbors saw him running away, too."

"What happened to him?" Lisa asked. "Where did he go?"

Tom shrugged. "That's the million-dollar question. Your guess is as good as mine. The cops would love to find him, but he's in the wind. They've been on the hunt for Nick ever since the murder."

"He's *missing*?"

"Yeah. He was on foot, too. The cops were all over his car, so he just ran. The sheriff put a squeeze around the whole town. I thought they would have nabbed him by now, but it's been ten days, and there's no sign of him. It's hard to believe he could still be hiding in Thief River Falls, so I figure he managed to get through the dragnet and steal a car. He's probably down in Florida again."

Lisa stared at the windshield, but it was almost completely covered in a light layer of snow. "I don't think so," she murmured.

"No? You think he's still around?"

"Yes, I do."

"You got any particular reason to believe that?" he asked.

Lisa didn't answer, and Tom lit a fresh cigarette. Number two. The smoke stopped going out the window and settled over the Camaro's interior like a cloud.

"Well, you could be right," Tom went on, when he realized she wasn't going to say anything more. "Maybe Nick is still holed up somewhere around here. He can't hide forever, though. And I'll tell you one thing. Nick better hope that the cops catch him before Denis Farrell does. This was his daughter. Believe me, Denis is out for blood."

29

Daylight was waning as Lisa slipped back through her old neighborhood. She made it to her house unseen, and when she was inside, she called for Purdue. He didn't answer, so she took the steps down to the cold, cluttered basement. She navigated through the maze of garage sale junk they kept down there to the tiny crawl space. Her heart felt a flood of relief when she spotted his face poking out from behind Madeleine's old Christmas decorations.

Purdue snaked from his hiding place and dropped to the floor. He wrapped up Lisa in a hug.

"You were gone so long!" he said. "I was afraid you were never coming back."

Lisa mussed his blond hair. "Don't worry about that. Wherever you are, I'll always come back for you. Why were you in the crawl space? Did someone come to the house?"

"I heard something outside, and I got scared. I didn't know who it was, so I figured I would hide."

"That was the right thing to do," Lisa told him.

The two of them went back upstairs to the main part of the house. Purdue went from window to window to peer outside as if he were a spy, and Lisa went into the kitchen to make herself a cup of tea. The kitchen was a match for Fiona's house, without the marble countertops and stainless steel appliances. There were knives on the counter, just like there had been at Fiona's, but none of the knives was missing. Lisa took Madeleine's butcher knife out of the block and thought about all the times she'd seen her mother cutting up chicken pieces with it and singing, "Alouette, je te plumerai" while she did.

When the water was boiling, Lisa brought her tea into the living room. She took a seat on the sofa and patted the cushion for Purdue to join her. The boy galloped over and sat with his legs underneath him. It felt right to have a boy running around the house. Her eyes drifted to the mantel of their fireplace, which was where they kept their family photographs, just as Fiona had. Except Lisa had turned all the photographs facedown when she came back into the house. Seeing them was still too painful.

"I explored the house while you were gone," Purdue told her. "I hope that's okay."

"Sure. It's fine."

He pointed at a copy of *Thief River Falls* on the coffee table. "I found that book in the bedroom upstairs. Is that yours? Is that the one about the boy who's lost, like me?"

"Yes. That's the one."

"Can I read it?"

Lisa shook her head. "Not yet. It's a little old for you."

Purdue fidgeted on the sofa. He looked at the book and then down at his lap. "Well, I started reading it anyway. I read the first part, about the boy in the ground who's talking to his mom."

"I wish you hadn't done that," Lisa said.

"Does the boy die?"

"No. I told you he gets rescued."

"What about his mom? She's dead, right? Like mine. You didn't say that in the book, but I figured that was it."

"Purdue, this is not a book for kids. It's a book for adults."

"What happens? Who rescues the boy?"

Lisa shook her head and didn't answer. She wanted to get away from the book; she didn't want to dive inside the plot of *Thief River Falls*. Not now. Then she heard an echo of Willow Taylor's voice in her head, and she realized she didn't have a choice. The more she tried to get away from the book, the more she kept finding herself in the middle of it.

Do you ever worry about someone bringing your books to life?

"Listen to me, Purdue, that first scene takes place in a cemetery," Lisa said.

"Uh-huh."

"Does that mean anything to you?"

"Like what?"

She tried to decide how much to tell him. To get answers without scaring him any more than he was. "I talked to a girl who was in one of the town cemeteries two nights ago. That was the night you came to my house. She says she saw someone in the cemetery, and she thought they were burying a body. I was just wondering if that stirs any memories for you. You know, like the boy in my book who was put underground."

His brow furrowed. "No."

"Nothing at all?"

"I don't think so."

Lisa didn't sense any deception from him this time. Purdue didn't remember what had happened to him, and if he'd been injured—if someone had struck him—then the trauma had blacked out his memories. So maybe he'd been at the cemetery and maybe not. There was no way for her to be sure.

"I'm going to say a few names to you," Lisa said, "and I want you to tell me if you've ever heard any of these names before."

"Okay."

"Fiona Farrell."

Purdue shook his head. "No."

"What about Nick Loudon?"

"No."

She hesitated. "Denis Farrell. What about him?"

"I don't know any of them. Who are they? What do they have to do with me?"

"Well, I don't think they had anything to do with you. Not until two nights ago. After that, I'm not so sure." Lisa reached into her pocket for the photographs she'd taken from Fiona's house. She took the wedding picture of Fiona and Nick, and she extended it to Purdue with her thumb covering Nick Loudon's face.

"How about this woman?" she asked. "Do you know her? Have you ever seen her before?"

"No."

Lisa moved her thumb away from the photograph. "What about him?"

Purdue's face changed instantly. He squeezed his eyes shut, as if he couldn't bear to stare at the man, as if his picture brought back memories of blood and death. Lisa knew. She'd suspected all along, ever since she'd heard about the murder of Fiona Farrell, ever since she'd found out that Nick Loudon was missing.

"That's him, isn't it?" she asked softly. "The man by the river? The one who looked like a football player?"

Purdue nodded.

"He's the one they tortured and killed?" Lisa asked.

The boy nodded again. He still hadn't said anything.

Lisa had one more photograph in her hand. It weighed hardly anything, and yet it felt heavy. "There's one more picture I want to show you, Purdue. I think this one may be hard for you to see, but I need you to look at it, and I need you to tell me if you know this man. If he was there by the water that night."

Still the boy said nothing.

She took the picture, and she covered up Gillian's face so that only her husband was visible.

Denis Farrell.

The county attorney of Pennington County.

She held the picture in front of Purdue's face and watched terror crease his features, washing away his innocence, bringing back that night as if he were in the midst of it again. As if they were holding him as he struggled to escape.

He knew the face. He knew Denis Farrell.

"Purdue?" Lisa murmured as the silence stretched out. "You have to say it out loud."

He pointed at the photograph with a trembling finger.

"Kill the boy."

30

"It was this man?" Lisa said.

She got off the sofa and shoved the photograph back in her pocket. She found herself moving restlessly around the room, touching all the little objects that made up her past. "He was the old man in charge? He was the one who told the others what to do?"

Purdue nodded. "Yes. He found me by the water. He pretended to be nice, but he wasn't. He asked me all sorts of things about who I was and where I came from, but I didn't trust him. He said the police were going to take me somewhere safe, but then I heard him say it to the others. *Kill the boy.* He didn't think I heard, but I did. He said it like an order, and then he walked away. He had a limp. I remember him limping when he left the others behind with me. That's the last thing I remember."

"Thank you, Purdue. I know that was hard for you."

"Who is he?"

Lisa asked herself how she could describe Denis Farrell to someone who didn't know him. Her judgment was colored by the fact that she'd never liked him. She resented the power he'd had over Danny and the way he'd tried to control both of their lives. Obviously, he'd done the same thing to Fiona. Denis expected the world to bow to him, and when it didn't, he needed to lash out at whoever stood in his way. For most of the past twenty years, that someone had been Lisa. The weight of his grief had fallen on her.

Even so, she felt sorry for him. Deep down, he was a sad old man caught up in his grief, and she of all people knew that grief could change someone. Turn them into someone new, twist around their minds until they didn't even recognize themselves. It didn't excuse what he'd done, but she wouldn't have wanted to walk in his shoes.

"He was Danny's father," she told the boy.

"Your Danny?"

"Yes."

"But . . . why would he hurt that man? Why would he hurt me?"

"Because that man hurt his family, and he was angry," Lisa said. "I understand that. I know how he feels. But Denis crossed a line, and now I have to find a way to stop him."

"How?"

"I need to go out again," Lisa told him.

Purdue got off the sofa and ran to her. "No! No, Lisa, don't do that."

"I have to."

"If you go out, we'll never see each other again. I know it. Something will happen. Don't leave me alone!"

"I won't let anyone hurt you, Purdue."

"But I want to stay together. I want to stay *with* you. Let's go away! Let's go to Canada! Both of us. Take me there, take me away from here, and we'll be safe. We can cross the street and hop on the train. Just like I did."

Lisa shook her head. "Denis won't let us leave. If we go, he'll keep looking for us. Sooner or later, he'll find us—he'll find *you*—and I won't let that happen. I need to stop him. I need to put an end to this. That's the only way to protect you."

The boy buried his face in her chest and hung on to her. She could tell that he was crying silently. She held him, stroking his hair, trying to comfort him. Then she felt his little body stiffen with resolve, and when he separated himself from her, he looked older than his ten years. He had that serious, quizzical face again, the face that seemed to understand the world better than she did.

"I told you that I would never be able to leave this place," he said.

"Don't talk like that. Nothing bad is going to happen to you. I won't let it."

"Something bad already did happen. I'm only here to run away from it."

"I can't change what happened to you before," Lisa said, "but I can *fix* this. I just need to gather more evidence against Denis. He's a powerful man, so I need something that will make people listen to me. Things I can take to Will at the FBI. I need to be able to prove what really happened."

"So where are you going?"

"I'm going to find the place where you were hiding two nights ago. I want to see if they left anything behind. Anything that proves what they did to that man."

"How are you going to find out where I was?"

"Well, actually, I'm pretty sure I already know. Denis owns a cabin by the river. Danny and I used to sneak in there all the time. I'm sure Fiona knew about it, too, and if she did, then so did Nick Loudon. I'm betting that's where he went."

Purdue nodded, but his voice was sad. "Okay."

"I won't be long. I promise."

"Okay," he said again.

"It's almost dark. Are you scared of the dark?"

"No. I'm not scared."

"Good. Remember the plan, okay? If you hear anything outside, you go back down to the crawl space in the basement. Stay there. Wait until I get back. I *will* come back for you. Nothing will keep me away. You got that?"

"Okay," he said one more time, but his voice had the strange artifice of a robot, the way it had in the very beginning. He sounded detached now. He was separating himself from the fear of what was going on, digging a hole for himself.

Lisa hugged him tightly. "Thank you, Purdue."

"For what?"

"For showing up at my house. You may not understand this, but I needed you every bit as much as you needed me. Sometimes things happen for a reason. I really believe that. It's not an accident that we found each other."

She turned for the back door, but the boy called after her.

"Lisa?"

"What is it?"

"If I'm not here when you get back, it's okay. Don't worry about me. I'll be fine. Really."

"Purdue, do *not* leave this house. Understand? You stay right here." She went back and knelt in front of him. "Are we clear about that? I don't want you getting any foolish ideas in your head, like hopping on a train and leaving me behind. Got it? You don't need to protect me. That's not what this is about. Adults protect kids, not the other way around."

"Not always."

"Well, maybe not always, but this time, that's the way it has to be. I'll be back as soon as I can, and everything will be okay. The only thing you need to do is not go anywhere. If you disappear on me, I'm going to be very upset. We're in this together, you and me."

"You and me," Purdue agreed.

Lisa kissed the top of his head. She framed the boy's face in her memory, just in case he was right, just in case something happened to her and all her promises were made of sand. Then she grabbed Madeleine's coat and headed for the backyard.

◆　◆　◆

Keri McDonnell had read *Thief River Falls*.

Actually, she'd read it twice. First she'd read it for herself, and then her book club had read it, too. It was probably her favorite book ever. So when she'd found out that the house she and her husband were renting was the same house in which Lisa Power had actually written *Thief River Falls*, she thought it was the coolest thing ever.

She remembered an interview in which Lisa had talked about writing the book out in the backyard next to the kiddie pool and the jungle gym. Whenever she was sitting out back with her seven-year-old daughter, she thought about Lisa in this same place, typing words into her laptop. It made her feel as if there was a connection between them.

Keri knew that Lisa's parents had died, and she knew that Lisa still owned the house next door, although it had remained empty for the past year. Sooner or later she assumed that Lisa would show up, if only to start getting the place ready for sale. She wanted to be there when she did, so she could talk to her. It wasn't that Keri was a creepy fan, but *Thief River Falls* was a mother's book, and Keri was a mother, too. She wanted the chance to tell Lisa how much it had meant to her.

The women in her book club thought she was crazy, but most of them had already met Lisa at the library. Keri worked evenings and weekends as an EMT, so she was rarely able to go to events.

Today, she'd kept a close eye on the house next door. She had a feeling, she just had a feeling, that someone was there. Once, when she glanced at the windows, she thought she'd seen the blinds moving. And outside, in the back, there were footprints in the snow. That didn't mean anything, because kids were always sneaking around the neighborhood yards playing games, but Keri was paying extraspecial attention to the house anyway.

Her kitchen smelled of chocolate chip cookies. She'd been baking for two hours, because her daughter, Emma, had a party at school the next day. Emma had been helping with the baking process, but her help usually consisted of sneaking spoonfuls of cookie dough when Keri wasn't looking. Now her daughter was in the family room, dancing with Elmo and running around on a sugar rush.

Keri checked her watch. One last batch of cookies was in the oven, but she needed to hurry. Her shift would be starting soon, and she still needed to shower. As she waited for the timer to ding, she grabbed one of the cookies off the cooling rack and munched it while gazing through the window at the neighboring house. She felt sad for empty houses. Houses were supposed to be lived in. They were supposed to have kids. She wished that Emma had a next-door neighbor she could play with.

Keri's eyes narrowed as she watched the house.

Was that a shadow? Was that someone moving around inside? She leaned over the sink and took a closer look, but she decided that her eyes were playing tricks on her. It was getting dark, and the wind kept throwing sheets of snow across the glass that made it hard to see.

Ding.

The cookies were done. She took them from the oven and moved them to the cooling rack, and then she washed her hands and switched into high gear. She didn't have much time. She flew into the family room, where her daughter was playing, took a few seconds to do a little dance with her and Elmo, and then said, "I have to take a shower, okay?"

"Okay!" Emma said.

"We need to go soon. I'll drop you off at Mrs. Allen's, and Daddy will pick you up when he's done with work. Are you ready to go? Do you have everything in your backpack?"

"Okay!" Emma said again, which meant she wasn't listening at all.

"Emma? Are you ready to go to Mrs. Allen's?"

"I'm ready!"

No, her daughter wasn't ready, but Keri just shook her head. Some battles weren't worth fighting. She headed for the bedroom at the back of the house and took the world's fastest shower. When she was done, she blow-dried her blond hair and shivered as she found fresh underwear in her dresser. Her uniform was laid out on the bed. She was half-dressed when Emma strolled in, carrying Elmo.

"Can Elmo come with me to Mrs. Allen's?" she asked.

"Sure," Keri said. *Sorry, Mrs. Allen.*

"Can I have a hot dog for dinner?"

"You can have whatever Mrs. Allen makes."

"I want a hot dog," Emma said.

"Well, I'll make hot dogs tomorrow."

"Okay," Emma said. "Oh, you missed that woman."

Keri stared at her daughter. "What?"

"The woman next door. The one you want to meet. She came out of the house while you were in the shower. I saw her."

Keri's blouse was half-buttoned. She ran to the bedroom window and peered outside, but no one was in the yard. "Are you sure?"

"Yes."

"How long ago?"

"I don't know. A couple of minutes."

"I can't believe it!"

Keri ran for the front of the house, where she shoved her bare feet into her husband's oversize boots. She opened the door and stomped awkwardly out into the yard. A leafy oak tree blocked her view of the street, but she hiked through the snow to the end of the sidewalk. Halfway down the block, she could see someone hurrying away on foot. Even at that distance, she recognized Lisa Power. She thought about shouting after her, but Lisa was already too far away. And she really didn't want to be a creepy fan.

Disappointed, Keri went back inside and kicked off the wet boots. Emma was waiting for her in the kitchen, eating another cookie.

"Did you talk to her?" Emma asked.

"No, I missed her."

"Maybe she'll come back."

"Maybe," Keri said. "Anyway, I need to get to work, and you need to load up your backpack."

Keri returned to her bedroom to finish getting ready. She saw her phone sitting on the nightstand, and on impulse, she grabbed it and dialed one of the women in her book club.

"Hey, it's Keri," she said when her friend answered. "You'll never believe it. I just missed Lisa Power. All year I've been trying to meet her, and I take a five-minute shower and blow my chance."

There was a long pause on the phone.

"You just saw Lisa?" her friend asked.

"Yeah, she was back at her parents' house. Emma spotted her."

"Was she coming or going?"

"Going. I know you two are friends. Do you know if she's back here for a while? I thought maybe I could leave her a note and see if I can bring over some cookies and coffee tomorrow."

"I really don't know," Laurel March replied. "I've been trying to find Lisa myself."

31

Lisa heard her phone ringing as she walked down Conley Avenue toward where the Camaro was parked. She'd meant to turn it off, in case they tried to track her through the cell towers. She grabbed the phone from her pocket to power it down, but when she did, she spotted a name on the caller ID that she hadn't seen in a long time.

Noah.

Her brother was calling.

She stopped dead on the street, listening to the phone ring, feeling it vibrate in her hand. She made no move to answer it. When the call went away, she couldn't even bring herself to push the button to shut the phone down. She stayed where she was. A minute later, she was still standing there, and the phone rang again.

Again, it was Noah.

Part of her wanted to take the call and ask him for help. Part of her wanted to take the call and scream at him. She didn't do either. She simply stared at his name on the screen and then waited until it disappeared. Not long after, a bell chimed, telling her that she had voice mail.

She didn't listen to it.

Lisa shoved the phone back in her pocket and continued to the end of the street to find the Camaro. It was dark now, and she didn't worry about being seen. Lights had come on in the houses around the neighborhood, but if anyone looked outside, she was nothing but a shadow. She got in the car and drove, but she could feel the weight of the phone in her pocket, reminding her that Noah had left a message.

The next band of snow arrived with the cold evening, falling in heavy wet flakes and gathering on the ground. She headed for the river, taking a roundabout route to avoid the main roads. She went east and south and then cut back toward the water on a rural highway. No other cars passed her coming or going. She thumped over railroad tracks and knew she was close to the point where Purdue would have climbed off the train in the pouring rain. Her headlights lit up the barren terrain he would have crossed. It must have been a long walk for a boy who had just lost his mother and had nowhere to go.

A long, miserable walk that ended at the bank of the Red Lake River.

Lisa knew the road she was trying to find. It was called Riverbend Trail, and she'd been there countless times, but she still had to keep her eyes wide open in the dark. She knew she was close when the pavement ended and turned to rough gravel under her tires, but even so, she almost missed the turn. There were no lights or landmarks out here; everything looked the same. She spotted a Dead End sign ahead of her, and she braked hard, turning right onto a cross street and driving through an inch of white slush. Fall trees loomed on both sides of the dirt road, and long driveways led toward riverside homes that were built a comfortable distance from their neighbors. She couldn't see the water, but it was close by. In the summertime, you could smell it from here, a little dank, alive with the whine of mosquitoes. She drove until the road curved like a horseshoe, and that was where she stopped. She turned off the Camaro's engine.

On her right was a long stretch of open fields under a dark sky. If she got out and followed it, she'd eventually wind up back at the railroad tracks. Without the fresh coating of snow, she probably would have seen Purdue's footprints in the deep mud. He'd come right past here. She was sure of it.

On her left was wooded land that led to the riverbank. The land belonged to Denis Farrell.

It was time to go back to the past.

Lisa opened the car door, but she hesitated before getting out. Her phone still felt like a lead weight, keeping her where she was. She took it out of her pocket again, and her thumb caressed the screen as she tried to decide what to do. Ignore the message. Delete the message. Listen to it.

What did Noah have to say to her?

What could he possibly say after all this time?

She put the phone on speaker, and she played the message. His voice filled the car, the oh-so-familiar voice in which she could hear echoes of Madeleine and her father and her brothers and herself. His words were halting and slow.

"Lis, it's me. Look, I know you're not answering, and I know you hate me. I don't blame you. I could make excuses for what I did, but none of them matter, so I won't bother trying. Not that you care, but things are different for me now. I'm living with a girl. Her name's Janie. We're good together. Ever since I met her, I've been thinking about coming home and trying to make things right with you, but I wasn't sure that I had anything to come home to. I don't know if I have a sister anymore. And I know that's my fault, not yours."

There was a long pause. Lisa wondered if Noah was done, but he wasn't.

"The thing is, you're in trouble. I know it. You never believed me about the connection between us, but it's real. I can feel you need help. You're sending out this—I don't even know what to call it—this primal scream, Lis. It's so loud, it's so raw, I want to cover my ears and run away again. But I'm not going to do that, not this time. I'm here. You may not want me, but I'm here. I want to help you."

That was it.

She could hear Noah breathing, and then he hung up the phone.

Lisa sat in the darkness. The Camaro was cold. The trees near her were a thick row of soldiers, guarding the riverbank. Hiding the old cabin. She didn't need to play the message again; it was already frozen in her memory. She told herself that it meant nothing. It changed nothing.

"You're right, Noah," she said out loud. "You don't have a sister anymore."

Lisa turned off her phone and got out of the car.

Noah leaned over the balcony of his third-floor apartment with his forearms propped on top of the railing. The complex around him was huge, more than half a dozen buildings and hundreds of units. He was never alone here. Whenever he looked out, he could see someone walking their dog or smoking a cigarette or see the glow of televisions through a dozen different windows. He'd grown up near parks and farm fields, where it was easy to walk half a block and feel like he was the only person in the world, but since moving to Janie's apartment in downtown Fargo, he'd discovered that he liked being around other people.

He knew that Lisa was the opposite. She didn't want anyone else close to her; she wanted silence and space. It had been that way since they were kids. Wherever she was right now, he was certain that she was by herself.

Janie interrupted his thoughts. She'd heard him leave the message. She sat next to him on the balcony, but unlike him, her back was straight and her knees were pushed together. She always sat with perfect posture. One of her calico cats perched on her lap and batted at her long brown hair, and she stroked its back with her purple fingernails.

"I'm proud of you, Noah," she told him. "I know that was hard."

"She won't call me back. I don't even know if she'll listen to the message. She might just delete it."

"Oh, no, she'll listen to it."

"How do you know?"

Janie shrugged. "I've read her novels. They're too personal. Too emotional. The woman who wrote those books would need to know what you said. She couldn't let it go."

Noah wasn't sure if Janie was right. He knew Lisa better than anyone on earth, and he knew she was stubborn as hell. Danny had always complained that Lisa kept a wall around the most sensitive part of herself and would never let anyone through the gate. You could love her, but you couldn't necessarily get to know her. Then again, maybe people could change. He'd been an introvert for most of his life, just like his sister, but Janie had brought him out of his shell. That was how he knew she was the one. He was going to marry her, and they were going to have kids. But something else needed to happen first.

He needed to make things right with Lisa.

"Do you think I'm crazy?" Noah asked.

"What, that you can hear your twin sister in your mind? That you can feel her talking to you? No, I don't think that's crazy at all."

"Lis doesn't even believe it herself."

"I bet she does but won't admit it. It probably scares her, so she pretends it's not real."

"She needs help," Noah said. "I know it. Something's very, very wrong in her life."

"Can you feel what it is?"

He shook his head. "No, it's like she's blocking it from me. I don't know—maybe she's blocking it from herself, too. The thing is, it's bad. I really think she's in danger. Whatever it is, I'm not sure she'll live through it."

Janie lifted the cat from her lap and gently placed it on the floor of the balcony, where it nuzzled her ankle. She extended a hand to Noah and pulled him closer to her. She placed both of his hands on the warmth of her swollen middle, where she carried their child. The son who would be born in three months. Noah was going to be a father.

It was one little ray of light in the darkness, after two years of hell. He could feel the growing life inside her, and after so much death, he had a profound new appreciation for life. That was another of Janie's gifts to him.

"I've already told you what to do," she said quietly. "Go to her."

"She doesn't want me there."

"You're her brother. You don't need an invitation."

"I might make it worse," he said.

"From what you've said, I don't think that's possible."

Noah nodded. Janie was right. He realized that his hesitation wasn't about Lisa; it was about himself. He was afraid to face his sister again after a year of silence, not knowing what was waiting for him.

"Okay. I'll head over there in the morning and see if I can get her to talk to me."

Janie said nothing. She was waiting for him to realize what he already knew. And he did. He knew what he had to do. The truth was obvious. Noah got up from the chair, and Janie watched him with a Mona Lisa smile on her face.

"I can't wait until morning, can I?" he said.

"No, you can't."

"Lisa needs me now."

"Yes, she does."

"I'll call you from the road," Noah told her, putting a hand gently on her stomach again and feeling life under his fingertips. "I'm heading to Thief River Falls."

32

The trees all spoke in urgent whispers, as if warning Lisa to turn back. She went slowly, navigating through tangled branches and listening to the in and out of her own breathing. The ground was soft, a shallow bed of snow and wet leaves yielding under her feet. The darkness of the night left her mostly blind, but her other senses were alert. She smelled no fire, no cigarette, no cologne. She heard no voices, no footsteps. If anyone was waiting for her near the river, they were well hidden.

She tried to remember the way in. It had been a long time, and everything looked alike under the dark sky. The outer woods were like a wall, but when she crossed that barrier, the trees thinned, spaced around grassland. The cabin was hidden somewhere in there. Danny's grandfather had built it, or maybe his great-grandfather, back when there were no homes along the river, only rustic forest for hunting and fishing.

Somewhere close by, water gurgled against the rocks. Lisa was near the river. She pushed her way to the very edge of the bank, where a ribbon of black water snaked through the channel. The temperatures weren't low enough yet to freeze the current in place. She stared at the water, overwhelmed by memories. She remembered skinny-dipping here with Danny during those long-ago high school summers. She remembered drinking whiskey with Danny and Noah around a campfire until she was sick. She remembered a moonlit night when she'd encountered a black bear up to its haunches in the river. It had shaken its wet fur, bared its teeth at her, and then lumbered peacefully away.

Lisa followed the path beside the bank. Purdue would have done the same thing, not knowing where it would take him. She knew the cabin was close by, because you could practically spit from the back porch to the water. Danny and Noah had both tried. Nestled among thick trees, the cabin was barely visible in the shadows. It was unchanged from her teenage years, although it looked smaller than she remembered it. She felt a keen sense of everything that had been lost in the time since then. Danny was gone. Noah had left.

She stopped where she was, waiting before she went closer, making sure she was really alone. Denis had no way of knowing how much Purdue had told her and how much the boy remembered of that rainy night. If he suspected that Lisa knew what had happened here, then he might have someone waiting for her. But the solitude of the area felt unbroken.

The cabin welcomed her back like an old friend. It wasn't large, and the decades had weathered the exterior. She wondered why Denis had never torn it down and started over, but maybe there was a little bit of sentiment in the man, despite everything he'd done. She found the front door and let herself inside, but she kept the lights off. She remembered that the interior was always nicer than the outside would lead her to believe. Plush furniture. A pool and gaming table. A fireplace. Always beer in the refrigerator and food in the cupboard.

She tried to stay in the present, but the past kept creeping into her mind. Music played from her memory's speakers; it was Third Eye Blind singing "Semi-Charmed Life" as she danced with Danny. Eighteen years old. The week after her high school graduation. Her gaze traveled around the shadows. She'd kissed him there, up against the wall under the old deer head. She'd taken off his shirt there, where the fire warmed their skin, and he'd done the same to her. She'd lost her virginity there, on the cushions of the sectional sofa.

Stop it!

The past was over. The past was dead.

She had to think like a thriller writer. She had to figure out the mystery of what had happened two nights ago.

Lisa turned on her phone again. She wouldn't be here long, not long enough for them to find her. When she activated the flashlight, she turned the phone around and squinted as a bright white beam shone in her face. A headache thumped behind her temples, as it had for two days. She quickly pointed the light at the hardwood floor, and when the afterimage disappeared from her eyes, she used it to search the small interior of the cabin.

She tried to put herself inside the head of a character like Nick Loudon.

He'd come back to Thief River Falls in a fit of rage. He'd stormed inside his old house and murdered his wife. Not just murdered her. Desecrated her. Defiled her. He'd left behind the body of Fiona Farrell for her father to find and fled on foot—to go where? Where could he hide in a town where everyone was looking for him? The cabin was the obvious spot. He could clean up. He could stay here for days undetected if he needed to. Stay until the heat died down and everyone had assumed that he'd slipped out of town.

What would he do first?

He'd shower. He'd be covered in his wife's blood and need to get rid of it. Lisa followed the white light into the cabin's one tiny bathroom and swept aside the curtain to expose a shower stall not much bigger than a phone booth. She'd showered here with Danny once, the two of them pressed together so tightly they could hardly move. He'd been behind her, his arms wrapped—

No. Let it go.

Lisa shined her light up and down the stone walls and into every corner of the travertine base of the shower. She had to get on hands and knees to get close enough. It was hard to get rid of blood, and there would have been a lot of it. Even so, she saw nothing on the smooth stone. The water had washed everything away as Nick frantically scrubbed evidence from his body.

But no, not everything.

She saw flecks on the grout in the far corner. A constellation of pinpoint flecks, so easy to miss. She crawled over and bent down to examine what was there. Her heart raced. It was only a trace of spatter, but she was sure it was blood. The pulse of the shower had sprayed some of the blood off Nick's skin and left a residue here after it dried. Nick had missed it.

It was the first real proof that Lisa was right. Nick had come here after the murder. Everything had happened right here in this place.

Lisa returned to the main room of the cabin. She shot the white light around the space, making shadows. Her imagination began to fill in the gaps. Maybe Nick had been foolish enough to go out near the river, and one of the neighbors had spotted him. Or maybe Denis had thought long and hard about his son-in-law and come to the same conclusion that Lisa had about where Nick was likely to run. The one thing she knew for certain was that somehow Denis had figured out that Nick was hiding here.

He'd staked out the cabin and waited for the right moment to move in.

Two nights ago.

The rain had been hammering down. Perfect cover. No one would stumble across them in the rain. No one would hear them go through the door; no one would hear them wrestle Nick to the ground, gag him, and drag him outside. In the beam of the white light, she could watch the action of the fight playing out in her mind. She could see their guns. She could imagine their shouts, muffled by the roar of the storm.

Nick panicking, trying to escape. The men chasing him down.

Four men. Deputy Garrett. Deputy Stoll. A ginger-haired killer named Liam.

And Denis Farrell. Denis was there, too. He had to direct the play. His daughter was dead, and he had no patience for the slow wheels of justice, for the insufficient retribution of a taxpayer-funded life behind bars. He was going to exact revenge on Nick Loudon.

Swift.

Immediate.

Brutal.

It would have come off without a hitch, too, except even a perfect plan couldn't expect the unexpected. None of them could have anticipated a runaway boy getting off a train, wandering through the muddy fields, and finding himself a witness to Denis Farrell's vengeance.

Denis's plan didn't account for Purdue.

Lisa went back outside and stood alone just steps from the river. The scene began to play out in her mind. A thriller scene. She needed to block out the action, where the actors were, how they moved, what they did. The first character was the boy. Purdue arrived first and made some kind of noise that drew Nick outside, so the boy hid in the weeds by the river.

Right over there.

She went past the cabin porch toward the black water. She could walk down the steps and practically wade into the current. It was so close. In her memory, Danny and Noah were arguing.

You can't spit that far.

Watch me.

Into the river? No way.

I said, watch me, I can do it.

Oh! Oh, close but not close enough. You lose!

Tall weeds grew on the bank, two feet high or more. They bent as the wind blew. She shined her light along the line of brush and saw a frozen spiderweb stretched across the green fronds. At the water's edge, she saw an area where the weeds were matted down. Someone had taken refuge here, so close to the water that he must have been partly submerged in the river. From the cabin side, with the rain drowning the clearing, Purdue would have been invisible.

But the boy could see everything.

She turned around. Where did they do it? Where did they tie him up? She eyed the trees that were closest to the cabin, illuminating each one with a white beam, deciding where she would torture a killer.

If I'm the writer, where would I put them?

She spotted an evergreen but rejected it because its branches were too low to the ground. A young oak had a trunk that was too thin. Another, larger oak was too far away from the cabin, too close to the property line. A neighbor might hear or see something and get curious. People around here knew the sound of guns.

Then she saw it.

An ash tree only twenty or so yards from the cabin's front door. It was straight as a telephone pole, thick and mature. The trunk would hold Nick tight and keep him on his feet when they looped the rope around it. They wanted him standing up, not sitting on the wet ground. Denis would have wanted to see his eyes. His mouth was gagged, but his eyes would have begged for mercy.

Lisa approached the tree.

She knew a little secret from her writing. Living things had an energy all their own. They could convey horror just by being there, and she could feel it as she got closer. This ash tree was alive, and it was part of the conspiracy. It was a murder tree.

She examined the gray ridges of the trunk. Five feet off the ground, she found the burn marks where the friction of the rope had eaten away the bark in two parallel lines as Nick struggled. You wouldn't know what it was unless you knew what it was. She aimed the bright light at the snowy ground. The whole scene took shape for her the way chapters of a book always did, taking over her mind. She felt sick. The violence was coming.

Looking at the ground, she knew they'd tried to clean up the evidence of their crime. When she kicked away the wet snow, she saw that the area was clear of leaves, clear of debris. They'd gathered up everything, right down to the wooden chips of bark that must have sprayed off the ash tree. The rain had taken care of the blood and left no clue of the horrible thing that had happened here.

But plans that looked good on paper still had to rely on humans, hopped up on adrenaline and fear. Humans made mistakes.

Someone hadn't counted properly.

They'd meant to count to ten, but they'd only gotten to nine.

Lisa spotted something on the ground, caught in the bulging roots of the tree trunk. Somehow they'd missed it. When her light passed over it, she thought at first that it was simply an acorn fallen from one of the oaks, but then she squatted and looked at it more closely.

When she did, she jumped back and slapped a hand over her mouth.

It was not an acorn.

It was a man's finger, sliced cleanly at the knuckle.

33

That was how the mystery began, with torture at the river.

Lisa wondered if Denis had felt anything at all, watching it happen. Probably not. No joy, no satisfaction, but also no revulsion. It would simply have been justice in his mind to watch Nick Loudon writhe, to watch him vomit into his gag and have to swallow it down, to watch fountains of blood erupt with each snip of Liam's clippers. There would have been no expression on Denis's face at all. He would have stood there like a statue outside the courthouse, patiently observing the story in Nick's eyes.

Disbelief. Panic. Agony. Madness. And finally nothingness.

Her gaze traveled from the murder tree to the river where Purdue had hidden away in the matted-down brush. The next chapter had taken place there. Denis had found him. Maybe he'd limped down to the water, turning his back on the coup de grâce from Deputy Garrett's gun. And there he was, a blond-haired, blue-eyed boy with a serious face. A boy who'd seen everything they'd done.

Lisa tried to imagine the horror of that moment. It must have felt to Denis that God was punishing him with a cruel joke, sending a witness to that exact place at that exact moment. *You think you're good, not evil? You think you're delivering justice? Then see if you can live with what you have to do now.*

She knew how Denis had gone about saving himself. How he'd chosen to protect his secret. She'd already given him the perfect plan. She'd laid it all out for him in *Thief River Falls*. Kill the boy. There was no other choice, nothing else to do, no opportunity for reprieve. *Kill the boy.* Then take both of the bodies to the cemetery, and bury them in a fresh grave.

Oh, how Denis must have appreciated the irony of bringing the events of her book to life. She'd painted him as a fictional villain, and now he had the opportunity to turn the tables on her. Now he was a real villain. A real murderer.

But sometimes life imitated art too well. The deputies were nervous. They didn't like the idea of murdering an innocent boy. They didn't hit him hard enough; they didn't bury him deep enough. Purdue escaped, just like the Purdue in her own novel had escaped. She understood now why they were so desperate to find him and get him back. As long as the boy was free, Denis and the others were at risk of being exposed.

Lisa knew what she had to do next.

She had to go to the cemetery and dig up Nick Loudon.

She left the cabin behind, which was like leaving her own past behind all over again. All the echoes. All the memories. She lingered in the woods, staring at the cabin and the river, wishing she could go back to those days, when she didn't know the horrors that lay ahead. All the loss she would have to endure. Then the white snow blew into her face, waking her up, and she had to go. She hiked through the trees back to the Camaro parked on the shoulder of the dirt road.

The darkness was complete out here. She couldn't see a thing. As she drove, the car's headlights felt weak against the sheer vastness of the dark land around her. She used the back roads to retrace her steps, avoiding the center of town. She made a stop at the house on Annie Street where she'd been hiding the Camaro, but she didn't leave the car there this time. Instead, she needed something she'd seen leaning against the garage wall.

A shovel.

It was heavy in her hands, with a pointed blade. The metal was rusted, but it would do the job.

She got back in the Camaro and drove to where Greenwood Street dead-ended near the railroad tracks. She parked the car. With the shovel clenched in her right hand, she hiked across the tracks and through empty parkland toward the cemetery only a few hundred feet away. The snow was still falling, huge cold flakes nipping at her exposed face. The world was white, like an avalanche falling over her. She crossed Pennington Avenue, where there was no traffic, and found herself back among snow-topped rows of tombstones.

There were so many graves. So many bodies. It took her a moment to orient herself and remember where she was going. The plot she'd seen with the overturned earth was at the far end of the cemetery, near the dense forest of the neighboring park and the path that led toward Dead Man's Trail. She pushed through the snow. The whistling of the wind filled her head, and she grimaced, because her headache was back. Really, it had never gone away.

When she spotted a faint indentation marking the curve of the sidewalk, she knew she was close. The street was nearby. Garrett and Stoll would have parked at the curb, not far from where they were taking the body. That wasn't the kind of thing you wanted to do over a long distance; it was hard to explain, even for cops. They would have had shovels, like her.

Her imagination told her the story: They'd dragged the body from the car. Purdue was with them. They'd found the freshly dug grave— a rectangular plot at the end of a row, so close to the trees that the branches could reach out and tap on your shoulder. When they got there, they began to dig it up.

She wondered at what point one of them had swung the shovel into Purdue's head.

Before they began to dig?

After the hole was ready?

She wondered which one did it. Garrett or Stoll. But their reluctance showed. Their hesitation won out. They hated what they were doing, and so they didn't do it well. The glancing blow drew blood and knocked out some of Purdue's memories, but it didn't kill him.

They put Nick in the hole. Then they put Purdue on top of him. And they filled it in. They buried him alive. Lisa shuddered at the horror of it. The thought of the boy underground made her sick with fear. It was the kind of thing that grew out of her worst nightmares. To wake up under the ground, unable to see or move or hear, barely able to take a breath.

She reached the grave near the trees. It wasn't hard to find, despite the deeper layer of snow. The uneven ground still showed the evidence of fresh digging. Lisa stood in front of the plot and realized she was crying. She felt overwhelmed, exhausted, almost unable to function. Her headache made a searing stab behind her eyes. She clutched the shovel in her hands and tried to plunge it into the ground.

Down there, a few feet away, was the body of Nick Loudon.

She knew it.

If she found him, she had all the proof she needed. She pointed the shovel at the ground and put her foot on top of the back of the blade. She just needed to push down and turn the dirt away. It wouldn't take long, but the shovel felt heavy in her hands. She found herself sweating, and she was dizzy at what she had to do.

Find the body. Bring him back.

"Oh my God, what are you doing?"

The voice startled Lisa. She dropped the shovel to the ground and spun around. On the sidewalk near the trees, two teenagers stared at her, open mouthed. Two girls, both young, probably no more than sixteen. One girl wore a white bubble coat down to her knees, and the other was dressed in a heavy army jacket with a rainbow-colored wool cap pulled down below her ears.

"It was you!" the girl in the multicolored hat screamed at her. "I saw you!"

"What?"

"You put that body in the ground!"

"No!" Lisa took a step toward them and held up her hands. "No, you're wrong!"

"Get away from me! I'm calling the cops!"

"No, wait!" Lisa shouted. "Don't do that! Stop, I need to talk to you!"

But the first girl didn't listen to her. She ran, stumbling through the snow and abandoning her friend. Lisa watched the teenager slip-sliding through the rows of tombstones, heading for the road. The clock was ticking now, leaving her no time to uncover the body. As soon as the girl called the police, Denis Farrell would be here. Nick Loudon would disappear for good. The evidence would be gone. They'd have Lisa in their hands, and soon enough, they'd have Purdue, too.

"Wait, listen to me!" Lisa called after her again. "You've got the wrong person. I'm trying to help!"

But the girl was already gone.

The other girl, the one in the white bubble coat, simply looked at Lisa with a curious expression. She didn't seem afraid, and she made no attempt to run. She was tall, with long blond hair and earmuffs over her head. Her hands were in the pockets of her white coat.

"It wasn't me," Lisa told her. "I didn't do this."

"Yeah, I know."

"You do?"

"Sure. I know who you are. You're Lisa Power. The writer. I'm a friend of Willow's. That's why I'm here. She told me all about what happened the other night, so I figured I'd check it out for myself. I mean, somebody burying a body in a cemetery in the rain at midnight? That's pretty wild."

"What about your friend?" Lisa asked.

"Oh, don't worry about her. I told her Willow's story. She freaked when she saw someone out here."

"She can't call the police," Lisa said. "I know that sounds strange, but it's not safe."

"I'll text her and tell her to knock it off. I'll say it was all a misunderstanding. She'll listen to me."

"Thank you."

"What are you doing here, anyway? What's with the shovel? Is there really a body buried there? I mean, duh, sure, there are like a thousand bodies out here, but Willow said she saw someone actually digging a hole in the ground. That's pretty creepy."

"I know it is. And yes, I think someone's buried out here who's not supposed to be here, and I think I know who it is. That's what I came out here to do. Find the body."

"Like in your book?" the girl asked.

"Yes, just like in my book."

"Is that where the boy came from?" the girl asked. "Was he in the ground? That was in the book, too, right?"

Lisa had to stop herself from jumping across the space between them and grabbing the girl by the shoulders. *What do you know about the boy?*

"Well, I don't know who he is or anything, but a lot of the kids were talking about him at school yesterday."

"What did you hear?" Lisa asked. "What were they saying about him?"

The teenager shrugged. "A woman on the other side of Pennington came across a boy wandering around the trailer park two nights ago. The park's not far from here. It's an easy walk from the cemetery. Anyway, this kid was hurt. He said he didn't know who he was. He didn't remember anything, his name, where he came from, nothing like that. So the woman took him over to the hospital to get him checked out. But the boy kept saying people die in hospitals, that he was going to die if he stayed there. He wouldn't get out of the car."

Lisa closed her eyes. *Purdue.*

"What happened to him?" she asked.

"Well, that's the weird part. A doctor came out of the hospital, and the woman flagged her down. The doctor got the boy calmed down and said she would make sure he was okay. She told the woman to go back home, that she had everything under control."

"So the boy went into the hospital with the doctor?" Lisa asked.

"I guess. Except the woman called the hospital the next day to see how he was doing, and there was no boy. He was gone. The hospital told her they had no record of him ever being there at all."

34

The hospital.

Somehow Lisa had always known that the road would take her back to the hospital. Sooner or later, that was where she had to go. She'd gone through those doors thousands of times in her life, and now she would have to go through them again. That was where she'd find the last piece in the puzzle about Purdue.

She sat in the Camaro in the hospital parking lot. The one-story brown-brick building sprawled over a flat lot in the middle of empty fields. It was night, but the parking lot was crowded, and people came and went through the doors. Emergencies didn't punch a clock. She'd worked the graveyard shift as a nurse for years, and there were nights when she'd have hours of boredom where she could take out her laptop and write, and there were nights when she'd spent the whole shift literally running from room to room to keep up.

Lisa waited for the right moment. It didn't take long. Two SUVs pulled up near the ER doors, and a crowd of people piled out of the vehicles, including a teenage girl who'd obviously injured her leg in some kind of high school sports accident. Several of the people with her were teenagers who wore uniforms from the local team, the Prowlers. Two adults carried the girl inside, two other adults called for help, and everyone else flooded into the hospital lobby with them, triggering what Lisa knew would be a chaotic scene of confusion and noise.

She got out of the Camaro and hurried across the snowy parking lot to slip into the hospital in the wake of the crowd. No one noticed her. The attendant at the desk was busy. Lisa put her head down and walked into the main corridor that led past the waiting room and into the treatment areas of the facility. The soft brown wood and ochre color on the walls was supposed to be soothing, but Lisa felt her heartbeat take off like a thoroughbred out of the gate. She could feel it beating madly in her chest, and to her ears, it sounded like the electronic beep-beep-beep of a heart monitor. She knew that sound only too well.

A nurse approached her from the other end of the corridor. Lisa knelt down, letting her hair fall in front of her face and fiddling with one of her shoelaces to avoid being seen. She made the mistake of looking up too soon and found the nurse staring right at her. The woman's brown eyes widened with recognition. The nurse didn't say anything or sound an alarm, but her shoes squeaked on the floor as she moved quickly away.

The nurse would tell everyone about her. Soon security would be looking for Lisa in the hallways. She thought about shouting questions after the nurse while she still had time.

Did you hear about the boy who disappeared two nights ago?

Did you see him?

Which doctor brought him in?

But Lisa didn't need to ask those questions. She already knew which doctor had brought Purdue in from the parking lot. It could only be one person. She remembered what Purdue had said about Laurel's reaction while the boy pretended to be asleep.

How did she look at you?

Like she knew who I was.

Lisa continued past the hospital rooms one by one. Most were empty. It was a quiet night. But she passed one room that was a hive of activity, and she found herself stopping to see what was going on. They'd forgotten to draw the curtain. A gray-haired man, easily in his eighties, lay under the white sheet of a hospital bed. A doctor and two nurses clustered around him. The doctor wore a white lab coat, and all three of them wore white masks. Something about the sheer volume of whiteness filled her with an inexplicable horror. White was the absence of color. White was the absence of life. The people in the hospital room didn't look like caregivers, like people who would save you and protect you. Instead, they looked like angels come to collect a body, come to usher you from death to the other side. It made Lisa want to scream. She closed her eyes and covered up her face with her hands, but she didn't see blackness on the other side of her eyelids. She saw white.

Everything was white.

She couldn't get away from white.

Lisa stumbled down the corridor. When she found an empty room, she went inside and shut the door behind her. She kept the lights off, because she didn't want white light. She went to the hospital bed and ripped off the white sheet and crumpled it up and stuffed it inside a drawer. She wanted nothing white in here at all, but she realized that she couldn't escape it. The whiteness followed her wherever she went, chasing her when she tried to hide. She sat on a window bench, and outside, white snow poured down through the white tower lights of the parking lot.

She pulled her knees up to her chest and wrapped her arms around them. She closed her eyes again. Her body was bathed in sweat, and her heart continued to race. Nothing felt real to her. Her lungs struggled for breath, and she was self-aware enough to realize that she was having a panic attack. She tried to coach herself to breathe more slowly, more deeply. She concentrated on her muscles and tried to relax them. Her arms, her legs, her chest. She opened her eyes to look for something she could focus on, and she picked the green EXIT sign outside the hospital's rear door. The letters glowed at her, telling her there had to be a way out of this situation.

She heard words in her head: *You are not going to die, my sweet.*

Madeleine's words. Madeleine's voice. Her mother had told her that with a musical little laugh, when Lisa was thirteen years old and in the hospital to have her appendix removed. She'd been so scared, and her mother was right there to give her comfort and tell her that everything was going to be fine. That was what mothers did when their children were frightened or in danger. They protected them. They saved them. That was their job.

You are not going to die, my sweet.

But Lisa felt as if she really were about to die. No, that wasn't even it. She *wanted* to die. She wanted to escape, to be done, to have this burden lifted from her heart. It was too much.

The door to the hospital room slid open.

The light went on, making Lisa wince at the brightness. Someone stood in the doorway, and it took her a few seconds to focus on who it was.

Laurel.

Laurel was here.

She wore her street clothes, so she didn't look like a doctor. She came into the hospital room and shut the door behind her. The two of them were alone. She took a seat on the long bench near the window on the other side from where Lisa was sitting. Seeing Laurel made Lisa want to run, but part of her also wanted to know what she would say to defend herself.

How do you justify betraying a friend?

"You don't look good, Lisa," Laurel said.

"No?"

"No, you don't. You're sweating. You're having trouble breathing. By the looks of it, I'd say you were having a panic attack."

"I don't need your diagnosis, Dr. March. I don't need anything from you."

Laurel let that remark sit there without challenging it. She kept staring at Lisa the way she always did, with her mind running in the background, showing nothing on her face. She was always so calm, so unflappable, so perfect with her hair in place and her long neck making her look like some kind of queen on the throne. Bombs could be falling around her, and her face would have that same expression.

"Do you want me to give you something to relax you?" Laurel asked patiently. "When did you last sleep?"

"If I sleep, where will I wake up? Underground, like Purdue? Or will I not wake up at all?"

"You'll wake up right here," Laurel replied. "I promise you, nothing will happen."

"Forgive me if your promises don't mean shit to me right now, Laurel."

Laurel didn't react to Lisa's cursing. She removed a pen from the pocket of her suit and rolled it rhythmically between her fingers. She had the look of a chess player who was trying to figure out the best move.

"Curtis is okay, by the way," Laurel told her. "In case you were concerned about that. There's no skull fracture and no concussion. Just a lump the size of an orange on his skull. You remember hitting him, don't you?"

"I remember him plotting to have the police kidnap me and Purdue at the airport," Lisa replied.

Laurel shook her head. "We need to end this. It has to stop, Lisa."

"It stops when Denis Farrell admits what he did. And when *you* admit what you did."

"What did I do?" Laurel asked.

"Two nights ago. That woman from the trailer park took the boy to the hospital and flagged down a doctor in the parking lot. It was you, wasn't it? You told her you'd take care of everything. How did you manage to get the boy inside without any record of it? Did someone help you? Wilson Hoke is the administrator here. He's in Denis's back pocket, always playing politics with the county board. Did Hoke find a way to keep this whole thing off the books?"

Laurel said nothing. She still had that same patient, infuriating look on her face.

"And then what?" Lisa went on. "What happened next, Laurel? How did it go wrong? Did you call Denis to tell him you had the boy? Did Purdue hear you talking on the phone?" Lisa nodded toward the window and the bright green EXIT sign outside. "He slipped out the back door, didn't he? There was a delivery truck parked out there, and he hopped on board. You lost him. That's when everybody really started to panic."

Lisa studied the parking lot again. Out past the fields, she could see cars on the highway. She was no fool. Deputies Garrett and Stoll would be arriving any minute to take her away.

"You think you can put the genie back in the bottle, but you can't," she told Laurel. "It's all going to come out. Do you really believe no one here knows about Purdue? The rumors are all over town, Laurel. People are talking about the boy who disappeared from the hospital. You think you can wave a magic wand and make people forget about that? What about the woman from the trailer park who brought Purdue here in the first place? Do you think she's going to let it go? She'll be back asking questions, just like me. She'll recognize *you*. Everything has gone too far, Laurel. You can't wish this away."

Laurel kept playing with her pen. "Yes, you're right. I've let this go too far."

"Then do the right thing and come *with* me," Lisa urged her. "We'll pick up Purdue, we'll drive to Minneapolis. We'll find Will at the FBI, and you can tell him what happened. About Denis, Fiona, Nick Loudon, about what they tried to do to the boy. Look, I don't know what influence Denis has over you, but I know how he controls and manipulates people. It's time to make it stop. It's time to fight back."

She could see Laurel's mind working fast. Laurel was smart. She'd always been smart. "Where do we pick up Purdue?" she asked. "Where is he, Lisa?"

Her friend said it so smoothly that Lisa almost trusted her again and walked right into the trap. She opened her mouth to say something, and then she snapped it shut again and closed her eyes and took another deep breath. "Oh, Laurel, why are you doing this?"

"I know you were at your parents' house today," Laurel went on. "Is that where you're hiding the boy?"

Lisa's eyes flew open, giving away the truth. "How do you know that?"

"You were *seen*, Lisa. You of all people should know that everyone recognizes you around here. You think you can come and go without the town knowing about it? Your next-door neighbor spotted you, and she called someone in her book club. As it happens, that was me."

"When? How long ago?"

"Enough time to send people over there," Laurel replied. "If he's there, we'll find him. That's the way it has to be."

Lisa's voice was a low, angry hiss of despair. "You bitch. We're talking about a *ten-year-old boy*."

"Settle down, Lisa. Don't upset yourself any further. Why don't you let me get you that medication? You need to relax."

But Lisa was already on her feet. She wasn't going to wait to be taken in, and she wasn't going to give up on a boy she'd sworn to rescue. She had to get home and see if Purdue had hidden in the crawl space. She needed to know if he was still there, or if the police had found him and taken him away from her.

Laurel stood up, too, blocking the way to the door.

"Stay here, Lisa. Please. I don't want you getting hurt."

"Get out of my way."

When Laurel didn't move, Lisa shoved her aside with a strength she didn't even know she had. She yanked open the door to the hospital room and ran for the rear exit just a few feet away. The white world welcomed her back as she crashed through the door into the blizzard of snow. Driven by adrenaline, she sprinted for the Camaro. Inside the car, she fired the engine, making the tires screech as she sped through the slush.

Lisa reached the highway and turned north. When she glanced in her rearview mirror, she saw the red lights of a squad car arriving at the hospital parking lot. They were looking for her, but they were too late.

She left the hospital far behind as she drove into the night.

35

The ruts in the snow at her parents' house told her the story.

The tire tracks were fresh. Lisa could see where the police car had parked, and she could see the boot marks where they'd gone to and from the doors in the front and back. She could see it all in her mind so clearly that she wished she could claw out her eyes. Deputy Garrett at the front door, Deputy Stoll at the back. The two of them storming into the house, hunting upstairs and downstairs, coming outside with a boy squirming in their grasp.

Tell me you made it to the basement, Purdue.

Tell me they didn't find you.

Lisa didn't bother hiding the Camaro this time. She parked at the curb and ran for the door. It was all darkness around her, no lights to be seen. She went inside the house, and she could smell the presence of strange men. The air was cold. Everything was still. Her eyes adjusted, and she could make out familiar shapes, things she'd known for decades. But nothing moved inside the house where she'd grown up. No one made a sound. No one was here. Even the ghosts of her family stayed away and left her alone.

"Purdue?" she called.

Her voice broke and grew plaintive. "Purdue, are you here?"

She knew where she had to go. The basement. If he was still here, that was where he would be. She didn't even bother with the flashlight on her phone as she made her way in the dark. The house guided her by feel, by years of experience. She found the old basement door that never quite closed right, and it squealed as she opened it. There was a light switch by the stairs, but she left it off. She didn't want light; she didn't want anything that was white. Darkness was fine. She took the stairs one at a time, descending underground, feeling the air grow even icier around her. Down here, there was no light at all. None. It was a black box, a coffin, a grave where you could be buried forever.

She inched toward the foundation wall.

As she did, echoes of her childhood caught up with her. She could hear the whisper of Noah's voice as they played the game and the heavy footsteps of their brothers upstairs, hunting for them.

"Where are we going, Lis?"

"I found a hiding place. It's the best hiding place ever. They'll never find us here."

"But where is it?"

"In the crawl space. Behind Mom's boxes."

"No! I don't like it there. It's too dark."

"Big baby, there's nothing to be scared of in the dark."

That had been a long time ago. Lisa had learned since then that there were plenty of things to be scared of in the dark.

"Purdue," she called. "It's me. It's Lisa. I'm here—it's safe to come out."

No one answered.

"Purdue. Please. Answer me, my sweet. Tell me you're here."

The basement was silent. As silent as a tomb. She had no choice now; she had to turn on the flashlight and fill the walls with a harsh white light. She lit up an old wooden chair. She lit up plastic bins stuffed with old clothes. She lit up children's games and books and broken fans and the dull steel of the furnace, and finally, she lit up the dirty concrete blocks of the foundation and the dark gap below the floorboards. She saw the boxes where Madeleine had written *Noël.*

She walked right up to the boxes and shined her light into the blackness. "Purdue?"

He didn't answer. He wasn't there. She knew he wasn't there, but she began to yank out the Christmas boxes anyway, ripping them from their places and dropping them on the floor, hearing the tinkle of glass as fragile ornaments broke. She was destroying her past, destroying what she had left of Madeleine, but she tore away every box until the crawl space was vacant. Until she could see the entire hiding place, where she'd huddled with Noah. The jutting nails in the floorboards that had ripped her clothes. The knots in the wood. The message scrawled in her childish hand on one of the boards in red marker: *Lisa and Noah were here.*

Empty.

The crawl space was empty. They'd taken him.

Lisa sank down onto the cold floor. She turned off the flashlight and sat in the total darkness. She couldn't see anything, and all she could hear was the sound of her hopeless sobbing. She cried and cried. She'd failed Purdue. She'd made this boy a promise, and she'd gone back on her word. She'd sworn to keep him safe, and now he was gone forever.

She had no idea how long she sat there. Her skin was frozen to the touch. She cried until she ran out of tears. She had thought the Dark Star that took away her family was the deepest, loneliest galaxy she would ever visit, but somehow, this was even worse. She felt in a trance. And she knew where she had to go, what she had to do. It was as if, for the past two years, there had been a sharpshooter poised near her, taking out the people in her life one by one.

Until there was only one target left.

One more bullet that needed to be fired.

Lisa got off the cold floor. She staggered back to the stairs, still in darkness, and made her way through the family house. First floor. Then the second floor. She was barely aware of what she was doing before she found herself in her parents' bedroom, with the closet door open. She stared at the metal rod stretching from wall to wall. She remembered opening the door that awful day, seeing her father hanging there, remembered screaming and screaming, unable to do anything but scream until Noah found her and dragged her away.

That old belt. That old brown belt he'd used. How many times had she seen him slip it through the loops in his corduroys? That old belt eventually became a killer.

Lisa had a belt, too.

She undid the buckle and took it off. It dangled from her hand, the hangman's noose. She knew how to do it, but then, she was an expert, because the picture of her father's face in the closet was burned into her memory. She could see exactly how the belt had been looped over the rod and tightened around his neck.

I failed you, my sweet.

She could feel them around her now. The ghosts. Gerald. Anton. Charles. Samuel. Madeleine. And Danny. There was room in the cemetery for another plot beside him. She took a confident step into the closet and swung her belt over the high rod. She needed a chair, and there was a makeup chair in the bedroom, so she dragged it into the closet with her.

Lisa climbed onto the chair and rested on her knees.

The belt was right there, waiting for her. All she had to do was tighten the loop around her throat and kick away the chair. Yes, she would struggle. People always did. It was an instinct. But that wouldn't last long.

She felt strange. She'd expected the ghosts to be happy with her decision. She'd expected to see their arms wide open, welcoming her, smiling, laughing, everyone together again. A dance of the dead. Instead, all she could see were shadows where their faces should be and hear them calling like the whistle of the wind through the old windows. *Nooooooooooooo.* That was what they said. That was what the wind said.

No.

Lisa knelt on the chair for a long, long time, but eventually, she realized she couldn't do it. She put the chair back. She retrieved her belt and strung it back around her waist. Then she sat on her parents' bed and wondered what to do. Her whole soul was consumed by emptiness, and she needed to fill it somehow. She needed to do something.

She found herself saying aloud, "Noah, I need you."

It took her by surprise. Then she said it one more time, and she realized she was crying again.

"Noah, I need help."

But that was foolish. Her brother wasn't here, and her brother wasn't going to help her. She could only help herself. And the way to do that was to keep her promise. She had to find Purdue.

She had to rescue him, even if it meant giving up her own life in the process.

Lisa got off the bed and wiped the tears from her face. She went back downstairs, sure of herself, sure of what she needed to do. She grabbed Madeleine's coat and went out of the house into the snow, not even bothering to close the door behind her. The Camaro waited for her, already shrouded by white again as the snow kept falling.

Tell me where you are, Purdue.

But she knew. A thriller writer always knew where the plot would take her next. If Garrett and Stoll had carried the boy out of her house, they wouldn't have taken him back to the cemetery. That plan was dead. No, they had to come up with another plan, and that meant going to the man in charge.

They would take Purdue to Denis Farrell.

She'd find the boy there. At his house.

Lisa hiked through the snowy front yard to the car, but before she got inside, she went to the trunk of the Camaro and opened it up. What she needed was right there, a gift from Shyla.

A fully loaded Glock.

Lisa took the pistol and caressed it in her hands. Then she shoved it into her coat pocket and steeled herself for war.

Noah, I need help.

He heard those words in his head as clear as a church bell. His sister was reaching out to him. Part of him was glad, but another part of him feared that Lisa had to be in the darkest of holes to turn to him for support. He knew what that was like. He knew how far down a soul could go, and he hated to think of Lisa—who'd always been the stronger one between them—suffering what he'd been through.

Noah emptied every other thought from his mind until it was as wide open as the flat nighttime fields bordering the highway. Then he concentrated on sending his sister a message. *I'm coming to you, Lis.*

He didn't expect an answer.

The rural roads around him were deserted. The night was pure black, with only his headlights to illuminate the highway ahead of him. Snow chased from one side to the other like a ghost. Up here, Canada inhaled and then blew its icy breath across the northern plains. Noah pushed the accelerator down, driving faster. The car was silent. No radio. Nothing to distract him. He needed to hear, to listen, to let Lisa in.

Where was she? What was she going to do?

One thing he knew about his sister. She would always sacrifice herself for someone else, no matter the cost. Noah remembered the last drive he'd taken with Danny, when they drove five hours to the Minneapolis airport for his flight to California. He knew Lisa wanted Danny to stay, but he also knew she wouldn't say a thing to change his mind. She had the power. She could have made him stay with two words, but she put his needs ahead of her own.

In the car, he'd asked Danny, "What if Lisa told you, 'Don't go'?"

Danny didn't hesitate. "I'd stay."

But Lisa didn't ask. Noah could have made him stay, too. He could have turned the car around and taken Danny home, and everything would have been different. Later, he wished he had, but it wasn't his place to say anything. Later, when they were crying together after the news came, he'd asked his sister, "Why didn't you make him stay?"

She said, "Because he needed to go."

That was what he felt from Lisa right now. She needed to go. Wherever she was heading, it was a dangerous place, and he was afraid that Lisa would end up just like Danny. Never coming home.

Ahead of him, Noah saw the next crossroad.

It was nothing special, two lonely roads meeting in a lonely place. He turned, feeling the tires skid. There was a road sign just ahead of him, counting off the distance to the next major town.

Thief River Falls.

Twenty-five miles.

36

Lisa stood near the riverbank behind Denis Farrell's house.

From where she was, she saw no lights or movement inside, but she knew Purdue was here. It was like a mother's sixth sense, part of the connection between them. She knew he was still alive. They hadn't killed him yet. She could feel his presence in the air and feel his consciousness in her heart.

She reached out to him: *I'm here for you, my sweet. I'm going to rescue you.*

Lisa bent down and picked up a heavy rock from the garden. Cocking her arm, she hurled it into the very center of the floor-to-ceiling window that faced the water. The tall pane of glass shattered. She stepped forward and punched out the remaining shards until the hole was big enough for her to climb through. Inside, she stood in the center of the living room carpet, with the fire hissing as white snowflakes drifted through the broken window.

All these years, and the house had changed very little. She'd been here only the one time as a teenager, when she swore at Denis in his office. Denis had never invited her again, and she'd had no interest in going. This was the enemy camp.

The chambered walnut door to Denis's office opened immediately. The man himself came through and closed the door behind him. The noise of the breaking glass had alerted him that she was here, but he didn't look alarmed. He said nothing to her as he came into the room, assisted by his cane. He was dressed in a suit and tie, as he always was, but he'd grown bent and old. She wasn't sure he'd ever been young, but the ravages of his life wore badly on him, especially those half moons under his eyes. A map of wrinkles was carved into his face. His wavy, pushed-back hair had grayed and thinned. Only his blue eyes were as alert as ever. Danny's eyes. That was the only thing the two of them had in common.

"Hello, Lisa," Denis said. He surveyed the wreckage of his patio window with a sour frown. "You could have just knocked, you know."

"Don't be cute. You know why I'm here."

"You're right. Laurel—Dr. March—already called and told me you might come."

Lisa shook her head. "Of course she did. You control her, too. Is there anyone other than me in this town that you don't control? I trusted Laurel, but that was a mistake. I told her everything. I opened my whole heart to her. Has she fed you all of my secrets for the past two years?"

"Not at all. Actually, she's much more loyal to you than you give her credit for."

"I suppose that's why she sent her husband as a spy to deliver me right into your hands."

"Why don't I call Laurel and ask her to join us?" Denis said. "She can explain everything to you, much better than I can."

"Don't bother. I already saw her at the hospital. I know she sent the police to my house. Do you think that's the end of it? Do you think I'm going to walk away and let you win? I won't do that."

Denis said nothing for a while. He just stared at her, as if he were looking for a way to get inside her head. Then he went over to a wet bar on the other side of the room. "Would you like a drink, Lisa?"

"No."

"I'm afraid I need one," he said, then removed a bottle of bourbon and poured a large quantity into a lowball glass. He retrieved ice cubes from the freezer, which he plinked one by one into the liquid, causing little splashes. "Are you sure I can't get you something? You look like you could use it."

"No," she repeated.

"As you wish. Gillian's drinking again, by the way. Grief will do that to you. She's taking the loss extremely hard, as you would expect."

"I'm sorry to hear that."

"Well, I suppose I should get all the alcohol out of the house, but what's the point? She's clever. She'll find a way no matter what I do. And frankly, I'm drinking my way through it, just like her. This has been devastating for me, too. You may not believe that. You probably think I have no emotions at all. But believe me, you couldn't be more wrong."

"I don't recall your shedding a tear when Danny died," Lisa said.

"Not in front of you maybe. That doesn't mean I didn't cry. He was my son."

"Yes, and he was going to be *my* husband. He was the love of my life. You didn't say a word to me after it happened. Not a word. Danny died, and you shut me out. At the memorial? You wouldn't even come near the grave until I was gone. To this day, I hear from your assistant or your lawyer, but never you. All because you blame me for taking him away from you and ruining The Plan. Somehow you could never get it through your head that Danny made his own choices in life. I didn't tell him to leave the law firm. I didn't tell him to come back to me. He did that all on his own."

"I don't blame you for any of that," Denis replied. He sipped his bourbon and stared back at her.

"You're lying."

"No, I'm not. Really. Was I angry? Yes. Danny could have done so much more with his life. He was called to greatness. Whatever he set his mind to, he could have achieved. But if he wanted to be a small-town fireman living with a small-town nurse, well, fine. I would have come to terms with that. Did I shut him out? Yes, and that was selfish and immature of me. I have to bear the guilt of knowing I never mended the rift with my son. But I don't blame you for that."

"Then what do you blame me for?" Lisa asked. "Why have you shut me out all these years?"

"Because you let him go!" Denis fired back at her, his nostrils flaring. "Two words, and you could have stopped him. Two words, and my son would be alive. I know him, Lisa. I know he doted on you, that he would have done literally anything you asked of him. Instead, here we are. Ten years later, and look at where we are now."

Lisa shook her head. "It was his choice, Denis. You know that. I didn't make him go. He *wanted* to go, and there was no way I was going to stand in his way. I'm a victim, too. Blame me if you want, hate me if you want, but I was proud of Danny for going out there and helping those people. I still am."

"Then we're in agreement," Denis replied. "I'm proud of him, too. But you're fooling yourself if you think this fight is a one-way street. You're part of it, too. Yes, I've used you as an excuse for my grief over Danny, but don't tell me you haven't done the exact same thing. You blame *me*. You hate *me*."

"I don't hate you."

"No? Please. You used *my* name in *Thief River Falls*. What a lovely joke, turning me into a monster."

"You didn't need my help for that," Lisa said.

"I'm not a monster, Lisa. I'm not the man you think I am. I'm just a father. I've done my share of things I regret—I'll admit to that. I haven't treated you well. But you've shut me out every bit as much as I've shut you out, and I think I know why. You blame yourself for Danny's death every bit as much as I do. You know you should have stopped him. To this day, you think you're being punished, don't you?

You think everything that's gone wrong with your life dates back to that one moment. The moment you let him go."

"We're done," Lisa snapped. She glanced over Denis's shoulder toward the house's front door. "You're stalling me, aren't you? You're waiting for Garrett and Stoll to figure out that something's wrong, and they'll come inside and rescue you."

"Do I need rescue?"

"That all depends."

"Really? On what? Why exactly are you here, Lisa? What is it you want from me?"

He was so cool. So calm. She didn't know how he did it, how any man could put up a front like that. She glanced at the broken window, where white snow had begun to make drifts on the carpet. She felt nervous and cold, wondering how much time she had before the deputies stormed inside. She'd let Denis play her yet again. It was time to bring it to an end.

"I'm here for Purdue," Lisa said.

There was no reaction on Denis's face. He sipped more of his drink, and there was nothing at all in his eyes. "Yes, I know. Laurel told me."

"Where is he?"

"We both know perfectly well that Purdue isn't here, Lisa."

"Liar."

"I'm not lying. We're alone, you and me. Well, except for Gillian upstairs. Why don't you let me pour you that drink, and we can talk through our differences? We both have things to say to each other. We're both hurting. Let's talk about it."

"No."

"I can't believe you'd deny me the chance to talk about him," Denis said.

Smooth.

He was unbelievably smooth.

Lisa reached into the pocket of her coat and withdrew the Glock, which she armed and pointed at Denis's chest. Again he didn't flinch or show surprise. There was no fear in his eyes. He kept drinking.

"Put that away, Lisa," he said.

"Where's Purdue?"

"I know you're not going to shoot me. The only thing you're going to do is hurt yourself. Or worse, get yourself killed. No one wants that. Put the gun on the floor, and let's talk."

"I'm done talking, Denis. I want the boy. I will do whatever it takes to keep him away from you."

"Yes, I understand that."

"Where is he?"

"You know where he is," Denis said. "Why don't *you* tell *me*?"

Lisa felt something crack inside her. She couldn't even define what it was. She crossed the kind of line from which you can never find your way back. She saw a mirror on the wet bar behind Denis, a pane of glass reflecting the back of his head and reflecting her own face, too. She didn't like what she saw, didn't like the person who was standing there, but she had come too far to let that stop her.

She pointed the Glock at the mirror, and she fired.

The noise was like a bomb in the closed-in space. The mirror exploded, showering them both with glass. Denis finally flinched, going pale with fright. He hadn't expected her to do that. He ducked, dropped his cane, and spilled his drink on the carpet. He put both of his hands slowly in the air.

"Lisa, for God's sake!"

"*Where is he?*" she demanded again.

Denis didn't answer. Even a gunshot didn't draw the truth out of him. But she didn't need him to tell her. She glanced at the closed door to his office, and she knew. Purdue was there. Purdue was waiting for her.

"Get down on the floor," she told Denis. "On your stomach. Spread-eagle. Don't move."

He did as he was told.

Lisa knew she only had a few seconds before Garrett and Stoll would break through the front door, or come around the side of the house and find the broken window. She needed to get Purdue and get away.

Now.

She ran for Denis's office and wrenched open the heavy door. Inside, she slammed it behind her and turned the dead bolt. Denis would always have a lock to keep his secrets safe. She spun around, and her breath flew out of her chest.

There he was. Purdue, tied to the chair. His eyes lit up with joy when he saw her.

"*Lisa!* You came back. You didn't leave me."

"Leave you? I would never do that. Now come on, we need to get out of here."

She ran to the chair and fumbled with the twine that kept the boy secure. Her fingers couldn't undo the knots. She pulled at it, but couldn't manage to free him. Sweat gathered on her neck. Outside, she could hear footsteps, and then someone's fist pounded on the office door.

It was Denis.

"Lisa! Lisa, come out of there!"

She ignored the noise. Her gaze flicked to the door that led out to the river, but she saw no one. That wouldn't be true for long. They'd be here any second. She studied Denis's desk for something, anything, that would cut the rope, and she spotted a pair of scissors stuck inside a misshapen ceramic mug, the kind of gift a child would make for a grandfather. She grabbed the scissors and used the blade to saw at the twine.

It came apart into threads, and then it broke.

She loosened the bonds that held him tight and pulled the rope away over Purdue's head. His arms flew around her.

"I love you, Lisa."

"I love you, too. Now let's go!"

She held his hand, and they sprinted for the patio door. Again she could see her reflection in the window; again she didn't like what she saw. It didn't matter. She pulled it open, letting in the storm. The backyard and the dark waters of the river were in front of them. When she took one more look back over her shoulder, she noticed an oil painting hung on the wall, and the sight of the painting made her heart break all over again.

It was Danny. He was still watching over her.

"Run, Purdue," she said.

37

Denis was sitting on the stairs that led to the upstairs bedrooms, with his hands on his knees, when Deputy Garrett came through the broken window into the living room. The police officer had his gun drawn, and his gaze flew to the mirror that had been shot into a thousand pieces. As he walked across the carpet toward Denis, his boots crunched on shards of glass.

"Are you okay, sir? What happened? I heard a gunshot."

Denis was still in shock himself and trying to work his way through it. "I'm all right, Garrett."

"What about your wife?"

"Sleeping like a baby. She slept through the whole thing."

"What happened, sir?" Garrett asked.

"It was Lisa Power."

"She *shot* at you?"

"Yes, she did." Denis shook his head. "Honestly, I never thought she'd go this far."

"Is she still here?"

Denis nodded toward the office door. "She went in there and locked the door. I can't hear anyone inside now, so I'm assuming she's on the run again."

As if to confirm his suspicions, the office door opened from the other side. Deputy Garrett began to raise his weapon, but he lowered it again when he saw Deputy Stoll in the doorway of the office.

"Lisa Power was here," Garrett called to his partner. "Is anyone in the office?"

Stoll had his gun drawn, too. "No, it's empty. The patio door's open. If she was there, she's gone now. There are footsteps in the snow heading away toward the river."

Denis pushed himself to his feet from the stairs. His legs were rubbery, and he grabbed for his cane and leaned his weight on it. He limped toward the fireplace and stood in front of it, hypnotized by the flames. His silence weighed on the deputies, who were both impatient for instructions.

"Sir?" Deputy Garrett said after a minute had passed. "What should we do?"

"Do we think she's still driving the Camaro?" Denis asked quietly.

"As far as we know. We've been looking for it, but with the darkness and snow out there, we haven't been able to find it yet."

Denis took another long length of time to process his thoughts. His mind kept replaying the gunshot that had roared past his head. The noise. The smell of the smoke. The cloud of glass. He ran his hand through his wild hair, and fragments of the mirror fell to the carpet.

"She'll be trying to get out of town," he said. "There are only so many ways across the rivers."

"What do you want us to do?" Garrett asked.

"Pull everyone in. Get every police car on the road. We have to keep her contained. Call East Grand Forks, Crookston, and Bemidji, and see if they can spare some men, too. And alert the border. It's possible she may head to Canada."

"Yes, sir." Deputy Garrett hesitated. "And what do you want me to tell them?"

"That we need to find her," Denis said.

"Yes, I know, but they're going to ask. What then? Do they confront her if they locate her? What are we supposed to do?"

Denis closed his eyes. The fire was warm on his face, but he could feel the chill on his back from the wind blowing through the house. "Tell them she's a threat," he said.

"Sir?"

"She fired a gun at me, Garrett! If anyone confronts her, she's likely to do it again. And we suspect she has more guns, don't we? That's what Curtis March said. Not just the Glock but assault rifles, too. This situation is explosive. I don't want this getting out of hand any more than it already is. We need to find her and keep her locked down."

Garrett nodded. "What do we do if she fires at our people?"

Denis rubbed his unshaved chin. He shook his head. "If she becomes a risk to anyone's safety, then we fire back. We have no choice. We treat this like any other active shooter situation. Now get moving, go, we need to locate her before she gets out of Thief River Falls. There isn't much time."

"Yes, sir." Garrett turned for the door but then stopped. "Mr. Farrell, did she say anything about the missing boy?"

Denis's gaze was lost in the fire again. He didn't answer.

"Sir?" Garrett repeated. "Did she say what happened to the boy?"

"No," Denis murmured finally. "I still don't know where Harlan is. I don't know where she took him."

The groundskeeper trooped through the snow that was filling up Greenwood Cemetery. He wasn't a happy man. It was late in the evening, and he'd already been at home in his pajamas with a Budweiser and an episode of *NCIS* on the flat screen when the public works director called him. Now he was back out in the cold. He wore a khaki parka with the zipper undone and the fur hood flapping behind him. He balanced the metal end of a shovel over his left shoulder.

The two people who were with him wouldn't stop talking. A mom and her teenage daughter. He'd already forgotten their names. As a general rule, Stan Erenstad didn't really like people talking. That was one of the good things about working with the dead. They weren't chatterboxes. He'd spent most of his sixty-three years living alone, with no one but a three-legged cat to keep him company for the past twelve years. He didn't talk to the cat, and the cat didn't talk to him, and that was a fine arrangement for both of them.

"Tell the man what you saw, Katy," Mom told the teenager, but then she didn't give the girl a chance to say a word. "Katy came home two nights ago with this story about someone digging up a grave over here. To be honest with you, we thought she was making it up. Let's just say it wouldn't be the first time that *someone's* imagination got a little ahead of the facts. When she was a girl, she had a story for everything, especially when she got into trouble. So when we caught her sneaking into her bedroom soaking wet, we weren't convinced by this story about being out in the cemetery."

"Uh-huh," Stan said.

"Mom, I told you, I was worried about Willow!" the teenager broke in. She wore a green army jacket that swam on her skinny frame, and she had a multicolored wool hat pulled down to her eyebrows. "She had a really weird Snapchat post about going to the cemetery, and it freaked me out. I wanted to make sure she was okay."

"Well, this girl Willow is definitely an odd duck," Mom agreed. "Sweet enough, but lost in her own world; do you know the type? Writers, I guess. She wants to be a poet, like you can make any money that way. Kids need to be practical in this day and age. Now quit dawdling, Katy, and tell him the story. Don't waste the man's time. We're out here because of you. Like I said, my husband and I didn't really believe this story of hers, but she came back home today and said she'd seen the same person in the same place back in the graveyard. She swore up and down she was telling the truth. That's why we called. My husband golfs with the public works director, and he called him up and said we don't really *know* that any of this is true, but it's strange enough that someone should probably check it out."

"Uh-huh," Stan said again.

"It's true," the teenager insisted. "It really happened."

Stan stopped in the middle of the cemetery and didn't hide his loud sigh. The two women kept going for a few steps before they realized he wasn't with them, and then they turned back. Stan slipped his shovel off his shoulder and leaned on the post. The snow kept coming down, which was normally one of his favorite things, because snow had a way of quieting the whole world. He really enjoyed going out on his back porch at midnight during a snowfall and listening to a whole lot of nothing.

"Okay, start over," he said. "What the hell happened?"

Mom opened her mouth to talk, but Stan held up his hand like a stop sign to silence her. "How about we let the girl tell it, okay?"

The girl, Katy, kept eyeing different parts of the cemetery. Her multicolored hat made her look like a rainbow ice pop. "Well, two nights ago, I came out here to find my friend Willow. She wrote this cool poem called 'Dance of the Dead,' and she let me read it. It's really good, but really creepy, because it's about a girl who goes to a cemetery when she's thinking of killing herself. So when Willow posted that she was coming out here, I got a little scared. I figured I'd go find her and make sure she was okay. I searched all over the cemetery, but I didn't see Willow anywhere, so I decided to go back home. Except before I did, I heard something weird, like somebody digging, which is *not* the kind of noise you want to hear in a cemetery at night. That's when I saw her."

"Who?" Stan asked.

"That woman. The writer. Lisa Power. She was burying a body out here."

"Burying a body? You're sure about that?"

"Yes, I'm sure! I saw her lift up the body in a sheet and put it in the ground and then start covering it up. I was thinking, wow, did she *kill* somebody or something? So I got out of there real fast. I told my parents, but they didn't believe me, even though it happened just like I said. I haven't been able to stop thinking about it since then. I figured I should do something, you know? That's why I came back to the cemetery tonight. I wanted to see if I could find where she put the body."

"And what did you see?" Stan asked, before Mom could open her mouth.

"I saw Lisa Power again! She was right back in the same place. She had a shovel with her, like she was going to dig up whoever she put in the ground."

"You're sure it was Lisa Power both times? I mean, the first night you said it was raining pretty hard. Maybe it was somebody else."

Katy's brow crinkled with annoyance. "No, it was her! I'm telling you, it was her! Everybody knows who she is. I figured she was coming back to get rid of the evidence. It was just the two of us out here, and she saw me, so I ran. I told my parents we had to do something right away. We had to get somebody out here to see what was going on."

"Well, we're here," Stan muttered, squinting into the snow. "You said this happened in the back of the cemetery?"

"I think so."

"Okay, lead the way. You know where we're going."

The teenager strutted forward, and Stan followed, with Mom bringing up the rear. He didn't figure the search would take long, because he didn't believe the story was true. This was going to be a wild goose chase. There was something about graveyards that had people seeing ghosts. It wasn't the first time he'd been dragged out here at night over nothing. He was already anticipating getting back home and thawing out in his hot tub and opening up another beer and seeing what Gibbs was up to on *NCIS*. He just hoped the DVR had recorded it.

They were nearly to the end of the cemetery, at the border of the woods, when the girl pointed her hand excitedly.

"There! That's the place right there!"

Stan did a double take in surprise. The teenager was right. In the last row of graves, in front of an elaborate marble headstone, the ground had been disturbed. Despite the blanket of snow, it was clear that someone had been digging here. He didn't know who or why, but there was no innocent explanation for anyone to be doing that without him knowing about it.

When they got closer, he was able to read the headstone near the disturbed ground. It wasn't for a recent burial. He checked the dates carved into the stone and saw that the grave under his feet was for a man who had died ten years earlier.

A young man. Not even thirty years old.

Stan always hated to see the young ones out here. He didn't like to see lives cut short. He murmured the name on the headstone aloud.

"Daniel Farrell."

A nickname was etched in the marble below. *Danny.*

38

Lisa had to avoid the police as she drove. They were at every bridge, every crossroad, watching for her like wolves in the snow. She felt trapped, forced to shift directions over and over. North, south, east, west, she couldn't escape from Thief River Falls. When she ran out of options, she stopped in a downtown parking lot on First Street to decide what to do. The other cars around her shielded her from view, but she had nowhere to go. She could see the Red Lake River bridge from where she was, not even two blocks away, but she could also see a sheriff's SUV parked up on the sidewalk near the water. Its flashing red lights were on, like a warning.

As soon as he spotted the Camaro, the chase would begin.

"Where are we going, Lisa?" Purdue asked from the passenger seat.

She didn't answer the boy right away. Her knee jerked nervously as she sat in the car, which grew cold as they stayed in the parking lot with the engine off. She chewed her fingernails, which she hadn't done in years. She felt like a jigsaw puzzle breaking into pieces.

"Lisa?"

"I don't know," she told him finally. "I don't know what to do. You'll be safe if I can get you out of town, but I just don't know how to do it. They've got us surrounded. I never should have fired that gun in Denis's house. Now he has an excuse for them to fire back. Shoot first, ask questions later. He can send all the other cops at us, not just the ones in his pocket. Oh my God, I'm so stupid."

"You're not stupid, Lisa. You rescued me, just like you said you would."

A sad smile took over her face. She looked at the boy sitting next to her. She felt an urge to reach out and straighten his long blond hair, which kept falling across his eyes. Those eyes. So smart, so blue, so curious. She realized how much he reminded her of Danny. It was amazing that she'd never noticed it before. The pictures she'd seen of Danny as a ten-year-old child could have been pictures of Purdue. Danny's hair, Danny's eyes, even some of Danny's expressions when he looked at her. Thinking about it made her own eyes blur with tears.

"Don't cry, Lisa. I don't like it when you cry."

"It's just that . . . it's just that I know I failed you, Purdue."

"But you didn't. It's not your fault. It's me. You should just let me go."

"I'll never do that. I can't."

She squeezed her fists shut and prayed for deliverance. For escape. For rescue.

And like a miracle, it came. The car window was streaked with wet snow, and when she lowered the window to see down the road, she spotted their salvation approaching from the west.

A truck.

A truck in the left lane heading for the First Street bridge.

"Hang on," she said.

Lisa fired the engine. The Camaro growled, ready for action. She took a glance toward the police car on the bridge and hoped the cop at the wheel wouldn't see her car as it crossed the street. There was no other way. She drove to the parking lot driveway and waited for the truck to pass, and with one quick burst of acceleration, she shot across the street into the right lane and took up position immediately next to the truck. She matched its speed as the two vehicles headed for the bridge.

The police car was on the other side. If she was lucky, the only thing he would see was the truck, not the car in the lane next to it. The truck rumbled onto the flat span, going slowly. Lisa slowed, too. Slush poured from the truck's tires and assaulted her windshield, and she had to run her wipers. On the other side of the concrete barrier, she could see the dark river water below them. She kept an eye on her mirror, expecting to see the flashing lights of the police car heading her way. But the ruse kept them out of sight.

The bridge wasn't wide. In a few seconds, they made it to the other side. The truck wanted to turn right, and the driver sounded his horn loudly, because Lisa was blocking him from the turn lane. She accelerated, shooting ahead of him and spinning around the turn onto Pennington Avenue. The truck followed, keeping her invisible to anyone behind them.

This area of town was so familiar to her. She knew every block like the back of her hand. And yet it felt foreign. Thief River Falls was her enemy now, and she had to find a way out. She drove past the landmarks of her childhood, past the houses of people she knew, heading out into nothingness again. The buildings disappeared. So did the trees. Fields took over, stretching to the dark horizon. She drove and drove. South of town, the lights of the airport runways showed up on her right, and she saw a FedEx plane waiting for takeoff. It was always strange, seeing large planes here in this small corner of the world. She heard thunder as the plane slowly gathered speed, aiming for the snow and the sky.

And still she drove, leaving everything behind. There wasn't a light to be seen anywhere, just her own headlights illuminating a small section of white pavement in front of her. She was out of town. They were free. Somehow she'd run the gauntlet and come out on the other side, and she could take the boy anywhere now. The sense of exhilaration filled her with joy.

But her relief didn't last long.

A cross street loomed ahead of her. She knew where she was, County Highway 57, a misnomer for a little dirt road dropped down between the farm fields. She didn't see the police car until it was too late. Its lights were off; it was nothing but a shadow parked on the shoulder. But he saw her. He couldn't miss her. Lisa slammed hard on the brakes, and as she did, the flashing lights of the squad car came to life. The Camaro skidded on the slippery pavement, and when it came to a stop, it was facing east down the dirt road. She accelerated, kicking up snow and gravel, staying in the middle of the rural highway. The police car followed. It was right on her tail.

"What's going on?" Purdue asked, sensing her panic.

"I think we're getting to the end of the line," Lisa said softly.

She sped due east. Her world was narrowed to the white light in front of the Camaro. Everything else was dark. The police car stayed behind her, not trying to stop her or force her off the road, but she knew he was on his radio, calling in backup from every direction.

The car thudded over railroad tracks, pushing her out of her seat. She spotted lights far off in the distance and heard the faint mournful cry of a whistle. A train was coming, only a few minutes away from the crossing. A train was heading north. To Canada.

"You were on your way to Canada," she said. "That's why you came here."

"Yes."

"Do you still want to see it?"

"Sure, I do."

"Okay then."

That was her plan. Get the boy on the train. Let him jump on board, let him travel with the night to faraway places, let him be free. All she needed to do was buy him time. And really, there was no other plan available to her anymore, because as she approached the next cross-road not even a quarter mile away, she saw more red lights. Police cars had slanted across the highway, forming a barricade. She was blocked from the back and blocked from the front.

Her headlights lit up a lonely building at the intersection. She saw a white tower and realized it was the steeple of a century-old Lutheran church, dropped down miles from anywhere. Her family had worshipped there. She remembered sitting in the wooden pews as a child and watching the light in the eyes of the people who stared at the altar. She remembered the minister talking about eternal life and wondering how anyone could really live forever.

It wasn't a large building, just the steeple and the slanted gray roof and a trio of windows on the walls of the small sanctuary. Evergreens made a U around the back of the building, creating a little grove that separated the church from the cornfield that butted up against it. There were no lights on inside. She had the strange thought that God wasn't home.

The police had the cross street blocked in front of the church, so Lisa spun the wheel hard. The Camaro swerved onto the shoulder and took flight across a shallow ravine where dead weeds grew out of the snow. The bumper hit the other slope, jarring their bodies with the impact, and then the wheels chewed into the ground and climbed from the valley with a roar. She turned the wheel again, feeling the car spin. She hit the brakes and jerked the Camaro to a stop just outside the church's white front doors.

"Inside," she shouted to Purdue. "Get inside right now!"

The boy ran for the church door. Lisa popped the release on the trunk and bolted from the car with the pistol in her hand. She pointed into the sky and fired. The noise of the gunshot froze everything around her. The police car that had been chasing her slammed to a stop, jerking across the highway. She saw the doors of two other police cars opening on the other side of the intersection. Spotlights swung her way, bathing her in white light.

"Stay there!" she screamed into the wind. "Don't come any closer!"

She could hear other sirens. More cars were coming. And somewhere out there she heard the whistle of the train again. The back door of the church led toward the evergreens and from there into the cornfield and from there to the railroad tracks. All she needed to do was give Purdue a chance. A chance to run. A chance to disappear like one small shadow into the night, where the police would never find him. Get on the train. Go to a new life.

It was an escape he had to make alone. Without her.

She would stay here, giving him cover. She would hold off the police until he was gone. Then they could do what they wanted with her. Nothing mattered once the boy was safe.

Lisa ran to the trunk and threw it open. She gathered up everything that was inside into her arms.

The assault rifle. The ammunition. An arsenal to hold them at bay.

She took it all with her and followed Purdue into the church.

39

Almost two dozen police cars staked out the two roads that made an L at the lonely corner outside the church. A handful of cops with guns drawn roamed the barren cornfields behind the trees. Intersecting lights from two sides erased the shadows and turned the black night to day. The evergreens bent as the wind blew, and waves of snow continued to pour through the light.

Denis Farrell was at the scene. So was the sheriff, who was on the front line with his officers. The media had heard the overlapping calls on the police radios, and they were on the other side of a perimeter a hundred yards away. Gawkers had begun to show up in the fields as rumors of the standoff went viral around town.

The mayor of Thief River Falls was there, too.

"Have we tried calling the church phone?" he asked Denis in a reedy voice. The mayor was a genial man in his sixties, with two little flaps of gray hair on his balding head. His black glasses were coated in snow. He kept taking them off and wiping them and shaking his head in disbelief at what was going on around him. "I mean, has anyone been able to reach her?"

"We called the church phone and Lisa's cell phone," Denis replied. "She's not answering either one."

"Well, there has to be someone who knows her, isn't there? The woman grew up in this town, for God's sake. We have to have someone who can talk a little sense into her."

Denis shrugged. "I talked to Laurel March at the hospital, and I explained the situation. She's on her way over here."

"Is this woman a doctor?" the mayor asked. "Or is she a friend of Lisa's? I mean, either way, I hope she can help."

"Dr. March is a psychiatrist," Denis replied.

"A shrink? Really?"

"Lisa's been seeing her for the past couple of years."

"Well, I'd like to say it's helping, but it sure doesn't look that way. Did Dr. March have any suggestions?"

"She said to do nothing until she got here," Denis replied. "We don't want to push Lisa and make her feel threatened. It's impossible to predict how she'll react if we do that. On the other hand, I'm worried that she may take matters into her own hands. She's got a lot of guns and ammunition in there."

The mayor wiped his glasses again. "You really think she's dangerous?"

Denis scowled and lost his temper. "Dangerous? Of course, she's dangerous! She broke into my house and took a shot at me tonight. She took a shot at the cops when she went off the road. Yesterday, she pulled a gun on two deputies at her house. She's holed up inside the church with assault weapons, and she knows how to use them. She's putting people at risk, and I don't care if she's mentally ill. You could say that about any mass shooter."

The mayor waited for him to calm down.

"I hear you on all of that, Denis, and you're right. The only thing I'm saying is this is *Lisa Power* we're talking about. Everyone around here knows her. And this isn't going to stay local. We're going to have national press on this, too. This is *news*, Denis. I'm already getting calls.

We need to take every possible step to make sure this situation doesn't get out of hand."

"It's already out of hand," Denis snapped. "Look, I know exactly who Lisa is. Believe me. No one wants to see anyone get hurt here, least of all Lisa herself. But that's up to her. The safety of the town and our police officers comes first. If we had some nobody hunkering down in that church with a rifle, you think we'd hesitate to take a shot when we had it? Of course not. The sheriff and I aren't giving Lisa Power any free passes. If she threatens our people, if she fires at us, she becomes a target, and we have to take her out. You know that's the only way to go."

The mayor exhaled long and slow. "Son of a bitch. I know what you're saying, Denis, but you need to think about what Lisa has been through. Not only is she *not* some nobody, she's also a woman who's just gone through the worst kind of loss that a human being can experience. We need to keep that in mind."

Denis held himself in check this time. He wanted to yell, but yelling accomplished nothing. And the fact was, he did know what Lisa had been through. He didn't like her, but he didn't wish her any harm. They'd been estranged for years, but she was still a part of his life. And a part of his family.

"I'm not casting blame on Lisa," Denis told the mayor. "I know how difficult this situation is for her and how impossible it is to accept. Remember, my wife and I are going through this, too. We're grieving, just like she is."

The mayor reached out and put a hand on Denis's shoulder. "Of course, you are. I wasn't trying to imply otherwise, Denis. You and Gillian have been through hell these past few days. This whole year, really, ever since the diagnosis. I can't imagine what this time has been like for you."

"Thank you."

"Is there any news of Harlan, by the way?" the mayor asked. "Did you find out where Lisa took the body?"

Denis nodded. He felt as if one weight had been lifted from his shoulders, only to be replaced by an even heavier burden. "Yes, I got a phone call a few minutes ago. They found him and took him back to the hospital. The funeral home will collect him shortly. So at least that mystery is solved."

"Well, good. One small blessing. Where was he?"

Denis stared at the church and thought of Lisa inside, making a fortress out of her guns and her grief. "She took Harlan from his hospital room to the cemetery. A groundskeeper dug up the grave tonight and found the boy's body there, wrapped in a sheet. Really, I don't know why I didn't think to send someone over there before now. I should have guessed that's what she would do. After Harlan died, she took him away from the hospital to be with his father. She buried him with Danny."

Laurel rushed to get ready. She had to get to the church.

She already had Lisa's clinical file open on the desk in her hospital office, and she'd been rereading every sentence of her notes from the past two years, looking for clues, looking for new ideas. She went over everything. Everything Lisa had told her about losing Madeleine and the rest of her family. Everything Lisa had told her about Harlan as her son's cancer got worse month by month. As the treatments produced no results, only misery.

Until two nights ago in the hospital.

Until the end.

Laurel felt helpless. She hadn't felt that way often in her career. She told herself that she'd guided a lot of patients through terrible loss, but she'd failed Lisa. She had never imagined the possibility of a crisis like the one Lisa was experiencing. She'd tried to contain it; she'd hoped she could reach Lisa before grief carried her across a line from which she'd never return. But Laurel was worried now that it was too late.

Lisa was ready to die for the child she called Purdue.

She turned off the lamp on her desk and grabbed her coat from a hook near the window. She needed to hurry. The office was dark, and the snow was like silver through the window. She pulled on her coat, but before she could leave, a shadow filled the doorway.

A man was there.

"*Noah*," Laurel said.

She crossed the short space between them and put her arms around Lisa's brother. She felt a desperate sense of relief seeing him, as if maybe there was still hope. Maybe with him here, Lisa could still be saved.

"I'm so glad you came," Laurel said. "Did Lisa call you? Do you know what's going on?"

Noah shook his head. He looked at a loss, not sure what to say. It had been more than a year since Laurel had seen him, more than a year since Noah had run away from Thief River Falls. Of course, Laurel knew what Lisa didn't, that Noah had been on the verge of suicide before he moved away. That he'd sat in Lisa's basement with a loaded gun in his mouth. The only thing Lisa knew was that a month after her brother had bolted from her life, her only son had been diagnosed with aggressive brain cancer, and she'd been left to deal with it alone.

"I don't know anything," Noah said, "but I can feel that Lisa's in trouble. Do you know what it is?"

"It's Harlan," Laurel told him softly.

Noah stared at her, his eyes widening with horror. He didn't want to hear it, and he didn't want to believe it. "Oh my God. You can't be serious. Not him, too. How bad is it?"

"He passed away two nights ago, Noah. Cancer. I'm so sorry."

Noah turned away from her and slammed one of his fists into the office wall. A keening, desperate wail squeezed from his throat. When he turned back, his entire face had dissolved into fury and tears. He could barely speak. The skin on his hand was a mess of blood.

"I thought the Dark Star was me," he murmured in a strangled voice. "I really did. I thought I was the curse, that I was the reason they all died."

"There's no such thing as a curse," Laurel told him.

"Well, I didn't believe that. I thought if I left, the tragedies would go away. And instead this happens. I leave Lisa and Harlan alone, and this happens. My God."

Laurel saw something different in Noah's face. Maturity. He'd aged more than just a year in the time he'd been gone. For a man who was nearly forty, he'd been mostly a child his whole adult life. With each loss in their family, Noah had grown more vulnerable, forcing his sister to shoulder the burdens by herself. Lisa had always been the strong one. But that was then. Laurel was staring at a new man. He was torn apart by guilt, but he wasn't running anymore.

She took Noah's elbow and led him down the gloomy hospital corridor. The overnight lights were turned low. They reached the empty room where she'd confronted Lisa earlier in the evening, and she stopped, because Noah needed to see it.

"He died here," she murmured. "This was Harlan's room."

Noah stepped inside. His gaze was drawn to the bed, and he inhaled sharply. "That poor, sweet kid."

"I know."

"What did my family do, Laurel? How did we piss off God like this? I can't believe it. I can't believe the Dark Star took Harlan, too."

"Lisa put him on a DNR order about two weeks ago," Laurel told him. "She wanted him to go peacefully. And he did. He passed away two nights ago in her arms. We'd known it was likely for some time, and I'd tried to get her ready for it, but some things you can never really be ready for. After the boy died, Lisa was alone with the body, and she had—well, she had a breakdown. She wrapped up Harlan in a sheet and took him away from the hospital. She took him to the cemetery.

She dug up the ground above Danny's grave, and she put Harlan there with his father."

"Of course she did," Noah murmured. "That doesn't surprise me at all. God, I can't imagine this. Lisa must be going through hell. I need to go to her. Where is she? Is she at home?"

Laurel hunted for a way to tell him. To explain. She felt choked for words, and Noah realized in her silence that something was very wrong.

"What is it?" he asked, his voice darkening with worry. "What's going on? Tell me."

"It's not over," Laurel murmured.

Noah took her by the shoulders. She could see panic rising in his face. "What are you saying?"

"She needs you, Noah," Laurel told him. "She needs you right now. The Dark Star isn't finished. It's trying to take Lisa, too."

40

The lights of the police cars flashed through the church windows above Lisa's head and lit up her face. She sat on the cold floor, her back against the wall, with a loaded AR-15 rifle draped across her knees. She wouldn't let it out of her hands. Her finger hovered near the trigger. The police could storm the church at any moment, and she needed to be ready to fire.

Purdue sat beside her, cross-legged, his hands neatly folded in his lap. He looked calm and unafraid, and she wished she could be like that herself. Her nerves were raw. Her muscles twitched uncontrollably. She could feel something black and ugly lurking in the shadows. It reminded her of the old Japanese fairy tale about the boy who took refuge in a church and drew cats on the walls to keep away a monster. Except there were no cats with them now. Just the monster, ready to come for her. That was okay. That was fine. The monster could have her, but she wouldn't let him have Purdue.

She knew they were in their final moments together. She hadn't had the courage yet to tell him that he would have to go and leave her behind. It was the only way to save him. And yet the boy was wise, and she suspected that he already knew the truth.

"There are a lot of people outside," Purdue said.

"You're right."

"Do they have guns?"

"Yes, I'm sure they do."

"Are they going to come inside?"

"Maybe. At some point. But before that happens, I'll probably have to go outside myself."

"Why?"

"To give you a chance to escape."

"But how will you get away?" he asked.

She smiled at him, hiding her sadness. "Don't worry about that. That's my problem, not yours. The main thing is for you to get to Canada. That's what your mom wanted. That's what I want for you, too. She was right. Canada is so pretty. It's wide open, and there are mountains and lakes and waterfalls and forests. It's like heaven. You'll see. It's just like heaven."

"I don't want to go anywhere without you," the boy told her. "I want to stay right here. Can't we just talk to them?"

"No. It's gone too far. The only thing we can do is save you. You're not going to die, my sweet. I promise you that. You are not going to die."

"How will I know when it's time to go?" he asked.

Lisa tilted her head and cupped her hand behind her ear. "We have to listen. There will be a train whistle. You can't miss it from here. It'll pass by on the other side of the field behind the church, and it'll be heading north. It'll take you up into Canada. The train stops here as it's coming into town, so you'll be able to hop on board. Can you do that? When we hear the train whistle, you'll need to slip out the back door and into the trees. No one will see you. And then you have to run, Purdue. Run until you get to the train, and then you just climb on and never look back."

"What about you?"

"I'll make sure no one follows you," Lisa said. "That's my job. To protect you."

"When we hear the train whistle?"

"Exactly. When we hear the train whistle, you run. Can you do that for me?"

"Yes," Purdue replied, but his lips puckered unhappily. "Why can't you come to Canada, too? You could come with me."

"Well, you can look for me up there," Lisa said, "and one day you'll see me."

They sat for a while longer in silence. Whenever there was a noise outside, she tensed, expecting the doors to burst open, expecting the assault to come. She prayed they would wait long enough for the train to arrive first. After that, nothing mattered. She shivered, because the monster in her head was getting bolder, getting closer, enveloping her in a dark cloud. She felt its breath on her neck like needles of ice.

"Lisa?"

"Yes?"

"Can you tell me a story?"

"Sure. I can do that. What kind of story would you like?"

"Tell me about the book you wrote. Tell me about *Thief River Falls*."

"That's a book for adults, my sweet," Lisa murmured. "Not for children."

"Tell me anyway. Please. I want to know what happens before I go."

Lisa reached out and put a hand over his. "Okay. I can tell you the story if you really want. *Thief River Falls* is about a lost boy. Remember? I called him Purdue, just like you. And it's the story of a lonely woman, too. A lovely, lonely woman."

"What's her name?" Purdue asked.

"I called her Madeleine. I named her after my mother."

"Was your mother lonely?"

Lisa smiled. "Oh, no. Not really. I mean, sometimes I'm sure she was, because she was very far from the place where she grew up. But that wasn't why I used her name. I use real names in my books when I want to feel close to the characters as I write them. And there was no woman I felt closer to than my mother. We were the only two girls in the family, so we had to stick together. Plus, my mother was the kind of person who would do anything for others, and that's what my Madeleine—the one in the book—is like, too."

"Madeleine," he murmured.

"Yes."

"So what happens?"

"Well, this boy Purdue arrives in Thief River Falls from Missouri. He's running away from home because his mother died, and he's on his way to find his uncle in Winnipeg. But he's on a train, and the train stops here for repairs. He's lost and sad and confused, so he gets off the train and begins to wander. He wanders through the cornfields in the pouring rain until he gets to a river. There's a cabin there, and he figures he can stay inside for a while. But instead, it's like wandering into a horror movie. There's a man hiding in the cabin who did a terrible thing, and some other men arrive to punish him for what he did. They torture him. They kill him. And the boy, Purdue, he witnesses the whole awful thing."

Purdue sat next to her, saying nothing, just listening to her as if this were some kind of Grimm fairy tale. She put an arm around his shoulder and nudged him closer, and he leaned his head against her.

"The men discover the boy, and they know he's seen what they did. He can get them in big trouble if he tells anyone what he saw. They're not necessarily bad men at heart, but they've let themselves become cruel. Revenge can do that to people. It can make you believe that the only way to deal with a monster is to become a monster yourself. And that's the wrong lesson."

"They hurt the boy, don't they?" Purdue said.

Lisa nodded. "Yes, they do. They hit him, and then they bury him in the ground along with the man they killed. But they don't realize that the boy is still alive. He's under the ground, but his mother is there with him in his head, and she tells him what to do. How to stay perfectly still. How to escape. And so Purdue digs himself out of the hole and wanders away from the cemetery. A woman in a trailer park finds him. She takes him to the hospital, but the first thing the hospital people do is call the police. Purdue sees the two policemen coming, and he realizes they're two of the men he saw at the cabin. So he does a smart thing. He runs away. He hops into the back of a truck, and when the truck stops, he wanders again until he finds himself outside a woman's house."

"Madeleine," Purdue said.

"That's right. It's Madeleine's house. She's a tough, sweet farm girl, but the kind of girl you don't mess with. She's an only child, and with her parents gone, she's just sort of existing from day to day, not really living. This boy, Purdue, gives her something to live for. The two of them click with each other. It's like they're meant to be together. Madeleine is determined to rescue Purdue, but as the book goes on, it's clear that Purdue is really rescuing her. Does that make sense?"

"I think so."

"At that point, the book becomes a little like a detective story. Because he was injured and buried alive, the boy has blocked out most of his past. He can't remember anything. So Madeleine and Purdue have to put the pieces back together to find out what happened to him. The clues lead them here to Thief River Falls, and Madeleine discovers that a horrible murder took place days earlier, in which a young wife was killed by her ex-husband. And the boy recognizes the man who killed her. It's the man he saw tortured and murdered at the cabin in the woods. So Madeleine understands just how serious this situation is. The people they're up against, the ones who want to find them, aren't just dangerous people. They're people with power in town. Police officers. The county attorney. It was *his* daughter who was killed, and he'll do anything to cover up the crime he committed out of vengeance. Madeleine knows she has to get Purdue out of Thief River Falls for him to be safe, but as they try to make their escape, the men track them down, and they're forced to hide away in a remote country church just like this one. They're inside, and the county attorney and his partners are outside. With guns. So Madeleine has to figure a way out of the trap that will keep Purdue alive."

"Wow," the boy said.

"I told you, it's scary."

"But I like it."

"I'm glad," Lisa said.

They were quiet again. Purdue still had his head against her shoulder. She wished, she prayed, that time would freeze like the Minnesota winters and slow down until every second ticking away lasted for days. But the white, snowbound world couldn't stay that way forever. The clock kept going.

"Lisa?"

"Yes?"

"Doesn't it seem weird to you?" the boy said.

"What's that?"

"Everything that happens in your book, it's just like everything that's been happening to you and me."

"Well, life is like that sometimes," Lisa replied. "My mother used to scare us as kids by telling us that if we dreamed too hard, we would bring our nightmares to life. Noah and I would hold hands across the beds at night in case we had bad dreams."

"Is that what's happening? Are we having a nightmare?"

"I don't know. The lullaby says life is but a dream."

The boy thought about this seriously, the way he did everything. Then he looked up at her with wide blue eyes. Danny's eyes.

"Lisa?" he said again.

"Yes, Purdue."

"Tell me how the story ends."

From the Novel

THIEF RIVER FALLS

BY LISA POWER

The train whistle screams in the distance, as lonely and mournful as a maiden who finds her true love turned to stone. It's time. Madeleine gets to her feet, watched by the religious paintings and stained glass of the church, blessed by Jesus on the cross. She reaches a hand to Purdue and pulls him up, too. The weight of separation is almost too much to bear. She sinks to her knees, throws her arms around the boy, and they cling to each other. They are as close as mother and son. Two days ago, she could never have imagined a moment like this, not in her life. Soon it will be over, but she regrets nothing. Not what came before. Not what has to happen now.

"Go," she whispers to the boy as she wipes tears from her face. "Do it just like we talked about. Go down the steps to the back door, and then wait. One of them will be watching the back, and I need to lure him away.

When you hear me shout, you count to ten. Slowly. As soon as you get to ten, go through the door and run. *Run*, Purdue. Make it to the train and don't look behind you."

"What about you?"

"Don't worry about me. Find your way to Canada. Find your uncle. You'll be safe. No one will be coming for you after today. I promise."

Purdue shakes his head. "I'm not sure I can do it."

"Yes, you can. I know you can. You're strong. Now go, my sweet! There's no time!"

The boy is torn. The back door leads out of the church, but the back door takes him away from her. He holds Madeleine's hands tightly, as if he cannot let go. She peels away his fingers and squeezes them. Her smile is hollow, but she fills it with love. Her eyes memorize his face.

"Go."

And he does.

She watches him fly as fast as his skinny legs can carry him, with his hair flapping like bird wings. She watches the boy until he gets to the steps and disappears, and then it's all up to her. She must draw the men to the sound of her voice. She must keep them away from Purdue.

Madeleine spins around. She aims the rifle in her hands at the church doors. She shouts as loud as she can so they can hear her. And so Purdue can hear her, too, and begin the countdown to his escape.

One, two, three . . .

"We're coming out!" she calls. "Don't shoot, we're coming out!"

But of course, she knows they will shoot her if they can. They must. They are desperate men.

"Don't shoot!" she cries again.

She goes to the church door. She tears it open, and her finger closes around the trigger of the rifle.

Eight, nine, ten . . .

The train whistle screams again, louder and closer. In her head, she can see the boy bursting through the back door and sprinting through the fields. It won't take him long to get to the tracks. She hopes he can see the train and feel its thunder. But he isn't safe. Not yet. First, the men must die.

Madeleine fires into the night.

She aims at any shadow she can see. She wants to kill. She wants to destroy these four men, these animals who would bury a boy in the ground.

There, behind the police car, is a flash of light, a burst of noise. One of them fires back at her, but the shot goes wild. She targets the spot; she fires again, and again, and again, and then she hesitates on the trigger to draw him to his feet. He stands to shoot, but she is faster. In the next instant, she fires once more, with deadly aim. Bullet tunnels through flesh, knocking the man backward. That one is dead. Clean kill. She cannot see which one, but he is in uniform.

One of the deputies. One of the traitors.

Madeleine moves quickly. She runs sideways through the rain, across the church lawn, toward the shoulder of the rural highway. Nearby is movement. Another man runs from her right, from behind the church; the noise and gunfire have drawn him forward and away from Purdue, just as she planned. They are close. He fires. She fires. They exchange bullets like greetings in a foreign language, but he is a nervous young man, unprepared for what it means to take a life.

He misses her entirely, while her bullet goes into his heart.

Another uniform. Another deputy. Two are gone, and two others remain.

Liam, the ginger man. The hired killer and torturer.

And Denis.

Madeleine makes a mistake now. There is something hypnotizing about the body at her feet, the man she has killed. She cannot tear her gaze away from him, and so she waits too long in one place. She is an easy target. A shot erupts behind her, an explosion that reaches her brain only after the pain comes. She looks down at herself, sees blood mixing with the rain, a red river on her chest. A bullet has passed through her shoulder, shredding muscle, breaking bone.

Madeleine sinks, as if falling to the ground, but it's a ruse. Instead, swallowing down the pain, she whirls around, firing the whole time, firing firing firing. She sweeps the air in a semicircle of bullets. Liam is there, with his wet red hair. He has nowhere to hide. She hits him, hits him again, hits him again. There are at least five bullets in his chest. His face has a look of shock and surprise. His heart is pumping out its last beats, and he knows he is done.

But not quite done.

There is enough hatred left in him to lift his pistol. He aims at Madeleine, pulls the trigger, rips open her stomach. The bullet has the kick of a rocket. The agony is like flame in her bloodstream. She gasps, but then she swings her own rifle up once more, pulls the trigger once more.

A red hole appears in the forehead of the red-haired man. He drops like stone.

Her vision grows cloudy. Darkness encroaches on her. This is more than the darkness of the night. The sharp pain grows dull. She has a sensation of floating, of flying, of the solid earth becoming lava under her feet. She is dying, but she refuses to die yet.

There is one man left. The last man. Madeleine tries to shout. She wills air into her chest, tries to croak out a name above the storm.

"Denis!"

Where is he?

Where is that old man willing to trade the life of a boy for his own sins?

"Hello, Madeleine."

Yes, he is right there. He is on the dirt road, leaning on his cane. He has watched the battle, watched his men die. They are gone, and he lives, but Madeleine is almost gone, too. They both know it. She grows dizzy, seeing the rain and the church turn upside down. It's raining on the sky. Her body is heavy, like lead, a weight she cannot sustain. Her legs wither and fall beneath her. She is on her knees now.

Denis has a gun, but he doesn't need to use it. He simply stands on the road, with the rain sweeping across him, waiting for the inevitable, waiting for Madeleine to die. She must fight back. She tries to bring up her own gun, right it, fire it, but it weighs at least a thousand pounds in her hand. She pulls the trigger. An explosion rocks her ears; smoke fills her nose. A bullet sears the ground, burying itself in the soft grass, the recoil knocking her sideways. Denis looks at her with a sad little smile, still saying nothing.

The wind blows. Not a strong wind, not even a gust, just a whisper of air, but it is enough to take her by the shoulders and lower her to the ground. She is on her back now. The sky is over her head, dark and violent. She stares at it, stares into the silver streaks of rain, blinks in confusion. A breath comes in; a breath goes out. Her lungs are in an ocean, sinking under a red tide of blood.

He is standing directly over her now. Denis. How much time did it take for him to limp down from the road through the tall grass and arrive at her feet? She was unaware of him moving at all. Time is slowing. Soon it will freeze altogether, never going forward, one second hanging in the scale without giving way to the next one.

Denis studies her like a scientist, curious about the moment of death, unmoved by her pain. His gray hair is wet and flat, his body gnarled, his expression not even malevolent, just inexpressibly sure of itself. The elite are accustomed to winning, to getting whatever they want. But he will not win this time. He is too late. Purdue is on the train.

She has no breath left to speak to him, but her triumph is in her eyes. *The boy is gone. You'll never get him.*

He simply smiles at her, as if he can read her thoughts. The train whistles again, like a cry of freedom behind the church, but something is wrong. Denis's head turns the way a snake's head swivels to watch its prey. When he looks back at her, she can see his eyes agleam.

Madeleine doesn't understand. Denis has lost; he should be bitter and angry. Then her head finds the strength to turn, and her heart wails when she sees him. Purdue. The boy stands in the weeds not even twenty feet away. He let the train go without him. He has come back for her.

They will die together.

She can't even summon the will to scream. To voice her despair, to shout to God, to say no, don't let this happen.

"It will be quick when the moment comes," Denis tells her calmly. "I promise you that. No pain."

He's talking about Purdue. He is talking about shooting him, killing the boy. This devil thinks those words will be of comfort to her, that somehow he is easing the struggle of her last breaths. Instead, it has the opposite effect. He transforms her into something superhuman. He gives her new life. Endorphins surge through her blood.

She is on her back on the wet ground, but the rifle is still right there with her. Her finger is still curled around the trigger. The heavy gun is suddenly weightless. A smile forms on her mouth, a smile that warns him of disaster, but he has nowhere to go, and he cannot move fast enough to get away. He is an old man. His mouth opens; his lips form an O of surprise, the last expression they will ever make. The barrel of the gun rises and spits flame. A single shot. A single bullet. It travels through his skull.

Denis is dead.

Relief floods Madeleine like a warm spring. She lets go of the gun and lets go of everything else, too.

Everything in her body relaxes. The pain vanishes. Her limbs feel as if they are becoming one with the soft earth below her. She stares at the sky, seeing something bright, a brilliant star that has somehow burned through the dark clouds. That star is where she is headed. She is going home.

We all die alone, she thinks.

But Madeleine is not alone.

Purdue kneels beside her, his young face pouring out tears that mix with the rain. He is holding her hand to his cheek, but she doesn't feel the touch of his skin. She doesn't feel anything at all.

"Madeleine," he begs, his voice choking up. "Please get up. Please don't leave me. We're safe. We can be together now."

Oh, my sweet.

Oh, if only we could.

She wants to tell him that everything will be all right. He will be fine. He will live. He will grow, he will thrive, he will love, he will marry, he will hold the hands of children of his own. She wants to tell him that life is about leaving, but that love is about memories. She wants to tell him about the bright star cascading through the night sky. There are so many things to say, so many lessons to share.

But that is for some other world.

This moment is for the angels.

She gives away her last breath without words, but she is happy at the end. Her eyes gaze into his young face for one final moment before the shadows come, and then they see nothing at all.

41

The train whistle screamed in the distance. It was time. This was the end.

Lisa could feel the vibration under the floor of the church, the earth trembling as tons of steel drew closer, and she knew that Purdue had to run. He had to get away, and she had to protect him as he did. She could draw their fire, the way Madeleine had. She got to her feet with the AR-15 loaded and ready in her arms. She extended a hand to Purdue, but the boy didn't move from where he was. He sat there, staring up at her with his big blue eyes.

"Purdue, you have to go now," she told him. "You have to run and get on that train. This is your way out. You'll be safe in Canada. I told you, it's so beautiful up there. I want you to see it."

"I really have to go?" he asked.

"Yes. I'm sorry."

"Like the boy in the book?"

"Exactly."

"But he didn't get on the train. He came back for Madeleine."

"Yes, but only to say goodbye. Then he had to leave. He went to Canada, and he was happy there. That's the end of the story."

"But Madeleine died," Purdue complained.

"I know."

"That's too sad. I don't like that. We need to change the ending."

"Life doesn't work that way, Purdue. I wish it did, but there are some things we can't change."

The train whistle sounded again, so loud it made Lisa cover her ears. She held out her hands again for the boy to take them. He needed to get up. He needed to run. But he sat on the floor like a statue. His eyes were wide and curious, staring back at her.

"Please," she urged him. "You need to run for that train. Go. I'll protect you. I'll make sure you're safe."

"By dying?" he asked.

"If that's what it takes."

The boy shook his head. "No."

"*Purdue.* You can't worry about me. That's not your job. I'm the one who has to rescue you. Don't you understand? I didn't get us this far only to lose you. I made a *promise.* I'm going to save you."

The boy smiled from the floor as he looked up at her. His smile was blinding. She felt utterly lost in the warmth of that smile and in the love that radiated from his eyes. All the cold went away. The church glowed around them.

"But you can't save me," he said to her.

"Yes. Yes, I can. I have to. That's my job. That's my responsibility. That's the only reason for me to be alive. If I can't save you, there's no point to anything. Your life is more important than mine."

"You can't save me. Don't you see? I'm already gone."

Lisa's headache throbbed behind her forehead, and she squeezed her skull with her hand as if she could force out the pain that way. "What are you talking about?" she asked the boy. "What are you saying?"

"You know."

"No. I don't. I don't know anything at all. All I know is that you have to get on that train."

"That was in the book," Purdue told her. "This isn't the book. The book is just in your head, Lisa. This has all been in your head. You have to let go of it now. You have to let go of *me.*"

"I don't *understand*."

"Yes, you do. You know. You've always known." The boy scrambled to his feet and tugged on her sleeve. "Who am I?"

"What?"

"Who am I? Tell me my name."

"You're Purdue," Lisa said.

"No, I'm not. I have a name."

"I don't know what it is. You never told me. You kept it from me. You hid it from me. You wouldn't tell me your name."

"Because you already know," the boy said.

"No." Lisa sobbed. "*No.* I don't."

"What's my name?"

Lisa wrenched away from the boy and backed up among the pews. She pointed to the rear of the church. "You have to go. Go now. I have to save you. We're running out of time."

"Who am I?"

"You're *Purdue.*"

"No. You know my name. You know who I am. Just say it. Please? What's my name?"

Lisa stared at him. She stared at this perfect boy in front of her. Ten years old. His whole life in front of him. Cities and rivers and mountains to explore. Smart as a whip, always able to make her laugh. Fascinated by everything. Jumping in the backyard while Lisa worked on her books. Playing hide-and-seek with Noah. Sitting in her lap as Lisa read to him.

"He's the most beautiful baby in the world," Madeleine had said ten years ago, a grandmother holding her grandson for the first time.

This perfect boy. The spitting image of his father.

The father who had never met him. The father who had never even known he was going to have a son.

Lisa thought, *Oh, Danny, I'm so sorry. I should have told you. I never should have let you go to fight that fire. I could have stopped you. Two words,*

297

and you would have stayed at my side. Two words would have changed everything.

"I'm pregnant."

The boy said it again. "What's my name? Tell me my name. You can do it."

Lisa broke apart, like ice breaking into sharp little diamonds. She struggled for breath. Her shoulders shook with the pain. Her head was in a vise, the pressure threatening to crack through bone. She didn't want to say it, but she had to say it. The name flew from her chest like a bird freed from a cage.

"Harlan."

"That's right. I'm Harlan."

"Oh my God. Oh, no, no, no, no. You're my boy. My baby."

"And what happened to me, Mom?"

Lisa shook her head. She couldn't face it. She couldn't go back to the hospital, with her arms around her child, feeling his body go slack as she held him. There was a monster here in the church, folding her into darkness. The strange whiteness of the past two days had fled, but what it left behind was pitch black. "No."

"You have to say it, Mom. You have to say it."

"I can't."

"It's okay," Harlan told her. "Say it. It's okay."

"You died."

"Yeah. That's right. I'm really sorry."

"Sorry? No, no, Harlan, you can't be sorry. It was my fault. I failed you. I should have been able to save you."

"You couldn't. No one could. Not the doctors. Not anybody. It's not your fault, Mom. But I have to go now."

Lisa felt it all coming back. All the memories, all the agony, all the tears, everything she had put in a box and hidden away for two days. Harlan was in her arms again as she carried him out of the hospital, still and somehow weightless. She remembered the rain as she dug down into the wet ground to bring her boy to his father. Danny was the only one who could protect him now, not Lisa.

And since then—nothing. Since then, she'd lived a different life. She'd disappeared into a world she'd created. She'd lived out the story of Thief River Falls.

Lisa clamped her eyes shut. The afterimage of Harlan's face shone in her head like a photograph. Her son, alive, standing in front of her, the way he never would again. Her son, saying goodbye.

She opened her eyes.

Harlan was gone. She was alone. She'd been alone for two days.

"No," she wailed, drawing out the word in all its finality.

The book was done. Purdue was back inside its pages. All that remained was her grief, which was a wide, deep canyon, sinking so far down she couldn't see the bottom. The only thing she could think to do was jump. She cared about nothing, least of all herself. Harlan was gone, and she had no purpose left in life. There was no one to save anymore. No one to rescue.

This was the Dark Star in full eclipse.

Lisa walked toward the church doors in a daze. She still had the rifle in her arms. She wrenched open the doors and was immediately bathed in the glow of spotlights. She was at the center of a whirlwind. Dozens of police cars. Dozens of people. Dozens of guns pointed at her.

And one man standing in the snow, apart from all the others. She held up a hand and squinted into the bright lights, trying to see who it was. Then she knew.

Noah.

"Lis, put down the gun," he said.

She was paralyzed. There was a hush over the scene, chaos freezing into complete silence. No one spoke. No one moved. The snow had stopped falling, and even the wind held its breath.

"Lis, it's me. It's Noah. I know about Harlan. Laurel told me everything. I know your heart is broken. I know your whole world is broken.

299

But we'll get through it. We'll put everything back together. You and me, like when we were kids. Just put down the gun."

Noah.

Noah, who'd run away. Noah, who'd left her alone. Noah, who'd abandoned her. She hated him. She hated her brother. Most of all, she hated that she could see herself reflecting in his eyes. It was like staring into a wretched mirror of all her own weaknesses.

Lisa raised the AR-15 and pointed it at her brother's chest. All she had to do was pull the trigger.

Noah screamed at the police. "Nobody shoot, nobody shoot, hold your fire, do not hurt her!"

And then to his sister: "It's okay, Lis. You want to shoot me? Shoot me. I ran out on you. Both of you. I wasn't there for you or for Harlan. But I'm here now."

Noah.

Noah, who'd grown up in the bed next to hers. Noah, who could read her mind and whose thoughts she could hear when she lay awake at night. She'd never admitted it to him. She'd never told him he was right. He was always with her. Noah, who'd introduced her to Danny. Noah, who'd been with her in the delivery room when Harlan was born.

Noah.

"If you'd stayed, you'd be dead, too," Lisa murmured.

"What?"

"Last year. You were going to kill yourself."

"I didn't think you knew that."

"I felt it," Lisa said. "I felt you put the gun in your mouth. I thought, *I'm going to come home and find your body on the floor.* I knew it. Instead, I came home and you were gone. I was glad, Noah. I was glad you ran away. I hated you for it, but I didn't want you to die like the others."

"I'm home, Lis. I'll never run away again."

He walked toward her through the snow. She watched him come. He climbed the wooden steps of the church and stood there with the barrel of her gun jabbing into his stomach. Gently, not rushing, he reached for her hand and peeled away her finger from the trigger and took the rifle from her. She let it go. She let everything go. He put the gun down next to him where it would harm no one, and as he did, she could hear the silence break into the thunder of footsteps as people ran toward them, the eruption of cheers, the blessings to God. Noah put his arms around her and held on, and she put her arms around him, at first stiffly, then as tightly as she'd ever held anyone in her life.

They stood there together like that for a long, long time.

Far away, from the railroad tracks behind the church, she heard a mournful whistle and felt the earth tremble as a train lumbered toward the heart of town on its way to Canada. And then, when the whistle went away, there was only silence.

42

Sunlight streamed through the window into the hospital room, which was brightly colored by bouquets of flowers. They'd come from around the world. So had cards, e-mails, and messages online. Thousands of strangers had sent prayers and condolences to her. It was easy to forget sometimes that a book went out into the world and touched people's lives, and Lisa was overwhelmed by the many readers who had reached back to her in the past week. They were like her family.

She sat patiently as Laurel checked her blood pressure and her pulse and listened to the beat of her heart. Everything was normal. She was on antianxiety medication and would be for a while, but the psychosis had receded. She was back in the real world, dealing with the loss of her son. There was a hole in her heart that would never be filled, but she had learned something in these days that she'd never understood before. She wasn't alone.

"It's odd," Lisa murmured. "I almost miss them."

"Who?" Laurel asked.

"All the characters from *Thief River Falls*. People like Mrs. Lancaster. Tom Doggett. Even a terrible person like Liam. They're all back in the book, but for a little while, they were real to me. They were alive. They'd been in my head for years, and suddenly they were actually there in front of me."

"It's a strange kind of gift."

"Everything got mixed up in ways I don't understand. The real world and my fantasies."

"How so?"

"Well, Fiona Farrell was just a character in the book. She doesn't exist. And yet in my head, she was Danny's sister, even though Danny was an only child. I don't know why my mind put it together like that."

Laurel smiled. "I guess you can probably thank Denis for that. He was a part of both worlds. He's real, but you put him in your book, too. So your brain blended reality and delusion."

"I guess so." Lisa was quiet, and then she added, "I kept seeing white."

Laurel's brow crinkled with puzzlement. "What?"

"Everything my head made up had something white in it. That was what made it different from the things that were really there. After a while, it seemed like everything became white as I went deeper and deeper. I wonder why."

Laurel tugged on the shoulder of her coat. "Lab coats would be my guess. Masks. I suspect that to your brain, white became the color of doctors. You began to associate white with the hospital. This is where you lost Harlan. Everything your mind invented was taking you right back here."

"The brain is a scary thing."

"It can be."

Lisa calmed herself with a slow breath. "Did you tell Curtis I was sorry for whacking him?"

"I did," Laurel replied with a grin. "He's fine now. I think he actually enjoyed being a bad guy. You may have to write him into your next book."

"I can do that."

"Me, too, in fact. I wouldn't mind seeing the name *Laurel March* in one of your novels."

"Okay, but no villains for you," Lisa said. "Maybe a slinky, sexy spy or something like that."

"Deal."

Laurel squeezed her shoulder. She headed for the doorway of the hospital room, and as she left, she had to make way for Noah, who was burdened down with more flowers and a bag stuffed with cards. Noah gave Lisa a smile, and she could see Madeleine in the curl of his lips and the twinkle in his eyes. And her father. And their brothers. And Harlan. Everyone who was gone was really still here.

"Hey, Lis," Noah said, his chirpy voice sounding like when they were kids. "More fan mail. You want me to write back to some of these people for you? You're going to need some help."

Lisa shook her head. "No, I'll do it myself."

"That's a lot of letters."

"That's okay. I want to do every one."

Noah dropped down onto the window bench next to her. "Sorry I was late getting here today. Janie and I are getting settled in at the old house. Whenever you're ready to blow this place, you can stay there, too. I mean, unless you want to go back to your house in Lake Bronson."

Lisa shook her head firmly. "No. If I learned anything, it's that I belong in Thief River Falls."

"Well, who says you can't go home again?" Noah replied. "Hey, by the way, I passed Denis and Gillian Farrell on my way in. Did they really come to see you?"

"They did. Little miracles are everywhere this week."

"How was it?"

"Honestly, we all cried together. We cried for Danny, and we cried for Harlan. It was good. Not only that, prepare yourself for the fact that we are actually invited to Thanksgiving dinner in the Farrell household this year. You, me, Janie."

"Get out."

"It's true. Denis apologized for shutting us out all these years. I don't know if Gillian made him say that, but it sounded sincere. He even admitted that he thought it was rather badass of me to turn him into a homicidal maniac in *Thief River Falls*. He asked if there was going to be a sequel."

"And is there?" Noah asked.

Lisa rolled her eyes. "Oh, no. That book was a stand-alone, believe me. After this week, I may start writing romance novels."

Noah looked away toward the door. He saw something in the hallway that Lisa couldn't see from where she was, and his face flushed. "Janie's here," he told her. "She can't wait to meet you."

"I can't wait to meet her, too," Lisa replied. "I love the idea of you getting married, you know. It's a new beginning, and that's what we need."

"Well, we sort of have a surprise, too. I didn't want to tell you before now. I wanted to wait to make sure it would be okay."

"Is it a good thing?"

"It's a very good thing."

"Okay, what is it?"

Noah waved at his fiancée outside the hospital room. Janie came in—carrying more flowers balanced in both arms—and Lisa understood the surprise immediately. She found her eyes drawn to Janie's swollen belly. Lisa didn't hear much of anything else after that. She was vaguely aware of Janie talking to her and telling her how much she loved her books and how much she loved her brother. But Lisa just kept staring at Janie and thinking about the baby inside her, and finally, Noah and Janie both noticed that tears had begun to fall down Lisa's cheeks.

"Hey," Noah said, reaching out to grab her hand. "Hey, are you okay?"

Lisa nodded. She was crying, but this wasn't sadness. This was something she hadn't felt in forever. Joy. She was overjoyed.

"I'm so happy for you two," she managed to say.

Noah beamed. "Thanks, Lis."

"Do you know if it's a boy or a girl?" she asked.

Janie glanced at Noah and then smiled at Lisa to give her the news. "A boy."

"And actually," Noah went on, "we already have a name picked out. He's going to be Danny."

Lisa just kept crying. It felt wonderful. "Danny," she said.

AUTHOR'S NOTE

Thanks for reading *Thief River Falls*. I hope you enjoyed this very emotional novel as much as I enjoyed writing it for you.

If you liked this book, be sure to check out all my other thrillers, too. Visit my website at bfreemanbooks.com to join my mailing list, get book club discussion questions, and find out more about me and my books.

Finally, if you enjoy my books, I hope you'll post your reviews online at sites like Amazon, Goodreads, Audible, and other sites for booklovers—and spread the word to your reader friends, too. Thanks!

You can write to me with your feedback at brian@bfreemanbooks. com. I love to get e-mails from listeners and readers around the world, and yes, I reply personally. You can also "like" my official fan page on Facebook at facebook.com/bfreemanfans or follow me on Twitter or Instagram using the handle bfreemanbooks. For a look at the fun side of the author's life, you can also "like" the Facebook page of my wife, Marcia, at facebook.com/theauthorswife.

ACKNOWLEDGMENTS

Every novel is the product of work by a team of talented people. I'm fortunate to work with some of the best in the business.

My editor at Thomas & Mercer, Jessica Tribble, has been a wonderful guide on the creative side of my books for several years, and she is also the efficient hand leading the entire publication process. I worked with a superb developmental editor on this novel, David Downing, whose advice was extremely helpful in getting us to the final draft. Copyeditors Susan Stokes and Laura Barrett caught all the little things that authors tend to miss, and they patiently put up with my jokes in the comments, too. The entire team at T&M are amazing professionals in putting first-rate books in the hands of readers, and it's a privilege to work with them.

My first reader on every book is my wife, Marcia. She is wonderful at challenging my preconceived notions, and she makes sure that my vision for the book makes it onto the page. My other advance reader is Ann Sullivan, who adds her own extremely helpful perspective on the first draft. Marcia and Ann both play a huge role in shaping the books, and given the uniqueness of *Thief River Falls* as a story, I relied heavily on their help and advice in making sure this novel achieved what I wanted.

My agent in New York, Deborah Schneider, has been my ally and advocate for more than fifteen years. I'm incredibly grateful to her and her colleagues at Gelfman Schneider, ICM, and Curtis Brown for helping me build relationships with publishers around the world.

Of course, I am especially grateful to YOU, the readers, for coming along with me on this ride and for taking my characters into your hearts. Thank you!

ABOUT THE AUTHOR

Photo by Malyssa Woodward

Brian Freeman is an Amazon Charts bestselling author of psychological thrillers, including the Frost Easton and Jonathan Stride series. His books have been sold in forty-six countries and translated into twenty-two languages. His stand-alone thriller *Spilled Blood* was named Best Hardcover Novel in the International Thriller Writers Awards, and his novel *The Burying Place* was a finalist for the same honor. *The Night Bird*, the first book in the Frost Easton series, was one of the top twenty Kindle bestsellers of 2017. Brian is widely acclaimed for his vivid "you are there" settings, from San Francisco to the Midwest, and for his complex, engaging characters and twist-filled plots.

Brian lives in Minnesota with his wife, Marcia. For more information on the author and his books, visit http://bfreemanbooks.com.